Praise for
Land of a Hundred Wonders

"I've been a Lesley Kagen fan ever since I read her beautifully rendered debut, *Whistling in the Dark*. Here she adds to what is shaping up to be her greatest strength as a novelist: She creates a most unusual narrator whose quirky innocence and frankness reveal more story than she is aware she's telling; it's deftly done and endlessly sweet. Set against the volatile backdrop of the small-town south of the 1970s, *Land of a Hundred Wonders* is by turns sensitive and rowdy, peopled with larger-than-life characters who are sure to make their own tender path into your heart."
—Joshilyn Jackson, author of *Gods in Alabama*
and *The Girl Who Stopped Swimming*

"Lesley Kagen has crafted a story that is poignant, compelling, hilarious, real, and absolutely lovely. Her characters are enchanting and will have you racing to the end of this terrific novel."
—Kris Radish, author of *Searching for Paradise in Parker, PA*

"A truly enjoyable read from cover to cover. . . . Miss Kagen's moving portrayal of a unique young woman finding her way in a time of change will touch your heart. And that, dear reader, is Quite Right indeed."   —Garth Stein, author of *The Art of Racing in the Rain*

"Lesley Kagen's lucid, confident prose shines on every page of *Land of a Hundred Wonders*, giving a unique and unforgettable voice to her moving and heartfelt story. The humor and passion of Gibby and her compatriots will stay with you long after you reach the end."   —Tasha Alexander, author of *A Fatal Waltz*

Written by today's freshest new talents and selected by New American Library, NAL Accent novels touch on subjects close to a woman's heart, from friendship to family to finding our place in the world. The Conversation Guides included in each book are intended to enrich the individual reading experience, as well as encourage us to explore these topics together—because books, and life, are meant for sharing.

Visit us online at www.penguin.com.

"With all the charm of *Cold Sassy Tree*'s Will Tweedy, Kagen has created an equally memorable, quirky character in Gibby McGraw. Gibby will make you laugh and touch your heart, proving that even someone who's Not Quite Right can still remedy the broken lives around her. For everyone who loved *Whistling in the Dark*, Lesley Kagen has worked her magic again in *Land of a Hundred Wonders*."
—Renee Rosen, author of *Every Crooked Pot*

More Praise for Lesley Kagen and
Whistling in the Dark
Chosen as a Hot Summer Read
by the *Chicago Tribune*

A Great Lakes Book Award Nominee

"Bittersweet and beautifully rendered, *Whistling in the Dark* is the story of two young sisters and a summer jam-packed with disillusionment and discovery. With the unrelenting optimism that only children could bring to such a situation, these girls triumph. So does Kagen. *Whistling in the Dark* shines. Don't miss it."
—Sara Gruen, *New York Times* bestselling author
of *Water for Elephants*

"[A] sophisticated charmer of a first novel. . . . What makes the novel appealing . . . is Kagen's literary style and her ability to see the world—and the truth—unfold gradually through the eyes of a ten-year-old. Sally's voice . . . is innocently wise and ultimately captivating. Sally and Troo are both finely wrought characters, achingly alive amid a few other splendid characters, such as a girl with Down syndrome."
—*Milwaukee Journal Sentinel*

"Every now and then, you come across a book with characters so endearing that you love them like family, and a plot so riveting that you can't read slowly enough to make the story last longer, no matter how hard you try. *Whistling in the Dark* is one such book. I absolutely loved this novel from the first page to the last!"
—Sandra Kring, author of *Carry Me Home*
and *The Book of Bright Ideas*

Also by Lesley Kagen

Whistling in the Dark

Land of a Hundred Wonders

LESLEY KAGEN

NAL
ACCENT

NAL Accent
Published by New American Library, a division of
Penguin Group (USA) Inc., 375 Hudson Street,
New York, New York 10014, USA
Penguin Group (Canada), 90 Eglinton Avenue East, Suite 700, Toronto,
Ontario M4P 2Y3, Canada (a division of Pearson Penguin Canada Inc.)
Penguin Books Ltd., 80 Strand, London WC2R 0RL, England
Penguin Ireland, 25 St. Stephen's Green, Dublin 2,
Ireland (a division of Penguin Books Ltd.)
Penguin Group (Australia), 250 Camberwell Road, Camberwell, Victoria 3124,
Australia (a division of Pearson Australia Group Pty. Ltd.)
Penguin Books India Pvt. Ltd., 11 Community Centre, Panchsheel Park,
New Delhi - 110 017, India
Penguin Group (NZ), 67 Apollo Drive, Rosedale, North Shore 0632,
New Zealand (a division of Pearson New Zealand Ltd.)
Penguin Books (South Africa) (Pty.) Ltd., 24 Sturdee Avenue,
Rosebank, Johannesburg 2196, South Africa

Penguin Books Ltd., Registered Offices:
80 Strand, London WC2R 0RL, England

First published by New American Library,
a division of Penguin Group (USA) Inc.

First Printing, August 2008
10 9 8 7 6 5 4 3 2 1

 REGISTERED TRADEMARK—MARCA REGISTRADA

LIBRARY OF CONGRESS CATALOGING-IN-PUBLICATION DATA:

Kagen, Lesley.
    Land of a hundred wonders/Lesley Kagen.
        p. cm.
    ISBN 978-0-451-22409-5
1. Women journalists—Fiction. 2. Women with disabilities—Fiction. 3. Kentucky—
Fiction. I. Title.
PS3611.A344L36 2008
813'.6—dc22   2008001062

Set in Janson text
Designed by Alissa Amell

Printed in the United States of America

PUBLISHER'S NOTE
This is a work of fiction. Names, characters, places, and incidents either are the product of the
author's imagination or are used fictitiously, and any resemblance to actual persons, living or
dead, business establishments, events, or locales is entirely coincidental.
    The publisher does not have any control over and does not assume any responsibility for
author or third-party Web sites or their content.

To my family

Acknowledgments

Heartfelt thanks to all *my* wonders:

Editor Ellen Edwards, who leaves no literary stone unturned, no matter what creepy thing may be hiding beneath. You are magnificent.

The amazing advertising, art, editorial, production, promotion, publicity, and sales teams at NAL and Penguin.

The inimitable Jeff Kleinman and the stellar crew of Folio Literary Management.

The readers, who have been nothing short of miraculous. Your lovely notes of encouragement have meant the world to me. Wish I could give each and every one of you a bag of dark chocolate–covered cherries.

The generous booksellers across the country who have made me feel welcome in so many ways.

English teachers and librarians, my earliest heroes.

Early readers and dear friends, the Flemings, Eileen Sherman, John and Marsha Bobek, Connie Kittelson, Hope Irwin, Susan Shimshak, Sharry Sullivan, Nancy Kennedy, Sara Schroeder, Eileen Kaufmann, and Robert Welker.

Restaurant Hama.

Mike Lebow, the wise guy.

Peter the Great, who makes me feel like I'm the honey on his toast.

And, of course, Casey and Riley, who make my world quite right with their every breath.

There are only two ways to live your life. One is as though nothing is a miracle. The other is as though everything is a miracle.

—Albert Einstein

Land of a

Hundred Wonders

A Deadline

Ya ever notice how some folks get well known for how they dress or hunt or even what kind of truck they drive? Along with my outstanding Scrabble playing, *I'm* well known for my newspaper.

Who: Me

What: Reporting

Where: Top O' the Mornin' Diner and Pumps. Cray Ridge, Kentucky, United States of America. Conveniently located at the corner of Main and Route 12.

When: Friday, August 13, 1973

Why: 'Cause if I don't get cracking, next week's front page is gonna have all the pizzazz of a piece of one-ply.

I put my favorite No. 2 back to work.

Welcome to Cray Ridge

You can set your watch by Miss Cheryl and Miss DeeDee showing up for biscuits and gravy every Sunday morning at

the diner. Miss Cheryl tells me she's a secretary. Her friend,
Miss DeeDee, has been experiencing some trouble with her vi-
sion, so they've been driving all the way from Paducah to visit
regular with Miss Lydia.

As you probably already know, an investigative reporter needs folks to write about. Late-breaking stories about trees, for instance, are few and far between. So when I'm not busy bussing tables, I'm allowed to interview subjects from all walks of life who later on become the *who what where when* and *why* of my stories. That's one of the things that's so rewarding about working here with Grampa at Top O' the Mornin'.

We're the last stop for refreshments before you hit Highway 75. You'll know the diner when you see it. Shaped like a shoe box, it's got tires washed white and lip-pink roses lining the entrance. Candy-cane awnings billow like crazy when the west wind kicks up. There's a counter inside with slick yellow stools, booths that sit four, and up at the cash register there's toothpicks—Take Two . . . They're Free! And since everybody knows what a tremendous part the good or the bad version of luck can play in your life, a rusty horseshoe all the way from Texas hangs lopsided above the screen door that creaks when you open it, but not when you close it. Just another one of life's little mysteries. (In case you haven't noticed . . . life is chock-full of 'em.)

This morning, like every morning, my grampa, who owns the place, is where he is most of the time when he isn't out on the lake. In the kitchen. Decked out in his white apron and cowboy fishing hat. He's wrassling up the breakfasts he learned to cook in that army mess, and damn, if there's anything that smells better on Earth than sizzling pork sausage, I wish somebody'd let me know. Oh, wait, I just remembered lily-of-the-valley smell . . . it's simply outta this world.

"Hey, Lois Lane, there's tables need your attention," Grampa yells, sticking his head through the kitchen peek window.

"Gimme a minute, Charlie," I call back. "Gotta get down a few more words 'fore this story flies outta my head."

Lois Lane is *not* my real name. Grampa's just making a joke due to his keen sense of humor. My real name is Gibson Mc-Graw, but most everybody calls me Gibby. I'm twenty, or maybe thirty-three years old. (I'll check with Grampa and get back to you on this.) I've been living with him permanent in Cray Ridge since the night three years ago, the kind of night anybody in their right mind stays home and is grateful to do so, me and mine were heading down here so I could start my usual summer stay. The rain was gushing down so bad it erased the highway line and our Buick sprouted wings more than a few times. And the sky wasn't the only one spittin' mad that night. The very last thing I can re-member my mama saying in her crossest of voices is, "We're not gonna outrun this storm . . . get off at the next exit and find us a motel . . . ya got talent at findin' motels, don'tcha, Joe? 'Specially the real cheap kind." Then my daddy bellowed back, "I'm warn-ing you, Addy . . . for the last time. . . ."

Little did he know how right he was. A wiper stroke later, we rounded a bend in the road and bounced off a stalled Champion bus, also from Chicago.

Thank the Lord for passing Dixie Oil trucker Mr. Hank Sim-mons, who found me wadded up on the edge of a creek and called for help on his 10-4 radio. I got three broken ribs, a gashed-up ankle, a cracked collarbone, and the *worst* of all—the left side of my head got dented. **Correction:** The *worst* of all was that I became an orphan that night. My mama and daddy made it out of that wagon, but not for long. (See earlier statement about luck. This would be a perfect example of the bad version.)

So that's it in a nutshell. All that I can remember, anyways, about the night I became what Grampa calls **NQR**, which is his pet name for **N**ot **Q**uite **R**ight, which means—brain-wise—I'm not doing so hot.

The Louisville Hospital sent him this letter dated July 10, 1970. I found it balled up in the glove department of his truck.

> *Dear Mr. Murphy,*
>
> *As a result of the brain injury she incurred in the auto accident, early indications are that your granddaughter is experiencing difficulties with word usage, reasoning skill, attention span and disinhibition. Currently, we're not certain if her memories are repressed as a result of the trauma or physiologically based. Only time will tell how much of the damage may be permanent or how much is*

The rest is ripped off in a jaggedy line. But what I think those hospital folks were *trying* to get at is:

Words and their meanings can elude me. **Elude: To avoid.** (I remembered that one last week when a catfish spent most of his morning *eluding* me, the little bugger.)

I'd never use the words "lightnin' speed" to describe my thinking.

Reverend Jack says my mind gets to wandering more than the Israelites.

I have an awfully hard time putting the brakes on my motoring mouth.

And my memory, well, it's sorta hit-and-run.

"The brain is mysterious," the hospital doctors told Grampa when he came to pick me up. "Current research indicates that keeping her mind *stimulated* may help regenerate the neurons and . . ."

"That right," Grampa said, blowing Lucky Strike smoke in their faces. (He also suggested the doctors do something I don't believe is humanly possible with their mysterious heads and their mysterious asses as he wheeled me out of that hospital so fast I swear, the wheelchair laid rubber.)

Now before you go off feeling sorry for me like most everybody else does, I want you to know that all is not lost. Though I'll confess to wavering at times, I haven't thrown in the trowel. Of course, I've been trying to better myself on a daily basis, but reaching this lofty goal wasn't of a vital nature 'til just recently. After Miss Lydia, my spiritual advisor, a woman of such astounding powers that she may chat whenever she wishes with those who have passed over to THE GREAT UNKNOWN, informed me of a horrible, heart-gutting situation. "Your mama's not resting in peace, your mama's soul is restless," she wailed over and over, her chest heaving.

Just in case you're not familiar with the goings-on of the dearly departed, what Mama's supposed to be doing is gazing down at her baby girl from on high, fluttering her wings in pride, her halo shooting off sparks of joy. She's *not* supposed to be pacing the stars, wringing her small but strong hands. Even though Miss Lydia tried to comfort me by telling me that it's not my fault, I don't believe her. That's exactly what she *would* say, her being the heart of Land of a Hundred Wonders. No, I'm positive Mama's restlessness is on account of me. Because I'm **NQR**.

So that's why #1 on my **VERY IMPORTANT THINGS TO DO** list is to prove that I *can* get **Q**uite **R**ight again. I figure I'm gonna have to set my hook into a heck of a plan in order to convince Mama. Ya know, something splashy. Like winning one of those public Scrabble tournaments they hold over in Appleville the first Sunday of every month. Or maybe reporting an awfully good story. It can't be something normal-like. It's gotta be something near miraculous in nature. Like me surviving the crash. Miss Lydia tells me all the time I'm a living, breathing miracle.

At the current time, I'm leaning toward that reporting of an awfully good story plan 'cause you're never gonna guess what I found on Browntown Beach this morning on my way to Land of a Hundred Wonders. Not the usual trout with what-the-hell-happened eyes. Not a soggy boot with gnaw marks neither. Or even a crushed-up can of Falls Beer. No. Could be I stumbled upon the kind of story that'll get lips flapping far and wide. I can perceive it all now. "I swear, the McGraw gal's better at reportin' these days than a twelve gauge," folks'll say, trumpeting my *Gazette* headline loud enough to be heard all the way up to the Pearly Gates. "Can you believe how much righter she's gotten?"

Lord. I believe I'll move that public Scrabble tournament plan to my back burner for the time being. Now that I've had a chance to think this through, this awfully good story plan appears to be the answer to my prayers! Yes, indeedy. *Start scouting for a nicely cushioned cloud to set your restless self, Mama. 'Cause that dead body? It's gonna be our ticket to* **Q**uite **R**ight *heaven.*

Black and White and Red All Over

Every Friday afternoon you can pick up a copy of *Gibby's Gazette* at Top O' the Mornin' and other important locations throughout Cray Ridge. Like Loretta's Candy World—Home of the Best Chocolate-Covered Cherries in the Universe and Beyond. Washateria keeps a stack near the detergent dispenser. And there's always a neat pile on the counter of Ye Olde Boo Store. (The *k* fell off a couple of years ago and Mr. Deacon, ye olde owner, isn't in any hurry to replace it. He gets a kick out of lecturing visitors that they'd be better off "quenchin' their thirst for knowledge" when they come sniffing around for bourbon and find nothing but good books instead.) In my humblest of opinions, the absolute finest of those knowledge quenchers is one called—**The Importance of Perception in Meticulous Investigation**. I used to be the editor of my high school newspaper, so I believe Grampa gifted me the book the day I got out of the hospital to keep my brain, like those doctors suggested, "stimulated."

Like always, we're busy at the diner, feeding the regulars and even the not so regulars. The fans are whirring overhead and the smell of frying eggs is strong when *Senor* Bender, a teacher of *Espanol* up at the high school, eases down onto his usual counter stool along with last week's copy of my *Gazette*. I can't waitress 'cause our customers get all kinds of irritable if I disremember and bring 'em home fries when they order grits, but along with wiping tables, I *am* permitted to get folks situated.

"How's the best-lookin' girl in Grant County this mornin'?" the *Senor* asks when I pass him the menu. (You can't tell just by looking at me that I'm **NQR**. The scar on the left side of my head is blanketed by the chili bean hair I got from my daddy and my celery-colored eyes are from Mama, so all in all, I believe I'm considered somewhat appetizing.)

"Why, I am just g-r-e-a-t," I say, showing off my outstanding service smile and superior spelling skills. "*Muchas gracias* for askin', you bastard."

"Gibson!" Grampa shouts outta the kitchen peek window.

Uh-oh. (The only time he calls me by my Christian name is when I've done something just the opposite.) "What?"

"*Home . . . home on the range . . . where the deer and the antelope play . . . ,*" Grampa begins singing so loud that I bet the folks in Mercer County are tapping the toes . . . "*where seldom is heard . . . a discouraging word . . .*"

Him doing that? That does NOT mean Grampa's a music lover. No. Sad to report, that singing is a secret code we got between us to let me know that I'm cursing and should quit ASAP. And it is too discouraging.

I bend down to explain to the *Senor* like I've been taught, "I was in a car crash that banged up my brain so now it's got a blue streak runs through it." Goodness, this man has real nice hair. Good and greasy. "Please accept my deepest of apologies. I'm workin' on it."

"Apology accepted, like always," he says after a sip of the coffee one cream I set down so carefully so as not to spill on the lovely shirt he's sporting. That paisley pattern's all the rage now. "So what's new in the world of investigative reportin', Gibby?"

"Lemme see," I say, trying to corral my thoughts. "Well, first off . . . I got an awfully hot lead, and second off . . . one of Miz Tanner's mares had a filly week before last. You're never gonna guess what she named it."

"*Que?*"

"Nooo." But I add on real fast, because I wasn't born in a barn, "But Kay is a solid guess and a real pretty name. Try again. Take your time."

The *Senor* short snorts, and says, "How about . . . ah . . . Gibby?"

"What?"

"No, I meant . . . did Miz Tanner name her new filly—*Gibby*?" he says. "After you?"

"How'd ya know that?" I ask, completely floored.

"Front-page news," he says, running his polished finger under the headline I musta wrote last week:

Filly Named Gibby! How Do You Like Them Apples?

Ya know, this is one of those moments it feels like no matter how good the plan, I'm not ever gonna get **Quite Right** again. Round and round and round I go. I swear, it's dizzying. If I could, if Grampa wasn't hawk watching me like he does, I'd run out the back door right this minute and hide in the crook of the pin oak, that's how weepy I'm feeling.

"Wait a minute now . . . go ahead and correct me if I'm wrong, but didn't ya just mention something about havin' an awfully hot lead?" the *Senor* asks.

Did I? I think I musta since he wouldn't make that up. The *Senor's* not that well known for lying. But what *was* my awfully hot lead? Bubby Heckler winning darts night at the Tap? No, no, that's old news. *Focus, Gib, focus.* It was . . . it was . . . that dead body. Yes! Lying on the beach near the jumping tree, the gnarled-up one kids yell "Geronimo" from before they tumble into the lake. But that body wasn't drowned. I've seen a drowned body before. No, the body I found this morning was not greenish like that other one, but it *was* puffy as hell 'cause it belonged to Mr. Buster Malloy, who is legendary large. And s'posed to be the next governor of the fine state of Kentucky.

Mr. Buster wasn't perspiring buckets like he usually did. He was cool to the touch on that toasty sand. Punctured something bad four times in the chest. His head dangling off his neck like a cherry twisted off its stem. Butterscotch candies tumbling out of his pocket, which was not unusual. He was well known for those candies. In fact, if Mr. Butter (that's what he was fond of calling himself) ever came upon you when you were just going about your business, he'd give a hearty laugh and say, "Lookee here, girl, look what Mr. Butter's got for ya. Sweets for the sweet that'll melt in your mouth." Never mind refusing him. He wouldn't leave you be until you stuck your hand in his deep pants pocket and rooted around. Another one of the things Mr. Buster was well known for—his thick ole eyeglasses—were smashed to smithereens next to his *corpus delecti*. According to Mr. Howard Redmond of New York City, New York, the author of **The Importance of Perception in Meticulous Investigation**—evidence is EXTREMELY important. Thank goodness, I also remembered to take pictures of that dead man.

So I got a body, and I got some photos, all's I need now for my awfully good story plan to work is to stay in focus. Plant the memory of finding Mr. Buster deep inside my brain so there's no chance of it gettin' blowed off like a dandelion wisp to parts unknown. (I'm sorry if this should occur from time to time. When it comes to my rememberings, I'm ashamed to say, it is apt to.) Once I get the chance to investigate that murder and publish the resulting story, I know that Mama will . . .

Wait just a cotton-pickin' minute.

Am I jumping to conclusions? Mr. Howard Redmond would be extremely disappointed in me if I was. In fact, in the chapter—**The Dangers of Jumping to Conclusions**—he warns specifically about doing just that. Maybe Mr. Buster wasn't murdered at all. Maybe it was nothing but . . .

"Gibby?" asks *Senor* Bender, tapping his cup for a topping off.

"Yeah?" I ask, pouring.

"That awfully hot lead you mentioned?"

"What about it?"

"Thought you might like to brag on it a bit," he says with a wink.

Well, for crissakes, everybody and their aunt Martha knows that you gotta keep a breaking story top secret. Poor, poor *Senor*. Looks like the only thing he's got going for him in his brain department is his real nice hair.

The Creek Don't Really Rise

Since we only serve breakfast at Top O' the Mornin', I flip over the GONE FISHIN' sign on the front door after the bells down the road get done clanging one time. There are two churches in Cray Ridge—Cumberland United Methodist and the one all the coloreds go to, First Ebenezer Baptist. Grampa is no longer a God-fearing man, but I walk on eggshells around the Ten Commandments. I cannot go to hell under any circumstances since I'm ascared of fire in a deathly way. To keep my bases covered, I attend the Methodist at least once a month, but get my daily dose of holy out at Land of a Hundred Wonders.

Our kitchen help, Miss Florida Smith, has already unknotted her apron and folded it square, because never mind that she's big as the state she's named after, she's neat beyond belief, and cleanliness is next to godliness in her book, which would be the Bible. Besides doing the diner's dishes, Miss Florida is also one terrific pie baker. If you think there can be something more soothing than the blueberry she does up this time of year, well, you'd be more'n dead wrong.

"See ya in the mornin', y'all. God willin' and the creek don't rise," she bellows out as she squeezes through the screen door.

(I know for a fact Miss Florida doesn't live close to Blossom Creek, but I'm not *ever* going to ask her why she always says that since the other thing this woman is well known for, besides her crusts, is a lack of patient explaining.)

"Stay dry," I shout after her, and then to Grampa in the kitchen, "I'm waitin' on you."

One of my other jobs is to pick up the eggs every afternoon over at Miss Jessie's farm. So after making sure the grill and the fryers are turned off, Grampa joins me in the booth across from the register and I watch while he scratches out the order on the back of a napkin. This is the same way it goes every afternoon when we close up shop, because my grampa, he's a big believer in routine. And keeping his nose to the grindstone. And a penny saved is a penny earned. (It's taken some hard studying, but I get the meaning of a lot of those kinds of sayings now. But there's *other* ones, like—don't throw the baby out with the bathwater—well, hell.)

"Check those eggs real carefully," Grampa tells me, sliding the order across the table. "Every once in a while Jessie likes to take advantage of me."

"Now you know that's not true." (I have recently begun to suspect that his memory, like mine, has sprung a couple of leaks. Proof: Whenever I ask him questions about the night of the crash, he answers, "Don't seem to recall.") "You know that Miss Jessie thinks you're a heartthrob with cowboy good looks."

"That right?" he says, lighting up a Lucky.

"I believe it is."

Sliding sideways and heading back toward the kitchen, he says over his shoulder, "That old woman might want to get her peepers looked into."

She certainly would. By you, Grampa, by you. Ya musta noticed Miss Jessie's gorgeous molasses eyes shuttered in shaggy lashes. She bats them enough at you. And she's not *that* old. Then again, him suggesting that Miss Jessie's nearing ancient might be an example of his keen sense of humor. He knows about a million and a half of those knock-knock jokes.

"Knock knock," he'll say.

And then I'm supposed to say back, "Who's there?"

"Little old lady."

And then I'm supposed to say back, "Little old lady who?"

With his mouth puckering up like one of those apple dolls the holler folks peddle to the tourists, he'll say, barely containing himself, "Why, I didn't know you could yodel!"

And then I'll say, "Me neither." That's right. I fall for it EVERY darn time since I don't usually get jokes anymore, which can be dismaying beyond belief since I've been told that once upon a time I was a girl with a lot of snap.

"How's next week's top story comin' along?" Grampa asks, pushing back through the kitchen swing doors with a bag brimming with what customers got too full to finish.

Pulling my black leather-like out from the cubby under the cash register, I follow him out the diner's back door. **The Importance of Perception in Meticulous Investigation** is small enough to carry along in my briefcase, which has everything I might need for a long day of reporting. After I break my awfully good story, when I'm **QR** again, and Mama's resting in eternal slumber, I'm planning to become a famous reporter in a city with a population larger than 2,723. I am intending to relocate to Cairo. (The one with the pyramids. Not the one west of here that rhymes with hay row.) I will tread where no other investigative reporter dares to tread. Rooting out tales in that desert sand. My camera and flashlight are also in my briefcase along with the other tools of my trade. My No. 2 pencils. My very important blue spiral notebook. And my pocket dictionary—in case I remember a word, but not its meaning.

Grampa heaves the garbage bag into the rickety Dumpster that sits out back. "I asked how you're progressin' on that story."

Miss Florida musta gotten picked up just a pinch ago 'cause the reclining chair under the pin oak is empty. I'm sitting down to stretch my sore legs straight when my dog scurries over, his tail ticktocking like mad. Miss Florida's been petting on him. He smells of Palmolive and pie.

"Gib?"

A few weeks after I got home from the hospital, Grampa and me were doing exactly what we're doing right this minute when we spotted this white wiry-haired pooch waiting on the back steps for us. He's bigger than a bread box, but not by a lot. With a chocolate-milk-colored stain spilling down his sides. Ears like one of Santa's helpers. Grampa said back then, "Well, what do we have here?" picked the pup up by the scruff, inspected for tags, and when he found none, said, "Ya need some responsibility, girl. This one's a Keeper."

"Gibby!?" Grampa shouts.

"Yeah?"

"The new story?"

I heard, I'm just stalling since I can't remember which one that is at the moment. My mind's too busy dwelling on dead Mr. Buster Malloy, the news of which I will keep locked behind my lips for the present time. I usually tell him what I'm up to, but this time, I don't want Grampa to know just yet. Hovering over me like he does, he'll try to warn me off in that no-nonsense voice of his. I know exactly what he'll say. "It's not safe gettin' tangled up in a murder investigation. Best you stick to reportin' about fishin' contests or birthed babies." He doesn't understand how crucial it is that I get **Q**uite **R**ight again. If he did, he wouldn't be telling me all the time that I shouldn't set my hopes too high. But believe you me, when I finally do break this murder story, not only will a certain someone's angelic wings bodaciously beat, but my grampa's brow will rise in pride as well. I don't know why, but I do know for certain that Grampa wouldn'ta spit on Mr. Buster Malloy if he was on fire. And Miss Lydia? Mr. Buster's sister? Grampa is not fond of her either. Fact is, he finds out I been spending most of my spare time with her up at Land of a Hundred Wonders—well, let's just say he won't be rushing off to buy me a sack of good times anytime soon.

"Focus yourself, Gib. Ya know the story I'm talkin' about. Miss Cheryl and Miss DeeDee? The two ladies that drive that red Corvair?"

Miss Cheryl and Miss DeeDee. Miss Cheryl and Miss DeeDee. "Oh, yeaaah." I took a swell picture of those gals sitting in front of the pumps. "I'm workin' on it."

"All right then," Grampa says, heading for the truck.

After I cozy up next to him on the bench seat, we wait until Keeper scrambles into the bed of the pickup, because second to raw eggs, he appears to enjoy fast air in his mouth. He also knows a couple of good tricks. And for some mysterious reason has got a white bandage running across the top of his head today.

"And awaaay we go," Grampa sings, turning up the radio and tossing gravel. He's always in a hurry like this when leaving the diner. Just like the sign on the door says, he's GONE FISHIN' every single day of his life, weather permitting. His daddy started him up when he was a boy in an Abilene river that ran clear and cold.

First things first. I can't bust my gut investigating the Mr. Buster story 'til I get this other one put to bed, else I'd have to listen to Grampa go on and on about the importance of finishing off what I started. I flip open my blue spiral notebook and get back to writing.

Since Miss DeeDee is going blind with cadillacs, I believe Miss Cheryl only lets her drive on the back roads.

Sneaky

Half the time my guts are up around my jaw and my bottom around my ankles when Grampa speeds around in this battered truck of his. Chrome hair smoothed back by the breeze. One hand jaunty on the wheel. "Ya got the egg order?" he asks, coming to a stop at the bottom of Miz Jessie Tanner's drive-up.

I slide the napkin out of my pedal-pusher pocket and read out loud, "Six doz." If he'd let me, I'd do nothing all day long but investigate and write my stories or ride through the woods stuffing my mouth with wild berries as I go, but Grampa says chores build character.

"Try to get Jessie to give you a coupla of those brown ones that ole Henrietta squeezes out, all right?" he says, hooking my bangs behind my ear.

"Knock on wood," I say, giving his fake leg that got stabbed in the war with a dirty bayonet a good whack. The army had to saw it off way back when so now he's gotta strap this one on every morning. Don't feel bad for him. The leg's got an attached black tie shoe and a sock with gray diamonds that he never has to wash, which I'd call a pretty good deal.

"Time's a wastin', Gib," Grampa says, anxious to get out on the water.

Snappin' shut my leather-like, I get out and wait for Keeper to join me. I don't go hardly anywhere without my dog.

Grampa shouts out the truck window as he takes off toward the cottage, "See ya at supper."

"Not if I see you later, you big baboon," I shout back.

As you can probably tell, I'm already busy working on improving my joking ability. (*All part of the getting **Quite Right** plan, Mama.*)

Tanner Farm is one of the spots in life that make it hard for me to see and breathe at the same time, it's that gorgeous. Once you get past the plumpy woods that run along the drive, the sky opens up to reveal paddock after paddock full of Thoroughbred horses chewing on the finest of bluegrass. That's what we call it in Kentucky for some unknown reason. But make no mistake, this grass is dollar green.

Halfway up the drive, I shout out, "Keeper?" 'cause he's taken off into the woods, probably sniffing for a spot to answer his call to duty, which he takes awfully to heart. "Finish up now, please. Miss Jessie is waitin' on us and we have bunches to do today."

"Hey," Billy calls, his voice wafting out of the treetops.

"Hey, you," I holler back.

You ever paged through one of those puzzles they put in the *Highlights for Children* magazine? They have them in all the doctors' offices. The artists of that magazine conceal foreign objects in a picture, like a candle in a curtain or a key snuggled up in a sofa cushion, and you're supposed to find it. You know it's there, but where oh where? Well, ditto with William "Billy" Brown, Junior, previously well known as "Little Billy." (After he got back home from the war, Billy wouldn't answer to that name anymore, but that's what he used to be called on account of his daddy being called Big Bill Brown.)

I don't remember a lot of details about Billy from before the crash 'cept that we used to run with the same crowd and when the stars came out we'd tell stories around a crackling fire. But one of the things Grampa has told me about Billy is that he used to possess his father's **Arrogance: Overbearing pride.** "The war has taught that boy, like it's taught many before him, that life is a delicate web, Gib. A thread is what we all hang by. That can be humblin'. And scary as hell."

I set my briefcase down so I got my hands free to retrieve the present Billy's left for me today. When he doesn't take his tranquilizing medicine like he should, he can't go into town. Billy says the pills make him feel numb and tired. Dry his lips out, too. But on the days he's able to swallow those pills down, he runs, and I mean leg-pumpin' *runs*, into Cray Ridge to buy me a little something and remains nearly calm. Sometimes I'll find a sack of chocolate-covered cherries lying in the scooped-out bottom of our secret stump. (My absolute favorites!) Other times, he'll leave me a story that has a snoopy reporter for the main character. Or a shiny ring, he's real fond of those. Once Billy left me a jar full of rice.

"Ya find it?" he asks, somewhere closer now.

"Got it." I bend down and draw a heart-shaped locket out of the stump, the sun making it glitter so. "Goodness! It's absolutely the prettiest . . . ," I start to say, but the sound of rustling and someone relieving himself in the trees shuts me up quick. It's not Billy I'm talking about here. Keeper neither. No. The both of them are much too mannerly to tinkle in the vicinity of a lady. I'll tell you who it is that's unzipped himself not ten feet away from me. It's the devil's right-hand man and the absolute scourge of me—Sneaky Tim Ray Holloway. (He tinkles a lot 'cause he drinks a lot. And is just about always waitin' on me.)

Hope he didn't hear me.

"Talkin' to yerself again, darlin'?" Holloway asks, clawing outta the thicket.

Shoot.

Just by the look of him you'd never guess that Sneaky Tim Ray's strong as hell. He's some years older than me with those kinda eyelids that can fool you into thinking he's taking a catnap when he's doing nothing of the sort. And then there's that glass eyeball that he'll tell ya he picked up in a bar fight, which if you ask me is not sanitary at all. But when he grins at me, like he's doing right this minute, it's with teeth that are curiously even and gloriously white. All in all, Miss Jessie herself has confessed to me that even though he is her cousin by marriage and has those real nice choppers, "The boy looks like he was rode hard and put away wet."

"Whatcha got there?" Holloway gives growling Keep the boot and grabs for my new locket, first one way, then the other. "You is standin' on my property so tha's mine, what ya found is mine. Give it to me."

"I will not," I say quite firmly, despite feeling quite shaky. The hooch smell coming off him is making my stomach flip. "And it isn't your property neither. It's Miz Tanner's. If you don't quit this sort of fibbin', ya do realize you'll be headin' to hell in a hand casket, correct?"

Holloway doesn't answer right off, too busy cleaning out his ear with his vibrating pinky finger. "Ya know, maybe you's right, darlin'," he finally says, swiping what he's mined through his slicked-back hair. "Maybe I *could* use some repentin'."

"Hallelujah," I say, because, boy oh boy, he really *could*. Not only is he a liar and a thief, he rubs on my chest when I'm up at the barn helping muck out the stalls in exchange for riding Peaches. He's warned me time and time again not to tell a soul. And I haven't. Not my best friend, Clever. Or even Miss Jessie. And especially not Grampa, who keeps me on a short enough lead line as it is. If he ever found out about Sneaky Tim Ray, well, he's still got one of his old Circle Bar B branding irons that he wouldn't at all mind putting to use on somebody's hide. And I can't let that happen. Sneaky Tim Ray has made it clear that if I tell on him, my Keeper might get run over by a tractor "accidentally on purpose." Or trampled by a horse. Maybe rat poisoned. "Let me put it to ya in a way that any idiot could understand," he's threatened over and over. "Lessin' ya wanna find that mutt on your back porch one mornin' stiffer than my pecker, ya better keep them luscious lips shut."

Giggling, Sneaky Tim Ray bows his head to commence his repentin'. "Dear Heavenly Father, please forgive me. I know I ain't been the best of your flock and I promise ya that—"

"Amen," I say, shoving my new locket deep into my pocket. "Well, best be on my way."

"Hol' up there a minute," he says, getting ahold of my shoulder and spinning me rough. "As ya jus' lay witness to, I've . . . wha's that, Lord?" He cups his ear heavenward. "Uh-huh . . . uh-huh . . . sure enuf." He takes my hands into his, real gently, like we're about to do the box step. "Ya know what He jus' tol' me, darlin'?"

I'm simply awful at guessing games so I can't come up with one thing the Almighty would have to say to this black sheep on the loveliest of days. The air's hanging heavy with the smell of cut hay and the aspen leaves are spinning. It's a cicada year. "I give up. What'd the Lord tell ya?"

"He told me to remind ya that it's your Christian duty to share these real nice titties with your brothers."

"The Lord knows damn well I'm an orphan and don't have any brothers," I say, batting off his fingers that've begun tiptoeing over the swell of my double D ninnies. "You're lyin' again."

"Why ya always got to be like this?" Sneaky Tim Ray whines. "A retard like you . . . who else is gonna wantcha? Ya should feel flattered I hanker for ya like I do."

The treetops are trembling.

"Let go of me. I ain't got time for this now," I yell, pretzling in his grip. "I gotta get those eggs for Grampa and ride and . . ."

"Maybe you's not the only one wantin' to go for a ride," he says, thick in the throat. And then real fast, for he is quick as only a small man can be, Sneaky Tim Ray shoves me to the ground and paws at my white blouse.

Don't worry. I'm not afraid. I know *exactly* what's about to happen.

A Friend Indeed

Billy comes rushing out of the trees in his camouflage outfit, his arms spinning like egg beaters and *wham!* Sneaky Tim Ray Holloway has been outsnuck. Billy is not only an expert at concealment, he's got some fancy Oriental moves he got taught in the army that can whip an enemy up but good. I've asked him recently to hold off on rescuing me until there is bodily contact in situations like these because **Q**uite **R**ight people know how to take care of themselves.

Getting up and brushing myself off, I tell him, "That was excellent timin'. Much obliged."

"My pleasure," Billy says, kicking Sneaky Tim Ray in the leg with his steel-toed boot 'cause it always takes some time for his stormy temper to wane. I don't believe he was quite so thunderous in nature before he attended the war. He was just as tall, though. I gotta crane my neck to get a good look at him 'cause I am not over six feet by three inches. I'm a lot shorter. And a little younger. He's twenty-three. (I did check with Grampa, by the way. I am not thirty-three years old. I'm twenty, but not for long. Got a birthday comin'.)

"Why didn't ya use that neck-choppin' move I taught ya?" Billy asks.

"I forgot." I pull down my blouse where Sneaky Tim Ray matted it up. "Next time I'll give him the neck-choppin' move, I promise."

He's so easy on the eyes, Billy boy is. Reminds me a lot of my absolutely favorite movie star of all time, Mr. Paul Newman, who, if you recall, played Butch in the movie *Butch Cassidy and the Sundance Kid*. That movie is a passion of mine. Clever's, too. (Even though she's my best friend, she goes more for Mr. Robert Redford; he's the blond one of 'em.) Billy's face is handsome and he's got brunette hair like Mr. Newman's, but he isn't anywhere near as calm under fire. No. Billy gets worked up enough, his words'll come out stuttery as a machine gun. And the slightest noise like a twig cracking underfoot can sound like cannons going off to his ears. He didn't used to be this easily riled. He used to be a cool-under-fire star quarterback. WILLIAM "LITTLE BILLY" BROWN, JR. shines bright on those football plaques that hang in the hallways up at Grant County High School. Come every fall, I write an article in the *Gazette* to remind everyone in Cray Ridge how proud we should be of our Billy.

"Got a little something for you, too," I say, removing the paper out of my briefcase. "This story's got your daddy in it. See?"

Billy won't look. His eyes are too busy searching the sky, the trees.

So I read to him, "Another winner for Big Bill Brown and High Hopes Farm."

"I heard about that race already."

"You did? Dried apple damn!" I do not care at all to be what is called by Mr. Howard Redmond of New York City, New York—scooped.

"I was up to the farm for most of the week," Billy says. "They got in some new colts and needed the help."

"You were up to the farm? Good job!" Since Billy's mama died birthing him and his daddy is ashamed that he came back from Vietnam with this nervousness sickness, it's a hard rope for Billy to tow being at High Hopes, which is one of the best racing stables in all of Kentucky. "Would you like a star?"

"Wouldn't mind a green one if you got it." He's got a row of 'em already stuck on his shirt pocket, next to that nice silver one the army gave him. I got this idea from my physical therapist at the hospital. Whenever I see somebody doing a good deed, I reward them with a star. Even though Grampa says goodness is its own reward, *I* say it never hurts to have something shiny. Yesterday, to the best of my recollection, I gave out two of them. One to Miss Florida for giving me an extra slice of blueberry pie and another to Miss Ruth at the library for recommending that *Jokes-A-Million* book.

"Ya workin' on any new stories?" Billy asks, stroking Keeper. Besides his couple of good tricks, my dog is well known for his spirit-lifting abilities.

"Nope," I say, wishing Billy'd look at me face-on. Those stormy sky eyes of his are really something to behold. "Nuthin' new to report."

"Did ya get a chance to look at what I left you in the stump?" he asks.

I dig down in my pocket and pull out the locket, let it twirl off my fingers.

"Go ahead and open it," he insists.

I do try, but sometimes my fingers on that left side of my body can still get shaky. Noticing I'm having a hard time, Billy lifts the gold chain off my fingers. "See?" he says, shy, showing me what's inside.

There's a picture of me on a palomino horse that I think used to be my favorite when I could still feel the cantering wind in my hair. It was taken back when I didn't live permanent with Grampa. Can't recall the horse's name. But golly, my dimples are deep. Another picture, one of Billy atop a tar black horse, sits on the other side of the locket. He's smiling, too, so that shot musta also been taken before he had to keep his eyes peeled every minute for pits full of steaks.

"Remind ya of anything?" he asks.

"Wish it did." I gather the hair up off my neck so he can fasten the necklace with the tips of his fingers. Billy doesn't go in much for skin touching. "Ya wanna come say hey to Miz Tanner?" I ask, because he really does need to spend more time with folks who are not me and Keeper and Grampa.

"Not today. Maybe tomorra," he says, sorta wistful, looking at the pictures one more time before he snaps the locket shut. "You, ah . . . feelin' all right about what happened?"

I glance over at sprawled-out and slobbering Sneaky Tim Ray. "Well, I'd rather he didn't jump out at me every single time I—"

"No . . . no. Not what *just* happened. I mean, about the other night." Billy points to the top of my legs.

I woke up yesterday with bruises on my thighs. Budding lilac now. "Oh, goodness. I've been wonderin' about those. How did I get them?"

"Ya don't recall?"

"No, I . . . wait a minute. Clever and me were up to the Outdoor a coupla nights ago. Could I have fallen or somethin'?" Movie watching is our favorite hobby. Shoot-'em-ups most of all. That giant sheet out there turns into something completely different in the summer, in the dark. Us two girls just about pass out with utter adoration gazing at those stars on the screen and God's up above.

"Yeah, that's right," Billy agrees real fast. "Ya musta fell. Ya know how uneven that ground is up at the Outdoor."

To quote Mr. Howard Redmond of New York City, New York: *An operative must pay special attention to the eyes of a subject during an interrogation. If they are darting, this is a sign of lying.* Billy's eyes look like leaves getting chased by a rake. What's this boy trying to hide?

Stretching his long self even longer, he says, "I got traps to tend to. See ya later."

"Not if I see you first, little old lady who," I yell out to his broad back that blends quick into the bushes that his laugh does not come back out of. Because Billy doesn't get jokes anymore neither. And since *his* sense of humor got lost way over on the other side of the world, there is little chance of him recovering it. Poor, poor Billy Brown.

Well, I suppose it's my Christian duty to check on Sneaky Tim Ray to make sure he's still breathing. Reaching into my leather-like for my compact mirror, I hold it under his nose until it clouds up, a trick mentioned in the pages of **The Importance of Perception in Meticulous Investigation**. He's fine. Well, maybe not fine, but he *is* still breathing. I turn to head back to the drive, but then, I swear, I don't know what crashes down on top of me at times like a wave. This overwhelming desire to commit such wickedness. I'm helpless to restrain myself. I'm **NQR**, you know.

I command, "Piddle," and Keeper readily obliges by lifting his back leg, smiling toothily at the steady stream spewing onto Sneaky Tim Ray's grimy ankle.

(Already mentioned to you that this dog knows a couple of good tricks, didn't I?)

Making Hay While the Sun Shines

Miz Tanner is sitting on the porch steps of her yellow farmhouse with Keeper, who scooted on ahead. She's distracting him with half a sandwich so she can check under his white bandage. I wonder why Billy didn't mention that bandage. Being of a medical nature, that'd be something that'd usually pique his interest. Guess beating on Sneaky Tim Ray piqued his interest more, which is exactly what is expected of him. It was my grampa who assigned Billy to guardian angel me.

"Hey, Miss Jessie," I shout, skipping up the last part of the drive, 'cause I always feel tail-waggin' happy upon seeing her.

"Where you been?" she yells back. "Your grampa just called. Said he dropped you off twenty minutes ago."

(He keeps a stopwatch on me 'cause I get lost. A lot.)

"I ran into Billy," I say, coming up and crouching down on the step below her. Miss Jessie's husband got thrown from a horse some years back and died on the spot, so just her and Sneaky Tim Ray live on the farm now. I'm not gonna tell her about this cousin of hers jumping me in the woods a little bit ago. No. That'd be purely foolish. Nuthin' bad can happen to my dog.

Miss Jessie sets the bandage back down on Keeper's head. Tamps the edges with her short-cut nails. "The stitches look nice and clean. Should heal up fine."

I remember now when Keeper got that cut. It was the night

when I came home late from Hundred Wonders, mussed up with mud and my dog in my arms. When Grampa yelled, "What happened?" all I could do was shrug, and say, "Miss Lydia doctored him," because I couldn't recall exactly *how* Keep's head got split open. Still don't.

Noticing my new locket that feels so cool and smooth between my fingers, Miss Jessie asks, "What do ya have there?" Her eyes widen when she sees what's inside. "I remember the day those pictures were taken. He's a good man, Billy Brown is."

Gee, I never thought of him that way. As a man. But he is now, I guess. He smells that certain way men do. A little gamey, I'd call it. And even if he takes time down at the creek in the morning to shave with his straight edge, by the afternoon his beard can get all prickery looking. Since he spends so much time cutting wood and hunting, he's also got muscles in his arms and back that look hard, but slick to the touch.

"Billy'd make some girl a fine husband, don'tcha think?" she says, giving me a mysterious smile. "Ya gonna ride today?"

I don't answer right off because I'm still wondering what that smile is all about, but to be quite frank with you, I get so tired asking people what this thing means or that, it really does wear me to the bone some days.

"Peaches?" Miss Jessie asks.

"No, thank you, ma'am. I had a helluva breakfast."

She strokes my hair and I do the same back to her curls, white as a wedding. "Hon, I meant . . . are you gonna *ride* Peaches today?"

"A course I'm ridin' Peaches today. But would you mind if we look at the filly first?"

"I already collected your eggs for ya, includin' a few from

Henrietta, so I don't see why not." Miss Jessie points behind her to a brimming wire basket, which I am mighty grateful to see and tell her so. (Just in case you're not familiar, chicken coops smell the exact opposite of how eggs taste.)

Leaving Keeper to his sun nap, I follow behind Miss Jessie's lean-as-a-pole-bean self toward the barn. "How's your grampa been?" she asks, all **Nonchalant: Unexcited.**

But she can't fool this investigative reporter. She's chalant as hell. Who wouldn't be? Grampa's got eyes the color of whiskey. Has all his own teeth, too. And he really does return Miss Jessie's affections. Maybe not quite as much as she sends out, because he thinks he's got to use up most of his love supply taking care of me, but I can tell he's got genuine feelings for her.

"Grampa's been fine," I tell her, giving the outside of the barn an admiring once-over. "Heavens to Betsy . . . what a terrific job the boys did!"

Vern and Teddy Smith, who are Miss Jessie's help, and younger brothers to dishwashing–pie baking Miss Florida from the diner, spent all last week painting the barn stop sign red, and I'm not sure, but I believe this is the first time I've seen it done.

"Where are the two of 'em anyway?" I pop open the clasp on my leather-like. "They deserve gold stars."

"Gave 'em the afternoon off," Miss Jessie says as we step inside the barn. "Florida needed some roof tarrin' done."

"Well, when ya see 'em next, could ya tell 'em—" I cut off, since there's nothing in this world, next to the smell of sizzling pork sausage and lilies-of-the-valley, that enters your nose as sweetly as a clean horse barn. Alfalfa hay and curly shavings and soaped leather mixing in with the perfume Miss Jessie calls oh de horse manure. Her breeding operation is a small one, but she does all right since she's got a nice stud named Handsome, who sired a Derby runner. She's also got a few retired racehorses she keeps for trail riding. Mostly nobody around here would keep a horse that doesn't earn its keep, but Miss Jessie, she's the kind type. Like allowing that vermin Sneaky Tim Ray to live with her. (I'm certain she doesn't realize that he's only laying low here at the farm until the trouble he instigated in Leesburg blows over. Even though he brags on it to me every chance he gets, I'm not gonna tell Miss Jessie that her cousin by marriage hoodwinked "some old bat" out of her cookie jar savings. Or that he is absolutely NOT staying here at the farm so he can help out around the place like he told her he would. It is a sad, horrible thing to be **Disillusioned: The condition of being disenchanted**.)

The barn's got twenty stalls lined up ten across ten. A tack room full of bridles and saddles and trunks full of medicine and traveling bandages. Washing sinks and hoses for watering. And a feed room with sacks of grain. Upstairs, there's a hayloft full of mice. That's where Sneaky Tim Ray sleeps and hides his hooch. Just to be safe, I close up my precious briefcase and slide it under the bushes outside the barn. In case Holloway comes to and wanders up here, don't want my leather-like getting disappeared by a certain someone who'd steal the gold outta your teeth if you fell asleep with your mouth open.

"She's down here," Miss Jessie reminds, 'cause she thinks I'll've forgotten the whereabouts of the filly, and she's right.

Snug in their stalls and busy picking at their afternoon hay, the horses *nicker nicker*, begging for something sweet when we walk by. Down on the far side of the aisle, backed against the birthing stall, are the old mare, Whinny, and her new foal, Gibby, named after me, that I got to see getting born. You know who helped deliver this baby? Billy. He's going to be a Vietnam veterinarian as soon as he gets over his nervousness sickness.

"Did you hear a rumor down at the diner this mornin' about Buster Malloy goin' missin'?" Miss Jessie asks, sliding open the stall door.

"Mr. Malloy has gone missin'? Really? How come nobody told me?" I ask, shocked. He's an important man around here. His disappearance would make a whopper of a headline in next Friday's paper. "Maybe I better not ride today. Maybe I should head over to the Malloy farm instead and have a look around for some clues. Mr. Howard Redmond of New York City says clues are real important to solvin' any mystery and that would include a missin' person, I believe."

Stopping her fussing with the filly, Miss Jessie says, "I don't think that's such a good idea, Gib. Ya better leave that sort of serious detectin' up to Sheriff Johnson. Pretty sure your grampa wouldn't want ya to get mixed up in something like that."

"All right," I answer, but I think I must be lying, which I am trying to do on a daily basis, since it's another good step in the right direction. **Q**uite **R**ight people lie. All over the place.

Done wrestling the halter on, Miss Jessie stands back and admires the baby, whose blaze is shaped like a question mark that makes her face seem curious. "She's a looker if I do say so myself."

"Will she race, ya think?"

"Sure hope so. Handsome is her sire and—" But then the barn phone starts ringing, and Miss Jessie says on her dash outta the stall, "Be right back. You keep pettin' on her. She's gotta get used to being handled."

"Okey-dokey," I say, going toward the filly on soft feet. I want to lay my cheek against her toasty neck 'cause these foals always smell delicious, but she shakes me off like a fly and darts under her mother for comfort, and her doing that, that makes the saddest feeling sweep over me. I work real hard at not allowing myself to miss my mama much, but sometimes the deep yearning for her seeps outta my heart and pools into a spot I've found is best not dove into.

"Well, this is gettin' more interestin' by the second," Miss Jessie says, bustling back down the aisle with a saddle and bridle that she sets down on the rack outside Peaches's stall. "Seems it's not a rumor anymore. Nobody's seen Buster for a coupla days. What's wrong?"

"Hay in my eye, is all," I say, sliding the birthing stall door closed behind me. I don't want her to tell Grampa I was crying. He wouldn't approve. "How'd ya find that out? About Mr. Buster bein' gone for sure?"

"That was Sheriff Johnson on the phone. Pull her out of the stall, Gib."

After getting Peaches hooked up in the aisle, Miss Jessie eases the saddle down on her scruffy gray back. I am hoping to ride horses again, but since the crash, I've had some balancing problems. This donkey is closer to the ground, if you get my drift.

"The sheriff's been up to the Malloy place and talked to his help," Miss Jessie says, fastening the girth tight.

"If Mr. Malloy has been missing for a coupla days, I think the help shoulda called down to the sheriff's station earlier. Would that be appropriate thinkin'?" (Reverend Jack, down at the Methodist church? He's *always* trying to get me to think "appropriately.")

"That certainly would be appropriate thinkin'," Miss Jessie replies in a complimentary way. "The field boss told the sheriff that Buster mentioned somethin' about going to a government get-together and he assumed that's where Buster's been. But whoever it was that he was supposed to be meetin' up with called the sheriff station this morning reportin' that he never showed up."

"Oh, my, my. The field boss assuming like that? That is such a big mistake to make." **The Importance of Perception in Meticulous Investigation** says that assuming anything is just about the worse thing anybody can do. You should never assume anything until you have the facts. "Are you by any chance having hot sex with Sheriff Johnson?"

"Lord."

I asked her that because when Miss Jessie and Grampa go out to dinner at Gil's Supper Club, and she's gussied up in that vanilla dress of hers that is cut on the low side up top, and the high side down below, well, I strongly suspect Grampa wouldn't mind spooning her up for dessert. But if my understanding is correct, hot sex is a one-per-customer deal, and if she's already having it with the sheriff, that would leave Grampa SOL. (Shit outta love.)

"No, I am not having hot sex or any *other* kind of sex with the sheriff," Miss Jessie snips as she fastens the last strap on the bridle. "And I better not see *that* tidbit in next week's *Gazette*."

"Fine, but ya best be careful," I warn. "He looks at you with a lot of lust, ya know."

"Oh he does, does he?" she says, still snotty sounding.

"Yes, he does. In fact, I bet LeRoy wouldn't mind one bit gobblin' you up whole," I say, swinging myself into the saddle. "Just like he does one a Miss Florida's pies."

Miss Jessie rests her hand on my knee, a mushy look coming into her eyes. "You and I both know that I already have feelin's for somebody, and that somebody is *not* Sheriff Johnson."

"I perceive that you are hot for Grampa," I say, gathering up my reins.

She gives Peaches a sharper than normal slap on the rump and says, "Well, *I* perceive this conversation has just drawn to a close. Git."

"Sometimes he calls out your name in his sleep," I say, steering out of the coolness of the barn into the muggy heat.

Miss Jessie chases me down. "What'd ya just say?"

"I said you are hot for Grampa."

"No, after that. Something about your grandfather callin' out my name in his sleep?"

I don't recall saying anything of the sort. "Are ya feelin' all right, Miss Jessie? As you well know, I have been trained in basic Red Cross. Maybe you're havin' a heatstroke. Are ya seein' stars? Do ya . . . well, speak of the devil." I point over her shoulder at the Grant County Sheriff car that's speeding up her drive. (Considering our previous conversation, him showing up like this doesn't look too good for her. Makes her look **Culpable: Blameworthy**, don'tcha think?)

"What in tarnation does he want?" Miss Jessie says, flushing flamingo.

"He wants to gobble you up—"

"Hush," she says out of the corner of her mouth as the car comes sliding to a stop next to the barn.

Watching the sheriff walk our way, I think about how he's always reminded me of a past-prime peach. With fuzzy orange hair on top and all over his arms, and while not exactly fat, he *is* real mushy around the middle. "Afternoon, Miss Jessie," he says to her with so much lust in his eyes it's practically squirting out. "Miss Gibby."

I say, "Good afternoon," but what I *want* to say is—it was until you showed up anyway, you rancid bully—and am real proud of my restraint.

"Like they say, two heads are better'n one. Got time to sort out Buster's disappearance with me, Jess?" he asks, offerin' his arm.

"Pardon me, Sheriff," I butt in, because Almighty God, the memory of finding that dead body this morning has just floated back into my mind! "Would ya know if Mr. Buster Malloy was well known for his swimmin' ability?" I will need this information for my awfully good story, because even though Mr. Buster wasn't drowned, but punctured in the chest and messed up in the neck, it would be an interesting background fact. I wish I had my blue spiral with me. I should be getting this down.

The sheriff, putting up a nice front for Miss Jessie, says to me in the dearest of voices, "And for what purpose would you be wantin' to know that information?"

"For the article I will be writin' about him once he turns up dead, ya big asshole."

"Gib!" Miss Jessie shouts, givin' me the cut-throat sign. (That's *her* secret code to warn me I'm cursing.)

The sheriff is waitin' on me to, but I won't give him my deepest of apologies, I won't.

"Well, now," he says, removing his mirrored sunglasses. "Guess ya got ahold of some bad information, Miss Gibby. Mr. Malloy is not dead. He's missin', is all."

I coulda corrected him, even mentioned that I got pictures of that dead man sitting in the camera that's inside my briefcase that's under those bushes in front of the barn, but I don't. Because at last summer's Cray Ridge Days, where there were running contests and buffet food, I overheard the sheriff remark to his deputy, "That McGraw girl's gotta be dumber than anthracite coal."

"Stay on the path," Miss Jessie calls to me as she and the sheriff head toward a shaded picnic table and a pitcher of sweet tea. I guess to put their two heads together and I hope that's all. "Like always, Gib, turn back when I ring the come-and-get-it bell."

"Turn back when I hear the bell. Got it," I say, heeling Peaches in the ribs.

Now, even though I am 100% lovable with mostly Christian thoughts, as I enter the backwoods, I'm gonna have to confess to thinking: Mr. Buster Malloy is too dead. And when I solve that murder and publish that story, by next week Friday, everybody in town will be reading the front page of *Gibby's Gazette*, their admiration piercing through the clouds and landing square in my mama's heart. We'll see then who is dumber than anthracite coal, Sheriff LeRoy Johnson. We'll just see about that. Ya big asshole.

Mr. Charles Michael Murphy

t's not until after I come in the cottage back door and set the egg basket down on our kitchen table that I realize that me and Keeper have come home without my black leather-like briefcase. I left it in the bushes back at Tanner Farm. "Doggone it," I shout, indecent mad at myself for forgetting.

"Where you been?" Grampa calls in a persnickety voice from the screened-in porch. He can get like that when he wakes up from a nap. "I just got off the phone with Jessie. She said you left more'n an hour ago."

"I . . . I . . ." I remember the lousy look Sheriff Johnson gave me when Miss Jessie went to retrieve my egg basket for me. I also recall Keeper yapping at snoring Sneaky Tim Ray when we snuck around him in the woods. But then . . . oh my goodness.

I will not tell Grampa. He'll only get red in the tips of his ears.

Like I mentioned earlier, I usually don't keep secrets from him, but in one of the chapters of **The Importance of Perception in Meticulous Investigation**, Howard Redmond states quite firmly that oftentimes, in the midst of an ongoing investigation, one must endeavor to conceal certain facts, so one might have to **Prevaricate: Stray from the truth.** Even from our loved ones if necessary. (For their own protection, you understand.)

"I went over to Miss Lydia's," I lie, stepping out to the porch.

Grampa's perched on the edge of the flowered wicker sofa. Rumpled up. "Please don't get mad."

Well, for godssakes, this is so UTTERLY discouraging. Why didn't I tell him I stopped by to see Reverend Jack at the Methodist church? Or bed-ridden-with-lumbago Nellie Wilson? Ya know, someone who'd make me look all saintly. Not someone like Miss Lydia, who's got squirrel skulls hanging off her trees that clang together when a storm's coming and make a much better sound than you can ever imagine. Not someone who Grampa despises.

Straightening up, Grampa shoves out through the screened door, letting it slam hard behind him. "I told ya time and time again to stay away from Lydia," he shouts back at me. "*And* Hundred Wonders."

Wish I could admit what I really did was go back to check on Mr. Buster Malloy's dead body on Browntown Beach. (The flies have gotten to him some.)

Not wanting to, because when he gets tempered like this, being around him's 'bout as much fun as batting a hornets' nest, I follow him out to our matching wood chairs on the lawn. I keep a stack of flat rocks under mine to use on perfecting my skimming skills. The lake's green and smooth as a chalkboard. Baby waves making their way through the cattails, always a fine place to catch pollywogs. And the cicadas are calling to one another from the woods, sounding as desperate as I'm feeling. "Those goddamn fish bitin' today?" I ask him.

"You're wanderin' off the subject *and* you're cursin'," he says, yanking his knife out from the leather sheaf that hangs from the tulip tree. Being a well-known whittler, Grampa was once asked by a museum in New York City to bring his figures up there for a show of folks art. I was about crushed flat when he told them, "I'd rather be skinned alive and pulled behind a buck-board of runaway horses." I'd been hoping to have lunch with Mr. Howard Redmond. I had a few questions for him about: **Surveillance**.

"Why don'tcha want me to spend time with Miss Lydia?" I ask, cocking my wrist and letting loose with a skimmer. "She was Mama's best friend."

"How many times we gotta go over this?" Grampa says, slic-ing hard on the donkey figure he's promised me for my birthday.

"Can we go visit Daddy's grave one of these days?" He's not buried alongside Mama and Gramma Kitty. He's Up North with his people. "I'd like to show him a coupla my best articles."

Grampa quits his stroking. Breathes in the aroma of the sweet-smelling roses that surround the cottage this time of year. "No."

I have asked Miss Lydia time and time again to have a VISI-TATION with Daddy like she does Mama, but she gets so agi-tated when I bring him up. Like Grampa, she harbors horrible feelings toward Daddy. I perceive that's because the both of them hold him responsible for causing the crash since he's the one that was driving. But I don't blame Daddy. I got a memory of him building me a soapbox derby car that he painted #1 on. "I've asked Miss Lydia to check and see if Daddy—"

"Lydia's off her head," Grampa says, back to hacking at the wood with a lot of vigor.

"What do you mean by that exactly?" I cannot imagine why he says that. Miss Lydia is one of the most completely right in her mind folks that I know, but I don't say that to Grampa. He'd only get more cantankerous than he already is, or worse, give me his famous silent treatment.

"Lydia was never right again after she lost her boy." As soon as Grampa says it, I can tell he wishes he could take it back.

"Where'd she lose him?"

"In the lake. He drowned."

"But you lost a child, too, and you didn't go off your head," I remind him, in case he's having another leaky memory moment.

"People'r different. Some can stand things. Some can't." His knife on the pine goes *sha . . . sha . . . sha*. Wood commas are dropping at his feet. "If I lost you . . . ," he says, so soft I can barely hear him.

"Now you're just bein' plain silly, Charlie. You won't ever lose me." I inch my lawn chair closer to his. "You're well known for being extremely organized."

"There is a world of danger out there, Gibby girl. Just like them cicadas, ya might think you got plenty of time to kick up your heels, and in fact, you got nuthin' of the sort." I know he's remembering about my mama 'cause he's got that particular lilt to his voice that is more soulful sounding than Mr. Otis Reading.

"Just because I am **NQR** does not mean that I cannot take care of myself, ya know." I fling my skimmer too hard and it sinks straight off.

Grampa shoves back on his cloud hair. His shoulders are wide, but he's lanky at the waist with hands that're full of hot grease scars. And he walks with a limp and a drag because of his fake leg, which must be hurting since he's been rubbing on where it's attached to his knee.

"Achin'?" I ask, setting my hand atop his.

"It's fine," he says, dropping his mad. "How you been feelin'?"

"Good as g-o-l-d." Wish I could, but I never bother telling

him anymore how I *really* feel. He'd only say what he always says. 'Bout me learning to play the hand I was dealt. Or the other one he's started up with lately: "It's time for ya to accept the fact that you're gonna need to saddle up and ride harder than most."

First off, I don't really enjoy card playing all that much, 'cept for the cribbage game Miss Lydia and me have every Wednesday morning after we pick flowers. And second off, I don't need to saddle up and ride hard. All I need to do is lope along. A nice easy pace. Giving me plenty of time to take in the scenery, just like Mama and I used to. Riding double, pressed together like one. A wildflower necklace lying warm against my neck. I know he's got my best interests at heart, but if I can be honest with you, my grampa's sort of a Gloomy Gus.

Resheathing his whittling knife that's so sharp I'm not allowed to go near it, he says, "Hungry?"

I listen in on my stomach. "Sounds like it."

When the weather is warm like it is, at the time of day the crickets and frogs tune up, we eat grilled perch or trout or whatever else has not outsmarted him that afternoon out on the lake. Sometimes with jolly red tomatoes, and just-picked sweet corn that's still got that clumpy dirt smell, and maybe some churned ice cream for dessert.

"Already got the coals heated," he says, heading toward the grill.

Upon hearing that, Keeper drops his stick at my feet, letting me know he's ready for his evening fetch and go. (This is his favorite hobby next to sucking eggs.) "Ready-set?" I shout, tossing his stick into the lake as far as I can, and when he brings it back, I throw it again, despite feeling awfully bad for loafing like this. What I should be doing is working on finishing up that Miss

Cheryl and Miss DeeDee story so I can get busy investigating the murder of Mr. Buster. I cannot tolerate the thought of Mama chewing her fingernails about me.

"Chows up," Grampa calls after a bit, walking our plates to the picnic table. "Wash your hands."

After sliding them into the lake and wiping them off on my jeans, I sit down across from him at the table he made from scratch. The cornbread is warm, the catfish crispy. "The sheriff was at Miss Jessie's today," I say, helping myself.

"Use your fork. What for?" he says, all of a sudden cranky again. Grampa does NOT care for LeRoy Johnson any more than I do. Says the man is a born and bred bully, same as his daddy and his daddy before him. And even though that's true, I also suspect that jealousy, sometimes known as the green-eyed lobster, might be rearing its ugly head tonight.

"Peaches and I had a wonderful ride this afternoon," I say. "And that new filly, she's really something."

"Gibby."

"Yup. And then . . ."

"Focus," he says, ripping a hunk off the cornbread and jabbing it in the clover honey. "Why was LeRoy up to Jessie's place?"

"Mr. Buster's gone missin'," I say, sliding a sliced tomato into my mouth that's sprinkled with dressing all the way from Italy. "The sheriff came by to talk to Miss Jessie about his disappear—"

"I heard there was some to-do up at the Malloy place," Grampa interrupts. His eyes look like the deposit slot down at the bank. "Don't be gettin' any ideas on using your powers of meticulous perception to go snoopin' around in this matter, hear? And don't talk with your mouth full."

"Why shouldn't I go lookin' for Mr. Buster?"

"Just don't," he barks out like the drill sergeant he used to be.

For what seems like close to eternity the only sounds are the far-off motors on the water and forks scraping against the tin plates cowboy Grampa loves so much because they remind him of stars at night that are big and bright deep in the heart of Texas.

Finished eating, he dabs at his mouth with his paper napkin. Says nicer, "Ya still wanna get the board out after we clean up these dishes?"

"A course I do, Charlie." I lay my hand on his whisker sprouts, rub 'em to let him know I forgive him using his hut-to voice. "Ya know, ya could—"

"Shhh. Hear that?"

"*Eeee . . . eeee . . . eeeeeee. Eeee . . . eeee . . . eeeeeee.*"

"Cooper's Hawk," Grampa says with a lot of know-how, because not only is he a whiz at whittling, he watches birds, and can tell the call of a red-throated loon from a common loon without even looking up. "Look, there he is."

The hawk's caught a breeze above the cottage next to ours. Something squirming in his mouth. I know, I know, it's all part of God's grand design, but I just can't stand seeing that kind of help-lessness, so I lower my eyes down to the Flemings' gray cottage. They were our neighbors for years and years, but they moved to town after Miz Comfort Fleming broke her hip when she fell on the slippery pier. They lease out their place now to strangers for extra money.

When Grampa mutters, "Useless," he isn't referring to the hawk. He means Mr. Willard DuPree, the most recent next-door renter who moved in right after Christmas, which is sort of a pecu-liar time to show up in Cray Ridge 'cause there's not much going on around here then. But Mr. Clayton Fleming told Grampa that Willard paid cash for a year in advance, so that was fine with him. Grampa does not fancy our neighbor one iota. First off, Willard smokes hemp. Even worse, he doesn't have a job, from what I can tell. In fact, most days our neighbor does nothing but lie around in the "contemplating" hammock he's slung up between two yellow-woods. Right this minute, I can see his behind pushing through the knotting and scraping the top of the grass that should've been mowed two weeks ago. This sort of **Indolence: Inactivity as a result from disliking work** can really get under the skin of a man like Grampa, whose calluses have calluses.

"Eat," Grampa says, lighting up with his Zippo. "You're startin' to look like a bedpost."

I take another sneak peek next door. Lord. Grampa would have an apoplectic fit if he knew that Willard has been attempting to teach Clever and me how to play strip poker, which I've come to believe doesn't have so much to do with cards as Willard taking the opportunity to show off his pecker that he has named Lord Sparky. Clever is dazzled. I suspect that the two of them might be having hot sex, which I think doin' before you're married is a lot like eating supper before sayin' grace. Contrary to common sense. But Clever, she dropped out of school in the ninth grade, so she is not entirely educated.

Grampa's stacking up his dirty dishes on one end of the picnic table, his cigarette dangling from his lips. "Ya feelin' all right? Ya seem on the distracted side lately. More than usual."

(Oh, if he only knew. Considering how he feels about him, my grampa's going to be thrilled to the nub when he finds out Mr. Buster is not missing, but dead. I can barely rein myself in from letting him in on the secret!)

"Stop frettin' about me and start sayin' your prayers, Charles Michael Murphy," I shout. "I got a feelin' I may go down in Scrabble history tonight."

Giving me a low-watt grin, he pulls open the screen door. "Don't forget to feed him," he says, and him and the dirty dishes disappear inside.

I got leftover catfish and a slice of cornbread on my plate for Keeper so I set it down in the grass for him. This time of day a breeze likes to tickle the lake so the tips of the willows are etching smiles near the shore. My bangs are ruffling.

Our neighbor calls over in his shovey accent, "Is he gone?"

"Yes, Willard, he is."

I attempted to write a **Welcome to Cray Ridge** story right after he moved in, but Willard dodged every single one of my questions, which I found odd since folks are usually quite enthused at the thought of seeing their name in the paper. What I eventually got him to admit was that his favorite color is gray and that he's from the New York area. That last part got me excited. I asked him if he knew Mr. Howard Redmond. Willard answered he might, but in his line of work he meets so many different people. "Ya don't say," I said. "And what line of work might that be?" Ya ever see a turtle reverse into his shell? Like that.

Remembering my neighborly manners, I holler over, "How they hangin', Willard?"

Only the hawk calls back.

"Willard?"

Nothing but the breeze in the trees.

He probably fell asleep. Willard does that a lot after he smokes hemp. He also eats Mallomars by the ton.

" 'Bout time," Grampa says, when Keeper and I join him at

the kitchen sink. Tied around his neck, he's got the Chief Cook and Bottle Washer apron that I gave him last Christmas. "Ya hear me? Do not go stickin' your nose into that tobacco farm's business."

"And why exactly would I wanna go sniffin' tobacco plants?" I ask, rummaging my hands around the soapy sink water.

Grampa shoots me one of his inspecting looks and must like what he sees 'cause he goes back to humming along with the singer who he admires beyond sense, Mr. Johnny Cash, who I do not care for one bit. I prefer the Beatles eight days a week, but Grampa won't let me listen to them because he says those boys are nothing but long-haired goo.

Doesn't take us long to finish up, there's just the two of everything. He hangs his apron on the nail, and says like he does every night, "Pour a coupla glasses while I get us set up."

Playing Scrabble is another one of the "stimulations" of my brain that Grampa tried out when I first got out of the hospital. When he was still hoping I could get **Q**uite **R**ight again. It's become a habit now. Every single night he gets out the board from the top shelf of the bookcase and we head out to the pebbly card table on the porch. At first I made words that looked like this:

Drg.

That's drag.

Or:

Whol.

That's wool.

So, of course, while I was still rehabilitating, Grampa whupped me good most nights. (Not to brag, but I believe I have turned that table on him but good.)

After getting down two of the leftover blue metal glasses we gave out last year at the pumps to folks using Premium, I top them off with his tart lemonade and follow him out to the porch. The last of the sun is skimming the top of the water. Soon the skeeters'll be out, which is why we have a screened-in. I pick the prickers out of Keeper's coat while Grampa takes the board out of the box, lights the brass lantern, and lets me blow out the match.

"I like your locket," he says, jotting down our names on the score-keeping pad.

I had completely forgotten about it. I open it up to show him the pictures of Billy and me from long ago.

"How's he doin'?" Grampa leans back in the folding chair and lights up another.

"You should quit smokin'."

"That right?"

"Yes, it is. I heard a New York City reporter, a Mr. Frank Reynolds, say on the television news that smokin' might cause cancer." There is a lot of tobacco growing in Kentucky. Around here especially. Our colored folks count on getting paid to pick that crop so they can feed their babies, so I hope I misunderstood that report.

"Reynolds, eh?" Grampa inhales deeper than usual. "With a name like that you'd think he'd be all for lightin' up."

That must be funny because he's apple-doll puckering.

"I gave Billy a star today," I say.

Grampa wriggles his hand around in the Scrabble box, searching for just the right tile. "Has he been spendin' any time up at his daddy's place?"

Grampa has affection for Billy and likes to keep track of *his* whereabouts, too. He believes that Billy should make up with his daddy, which I think Billy might be willing to do if only Big Bill

Brown did not look at his son in a way that squeezes whatever gumption his boy's got left right out of him. Why ever does he do that? Even the most ignorant of us know that kin is the most important thing in life. If *they* don't love you and accept you for what you are, you might as well go hunting without a gun.

"Billy told me he was up to High Hopes just this week," I report.

Grampa picks out his first tile. "Y."

"I can't remember why."

"No, I meant . . . what'd you get?" he asks, leaning across the board. I show him my *D*. "Low letter goes first. That means you."

"For crissakes, I know that, Charlie."

Nature's started up its nightly concert. This time of night the lake reeks of leftover gasoline and heat and . . . uh-oh. Hemp. I can tell Grampa is smelling it as well. His shoulders are bookending his ears. Don't want him getting all crabby again, so I make my move.

"Double word . . . twelve," he says, jotting it down. "Where's your briefcase at?" He reaches across the board and adds on an l-y to my d-e-a-d.

"I don't know." I add on *m* and *n* on top and below the *a*, making it deadly man. "That's twenty-five points, right?"

Grampa takes a last pull off his cigarette and snubs it out on the heel of his boot. "Ya gotta be more careful with your things. That camera wasn't cheap."

We got some cash from the Champion Bus people after their driver stalled out his bus in the middle of the road and Daddy ended up bouncing off the back of it. But Grampa's right, that's no excuse to be careless. He says he won't live forever, and that money will take care of me when he's gone. My stomach clenches badly when he brings it up, at dusk mostly.

Studying the board, I say, "I'll look for my camera tomorrow." Even though I know where the briefcase is, and that the camera's inside it, I don't tell him. See that? That's something I've perceived to be different in my mind recently. Like this afternoon with the sheriff? When I didn't tell him how I already found Mr. Buster dead on Browntown Beach? I think that shows that I'm getting more **R**ight already and it's a good thing. But I've also perceived something else *not* so good going on lately. Unsettling thoughts are creeping around up top. Nudging me, whispering how wearisome Grampa's bossy ways can be sometimes. *Wouldn't you just love to cut loose a little, Gibby? You're not a child, you're a grown woman!* Christ Almighty, that makes me feel ungrateful. All that old man has done for me, and here I am thinking these willful thoughts. I should be horse-whipped.

"*I keep a close watch on this heart of mine. I keep my eyes wide open all the time,*" Mr. Cash bellyaches out from the parlor.

Grampa says, "As usual, that man is full of good advice," while he searches the board.

"Do you think you and Miss Jessie would ever get married?" I've just laid down w-e-d.

He draws his hand up onto his chest with an agitated look. Swallows down some of the TUMS he keeps in his trouser pocket. (He's got a fondness for greasy hush puppies.)

"Ya know, one of these days I'll get **Q**uite **R**ight again and I'm gonna wanna start livin' by myself," I say, glancing upward and winking at Mama. "And when that day comes, it'd be nice for me not to have to worry about you anymore." After I move to my own apartment in Cairo, I wouldn't enjoy those walks in that wavy desert heat half as much unless I knew Grampa had some company to keep. "It'd be nice for you to be spoonin' with Miss Jessie in that big brass bed of hers, don'tcha think? She's quite fond of Scrabble. I asked."

"Don't get your hopes up on *neither* one of them subjects," he says, irritable again because loud from next door, Willard's favorite musical group is complaining about getting no satisfaction.

Grampa cups his hands and bellows, "Turn that caterwauling down, ya jackass."

Willard obeys straight off because even *I* know that smokin' hemp is against the law. Willard knows full well that Grampa *could* turn him in to the sheriff, but not that he *won't*. "Grown men should know what's right and what ain't right in their hearts. Shouldn't need no laws or a blowhard like LeRoy Johnson to remind 'em," is what my old cowboy lectures whenever the subject comes up.

Two lemonades and a bowl of strawberry ice cream later, Grampa is tallying up the score. "Two hundred twenty-seven to one hundred fifty-four."

"You or me?" I ask, trying to get a look at the score sheet.

"Don't matter who won," he says, scrunching up the paper in his fist. (Poor, poor Grampa. Isn't that what folks *always* say when they lose at something?) "You sleepin' out here tonight?"

"I am, but not right off. I gotta finish up my story." I reach behind me for my extra blue spiral notebook that I keep under my porch pillow. Wish to hell and back I hadn't forgotten my leather-like up at Miz Tanner's.

"Not too late," Grampa says.

"Nightie-night, Charlie. Think about what I said about Miss Jessie's big brass bed."

He walks stiff into the house. He'll splash water on his face in the bathroom. Sit down on the wooden chair next to his bed and unstrap his leg. Have a sip of peach schnapps. "Be sure to brush your teeth and say good night to you know who," he says, out of the darkness.

He means Mama. Grampa's hung her paintings all over the cottage walls to help me remember more of her. She was well known for her dreamy watercolors of horses, rearing and playing, kicking and galloping. Mama was an artist. A woman of **Refinement: Elegance.** Grampa tells me her paintings still sell for a pretty penny up in Chicago. Because she is dead, that makes them worth more, which pains me some days, so bad. There's photographs of her, too. Winning blue ribbons for her art. Holding a fish on the pier that's bigger than she is, with the kind of smile that makes you wanna smile back. My mama was my grampa's only child and the love of his life. Though I probably loved my daddy as well, I know she was mine, too. If only I could net more than a handful of memories of her. Like the feel of her powdered cheek on my fevered forehead. The way her velvety braid tickled the tip of my nose when she tucked me in. Some nights, when I can't take not remembering her anymore, I lay my face onto the grazing mare and filly painting above my bed, hoping to feel something she left behind. But I should be fine tonight. I got my story to keep my heart out of that longing territory. And a job to do.

As Clever Does

Plumping up my pillow, it's just me and Keeper and my extra blue spiral out here on the porch now, nobody to bother me for a while. I can't stop dwelling on Mr. Buster and his twisted noggin and how that would be so useful as an investigator to have eyes in the back of your head like that.

Focus, Gibby. Focus on the Miss Cheryl and Miss DeeDee story. It's almost done and then you can get busy investigating on Mr. Buster. I press my pencil to my pad, wishing I had my favorite No. 2. Love that worn rolling feeling.

Miss Cheryl and Miss DeeDee have been visiting Hundred Wonders every Sunday afternoon for over two months now. Miss DeeDee cannot believe the improvement she has been experiencing in her eyesight.

I scooch Keeper over a bit. He's such a bed hog.

Miss Cheryl, Miss DeeDee's good friend, has this to say about their visits. "If I hadn't seen it with my own eyes . . . well, it's a miracle."

Miss Cheryl's right about that. Miss Lydia *can* perform miracles. During our VISITATIONS, and I'll swear to this on my Bible, I can feel Mama's presence so strongly. Miss Lydia makes Mama come alive again for me at Hundred Wonders.

From outside the porch, there's a *rustle rustle* and a *snap*. Clever is much earlier than usual. (I am not sure if I have mentioned this before, but her given name is Carol Lever. I saw it written down like this before I was properly introduced to her—C Lever—and I assumed, proof once again that the road to hell is paved with good assumptions, that her name was Clever. She liked it, so it stuck.)

"Whatcha doin'?" she asks, separating the bushes and sliding up to the other side of the screen. She's fussing with a sweetheart rose. She almost always has got one pinned to her hair. Her and Grampa love those flowers to death. If I was writing an article about Clever for the *Gazette* and had to come up with a hobby of hers, besides western-movie watching, of course, I'd say it's either tending the gardens along with him, pruning and watering and pinching and all. Or attending funerals. (She finds the newly dead real interesting.) Or stealing. Clever is what one might call light-fingered.

"I was tryin' to get a few more words down in this story 'fore you showed up," I tell her through the screen.

" 'Bout this evenin' . . . ," she says in a drawl so finger-lickin' sweet you could frost a birthday cake with it.

Almost every night that I can remember, and some I can't, we perform what Clever has dubbed **Gadabouts: Reckless adventures or escapes from confinement.** This can mean anything from us taking the boat out on the lake during an electrical storm to trespassing where we're not supposed to. Sometimes Billy still pals along if Clever gets it in her mind that she wants to steal something bulky, like that Jim Beam liquor sign off the highway. The girl truly excels at coming up with spine-thrilling activities.

"What'd ya have in mind?" I ask her since there is no sense in my resisting. Clever is the boss of us this time of night and she has been since the old days. Only it was the four of us gadding about back then. We tried to come up with a good nickname for ourselves, you know, like, the *Four* Musketeers or Running *Four* Cover. Something snappy like that, but me, Clever, Georgie Malloy, and Little Billy could never agree, so we just quit trying. And then Cooter Smith, Miss Florida's grandbaby? He started to tag along with us, so even if we coulda agreed upon one of those *Four* nicknames, it wouldn'ta worked out.

"We could play some cards with Willard," Clever suggests, raggedy-looking in the lantern light. She's a slip of a gal with tawny hair to her shoulders that waves like a piece of corrugated tin. Shallow-water eyes. Same age as me. Her front tooth's chipped and her nose's got a bump up top from when she fell off the side of the Leghorns' silo during a previous gadabout.

"Can't play cards tonight. I really gotta get this story wrapped up," I say, pressing my eraser to the paper. "What's new?"

"I mighta fallen in love."

This is NOT hot off the presses. Clever falls in and out of love faster than Miss Elizabeth Taylor. (That's where I got my idea to move to Cairo, by the way. From that movie *Cleopatra*.)

"And," Clever says, "Mama kicked me out of the apartment this mornin'."

This also happens on a semiregular basis. Mostly right after Janice gets herself a new love interest. Grampa says the Lever girls remind him of oil and vinegar dressing. They're hard to keep together and separate easy.

"Ya know, if I were you, I might try blendin' better with my mama," I say.

"Well, ya ain't me, are ya?" Clever shoots back.

In my way of thinking, even a bad mama is better than no mama at all, but I know better than to say that out loud. Everybody knows that Janice Lever, although a top-notch waitress at Top O' the Mornin' Diner, the kind that can carry two dishes on each arm, stinks to high heaven in the mothering department. But if somebody else besides *her* insults her mama, Clever'll give 'em an Indian burn that stings like the dickens.

"Ya stayin' here with us then?" I ask. She's been living off and on with either Miss Florida in Browntown or here at the cottage since she was little.

"Believe I'll stay over at Willard's." Clever picks out the last cigarette butt from the bag she keeps in her rolled-up sleeve. She steals the leftovers outta the ashtrays down at the diner when she can. "For now, anyways."

"Mr. Frank Reynolds from ABC News in New York City says smokin' can give you cancer."

She holds a match to the tip, breathes in. "Gettin' cancer is the least of my problems," she coughs out. "I'm . . . ah . . . in trouble."

Also not breaking news. Probably she's in Dutch again with her boss over at the ice-cream stand. That's fine. If she gets herself fired, maybe Mr. Cubby, the taxidermist, will hire her. She's been wantin' to work for him.

"I'm knocked up," she says.

"I know how you favor those knock-knock jokes much as Grampa," I say, swiping off eraser crumbs. "So I'm real sorry, but I don't have time to be honing my sense of humor right now. It's vital I get this story done."

"Being knocked up don't have nuthin' to do with a joke. It ain't funny."

"Well, what does it have to do with then?" I ask, fussy. Besides feeling like a full-out failure when I don't understand what something means, I fear Mama's gonna wear her pacing feet to the bone if I don't figure out who murdered Mr. Buster soon.

"Knocked up means"—Clever stops to hawk and spit—"I'm gonna . . . I'm gonna have a baby."

"You're *what*?" Whipping my face to hers, I can tell she's expecting me to say something more, but what would that be? I have no idea what the "appropriate" thing is to say in a situation like this. Would it be, "Congratulations"?

"Mama says it's gonna ruin my life the same way I ruined hers. She agrees with Willard, who says I should give it away."

"Give *what* away?" I ask, completely confused.

Her words sound like they're wrapped in tissue paper when she answers, "The baby."

"You can do that? Like . . . like . . . they give away those free samples of fudge at Candy World?"

"Willard says there's a social place in Lexington that'll take it. If I give it away, he'll let me stay with him long as I want. Maybe even take me to New York when he goes back."

A social place? I consider myself to be fairly knowledgeable in the social ways. This does not sound like anything I know about.

"Ya don't wanna play cards. Ya wanna go to Browntown?" Clever asks, shooing off the baby subject and moving back onto the gadabout subject. "I could get a little hooch off Cooter."

Just in case you don't know any Negroes, you definitely should get to. I am acquainted with quite a few of them because Miss Florida Smith, our helper at the diner, she is the Queen of Browntown even though the rest of Cray Ridge does not treat her like royalty. Except for when they are eating some of her pie. I am not allowed to go over to Browntown at night anymore. Miss Florida told Grampa last week to keep me away until things simmer down. But staying away, it breaks my heart. The way that place smells of barbecue and how the houses are hugged together so close that you can hear when somebody is mad at somebody or when they're giving each other a little sugar. All the little children running around with their nappy hair and dusty toes. And that music. That low-down music.

But . . .

Grampa was clear on the subject, and if he finds out I was over there, he won't call me Gibby girl for a week. He'll call me Gibson, and only if he has to tell me to do something of an emergency nature. *The hell with him!*—the creeping thoughts are nudging—*Go! You love Browntown. And you might could come across an awfully good story.* Yes. It'd be worth getting into trouble for an awfully good story. That's exactly what I need right about now. This Miss Cheryl and Miss DeeDee article is feeling a mite stale.

"Gib?"

"Yeah?"

"I'd be a good mama," Clever says, real wretched.

"I know, I know you would." She has always been good with the little ones. Gives them free cookie cones, which is one of the reasons she's always in Dutch with her boss.

"Knock knock," I say, 'cause besides offering her a steaming bowl of chicken noodle soup straight out of the can, or five dollars, it's the only other way I know to cheer her up.

"Who's ttthere?" she says, struggling.

"Butch." That's her nickname for me. It's from our special movie.

"Bbbutch who?"

"Butch Cassidy and the Sundance Kid. The both of 'em. Right there. On your doorstep. Wouldn't that beat all?"

She fans her hand out on the screen. I do the same. Her heart is pounding in her thumb.

"Come with me," she says, snorting up the sad.

Even though she's pretending she wants to go to Browntown

to get some hooch off Cooter, that's not what she really wants. Even though Clever's been busy with Willard for months, when the going gets rough, she'll run to Cooter lickety split. The two of them've been running hot and cold for forever. And if she can't locate *him*, she'll settle for a different kinda lovin' from Miss Florida, who's been a second mother to her.

"Well?" Clever says, snotty now 'cause she'd prefer having her eyes pecked outta her head by hungry crows than say *please*. "I ain't got all night."

(You gotta admit. She's irresistible.)

"Oh, all right, Kid." That's my nickname for *her*. I set my blue spiral back under my pillow, lower the lantern wick, and slip on my sneakers. Keeper and me are extra careful with the porch screen door, praying nature noise will cover up its squeak.

Once out on the lawn, I call softly into the dark, "Where are ya?"

"Down here," Clever calls back. "At the pier."

When I join up with her, she reaches for my hand and holds it firm across her belly. I cannot believe I haven't noticed how round and hard it's become! Have my powers of perception taken a vacation? Then again, she *has* been wearing a lot of these flowing-type outfits instead of her usual short-shorts and T-shirts. Something strong ripples under my palm. "For crissakes, what the hell did you have to eat tonight?" I ask, taking my hand away quick. "It's really comin' back on ya."

"That's not supper, that's the baby movin' around. It squirms like that day and night. Don't ya know one thing about how this all works?"

While certainly not an expert, I did see that filly getting born just a couple of weeks ago. "I know *some*."

Clever looks awful disappointed. She counts on this investigative reporter to keep her up on current events. "Well, knowin' *some* is knowin' more'n me," she admits. "The only thing *I* know is one of these nights I'm gonna wake up in fits of pain and after a while the baby'll slide out."

Poor, poor girl. She probably doesn't know what a mess this birthing is going to make either. "When that night comes, ya might wanna change into some work clothes, kiddo," I explain as she undoes the rope that's holding the boat safely to the dock.

We'd usually take the path through the woods over to Browntown, but Clever, being weighted down with child, has decided the boat would be quicker, I guess. Keeper and her are already snuggling close on the middle plank, so I set myself down next to the outboard. A wide moonbeam is making the lake look unzipped.

"Don't start the motor up. Grampa might hear," Clever bosses. "Row."

For once, she's right. **The Importance of Perception in Meticulous Investigation** clearly states: *At times it may be crucial for an operative to commit an act of subterfuge. Think like a leopard.*

The Gadabout

Once we're up close to Browntown Beach, I pull the oars into the boat and we glide the rest of the way. Clever splashes into the lake first, followed by me, with Keeper bringing up the rear. It's so damn sultry tonight, even the frogs are complaining. And the cicadas, well, they don't appear to know the meaning of the words "enough already." I'm beginning to get that wormy feeling in my stomach. Maybe I shouldn'ta agreed to this. We pulled up the boat not too far from where Mr. Buster is rotting away.

Clever taunts, "Race ya," and rushes off toward the trees that the colored music is dripping out of like sap.

Should I tell Clever, my dearest and oldest friend, about finding his dead body? She could have some ideas. Every once in a while she gets a bright one. Like how she figured out how to get us into the 57 Outdoor for free by outfitting me in a two-sizes-too-small angora sweater. Our thumbs and my double D's stuck out quite nicely on the highway. (I wouldn't recommend the trunk of a Fairlane as a mode of travel, but *Paint Your Wagon* was worth every bit of that greasy ride. That Mr. Clint Eastwood certainly's got an awful lotta mumbling charm.)

Then again, if I tell Clever about finding Mr. Buster, I might as well go ahead and plaster the news on the billboard outside of town, because as much as I love her, and I do with every inch of myself, the girl is NOT well known for her secret-keeping ability. No. There'd go my investigation, and writing my awfully good story is still #1 on my **VERY IMPORTANT THINGS TO DO** list.

"Gib?" Clever's hurrying ahead down the path that runs along the shore, still impressively swift despite her swollenness. "What's takin' ya so long?"

I can't see her face, but I don't have to. I know it's radiating excitement, and if you could see her heart, it'd have a crazy ole grin plastered across it. Clever gets like this whenever she's near Browntown. Wilder.

"Be right there," I yell, true to my word, 'til a mewling sound coming out of the bushes next to the path stops me cold. Lifting up the low branches, I can see a tabby kitten huddled in the dirt, looking scared as can be. I recognize her as one of Miss Lydia's from her cat Sheba. How'd she get out from underneath the porch? Shame on her mama.

"C'mon," Clever shouts from farther down the path, her head bobbing through the bushes.

"Come back here," I holler. "I found somethin'." I'd like to think the reason she keeps going is that she can't hear me, but more'n likely, it's 'cause she's so charged up. Well, I can't just abandon the poor thing. There's snakes and possums and all sorts of critters livin' it up in these woods at night. Don't know if they lick their lips for kittens or not, but don't think I'll take that chance. "C'mon, Keep. We gotta make us another stop first," I say, veering down the path that leads to nearby Land of a Hundred Wonders. I must also confess to some selfishness right here on my part. Because if Miss Lydia is still up and about, which she will be since she hardly ever sleeps, I figure she'll let me have a quick VISITA-

TION with my mama, after which I will feel cherished. When we're done, me and Keeper'll take the trail behind her barn so we can reunite with Clever.

"Hurry up," I tell Keeper, who's dragging behind me. He is not at all fond of felines, so he's low growling. I got the kitten up close, snuggling into her fur the way you do. "*Shhh . . . shhh . . . shhh . . .*" I'm croonin' over and over, when outta the dark comes a voice I know only too well.

"Well, lookee here."

"*Sh . . . it!*" I squeal, tripping, almost falling. "Ya 'bout scared the wits outta me!"

"Don't you mean what wits you got left?" Sneaky Tim Ray says, the stink of him permeating the air. It's not only the usual hooch smell, it's something else real off-putting. Keeper's full out snarling.

I say, the fright of it all giving me heart-pumping bravery, "I'm warnin' you, Holloway, quit poppin' out at me like that or I'll . . . I'll . . ."

Swaying back and forth like a strong wind's gotten under his skin, he says in his snidest of tones, "You'll what, darlin'?"

"I'll . . . I'll . . ." He's right. What *will* I do? I cannot thwart him. He'd hurt Keeper "accidentally on purpose," the way he's sworn to do. "What do ya want?"

"Saw y'all boatin' along the shore," he says, swigging down a swallow from his jug. "Ya could say we's your welcomin' committee."

We? What does he mean, "we"?

Who *is* that towering behind him in the shadows? "That you, Cooter Smith?" I ask, hoping it is 'cause me and him go way back. Not only as gadabout friends, but after his mama and daddy disappeared, Miss Florida asked Grampa to take Cooter under his wing. Growing up, I can't tell you the number of nights I fell asleep listening to the two of them out on the lawn practicing birdcalls. For old times' sake, I sing to him, *"Oakalee . . . oakalee . . . oakalee."*

"Gib." Cooter steps forward and nods, barely.

Lord, what is that citified thing he's done with his hair? Looks as sleek as a fender on a funeral car.

"Whatcha got there?" Sneaky Tim Ray pries my arms apart with only-God-knows-where-they-been fingers. "Awww. Ain't she precious." He runs his hands down the kitten's spine, wrenches her outta my arms. "Ya know, you and me have a lot more in common than ya might realize, darlin'. Bet you didn't for instance know that I love pussies, too," he says, laughing cruddy and flinging the kitten into the woods.

When I start after her, Holloway cinches me around the waist. "Not so fast. You 'n me got some unfinished bidness to take care of."

Cooter, shifting from foot to foot, says, "We ain't got time for this. Leave her be."

" 'Fraid I cain't do that," Sneaky Tim Ray says, wrenching my hand to the front of his stained bibs. "The south has risen again."

Cooter brushes past me mad as hell, leaving behind the smell of chewed bones and coffee grounds and orange peelings from the Browntown dump. He's gotta work there because Sheriff Johnson spreads awful tales about him so nobody else will hire him anywheres else. (There's a feud between Cooter and the sheriff that is perpetual. You ask anyone, they'll tell you how much LeRoy despises "that uppity Smith boy.") "You comin'?" he calls back to Sneaky Tim Ray.

"That's the plan," Holloway says, breathing faster now. But it must be important wherever they're going 'cause he's glaring at me, then back at the woods that Cooter disappeared into, and then back at me, finally spitting out, "Fuck," as his hand darts up to my neck. He thumbs the indent of my throat, tears off my new locket. "I'll jus' take this for a consolation prize. Ya know what tha' means, don'tcha?"

I'm pretty sure it means I wish I was back at the cottage with my grampa.

"I'll catch you on the flip-flop, darlin'. Don't think I won't." He takes a swipe at my ninnies and yells, "Hold up, Smith," and off he goes into the trees.

God*damn* that Holloway!

After I'm sure that he isn't going to double back, which he's pulled on me more than once, I head over to where the kitten landed, but Keeper's stopped fussing, so she musta made her way back home. Ya know one of the things I pray for each and every night without fail? That Sneaky Tim Ray'll fall into a pit of quicksand right before my very eyes. And when he starts begging for me to hand him a branch, I'll break one off the closest tree and wave it just outta his reach, saying, "Remember that time in the woods? In the barn? All those times ya took advantage?" (I'm lettin' you know right now, I ever get a chance to avenge myself, I'll eye-for-an-eye do it.)

Clever is calling again, "Giiibby."

"Over here," I try to yell back, but Sneaky Tim Ray's stench has clenched tight in my throat.

"There ya are," she says, skipping down the path toward me. "Look who I found."

My, oh, my. If I had my camera with me, if it wasn't lying

under those bushes in my briefcase over at Miss Jessie's, I'd click off a picture of Miss Florida Smith. That'd make a good human interest shot for the *Gazette* during L&N Railroad Days, that's how much she resembles one of their locomotives.

Miss Florida yells, "What in tarnation ya doin' here?"

"I don't remember," I yell back.

"Are you crazy comin' over here in the dead of night? If your grampa finds out, ya know what kind of trouble y'all'd be in?"

Clever says to her, "Don't be so mad. It's my fault. I made her."

"Why don't that news surprise me none?" Miss Florida gives us both a real crummy look and commences chugging back toward her house.

"I saw Cooter," I say, thinking that'll slow her down some because she loves her grandbaby to bits.

"Ya saw Cooter?" Clever says, real lively.

Miss Florida asks me, "He alone?"

"No, he was not. He was with Sneaky Tim Ray, who told me the south—"

"Oh, Lord. Sure as the day is long, that no-account Holloway has gone and got my Cooter into something he shoun't oughta be into," Miss Florida laments.

I almost say: Well, of course he did, but I dare not get Miss Florida any more worked up. She's already steaming.

No denying the paint could use some refreshing, and a couple of the windows are black-rotted, but Miss Florida has washed many a dish and baked hundreds of pies to save up for this little white house that stands at the edge of Browntown.

"I swear, you two gals have less sense than a penny," she says, hiking herself up the porch steps. Her younger brothers, Vern and Teddy, are off to the side in ladder-back chairs and well into a game of dominos on a TV tray 'neath the bug light. Keeper's already curled himself up at their feet, thumping his stump to the top-hat sound that's riding down the road above one of those blues tunes that get me all choked up whenever I hear their moody sweetness.

Miss Florida does not miss a beat. "Boys, wind that game up now. I need for y'all to take these girls home," she says, just about pulling her screen door out of its frame. "I'm fixin' to call Grampa to tell him you're on your way."

I say, "For chrissakes, don't do that," but she's already speeding through her sharply decorated parlor. Besides a green brocade sofa, she's got a rag rug she made herself, and golden lamps she got from a catalog that sit on two matching spool tables. And she must have a pie in the oven because something smells divine. "Please, please, don't call Grampa," I say, when we catch up with her. "Clever is knocked up."

"What?" Miss Florida says, bringing her face close to mine and then jerking it toward Clever's stomach. For a bit, it's like an ice storm swept through and froze us all up. Except for Vern and Teddy, who are bickering hotly about something outside the window.

"Knocked up means Clever is goin' to have a baby," I try to explain, but before I can, Miss Florida yells, "Mercy," and collapses into her red watching-television chair with a crashing *thrump*.

"And Mr. Buster Malloy is dead and after I solve the crime and write my awfully good story for the *Gazette*," I say, "Mama will finally be able to rest assured 'cause she'll see I'm gettin' more **Q**uite **R**ight and that I can take care of myself and . . ."

Damn.

Clever and Miss Florida chime in together, "What?"

Hat's out of the box now, no sense denying. "I said, Mr. Buster Malloy is dead and—"

Miss Florida interrupts with a wave of her hand. "Lord knows, there's plenty of good folks wish it upon him." Mr. Buster is known countywide for paying dirt cheap and not supplying near enough shade breaks to the colored men bent over those tobacco plants from sunup to sundown. "But Buster ain't dead. Talk at the diner is he's missin', is all."

I can tell by the sassy look on her face that Clever doesn't believe me either. Good by me. According to **The Importance of Perception in Meticulous Investigation: Breaking News:** *One of the most important aspects of solid investigative reporting is the ability of a reporter to keep a story under wraps until he has gathered the proper substantiation of said story.*

Miss Florida groans, "Why din't you tell me you was pregnant? Thought ya just been eatin' too much barbecue." She jabs her finger at Clever, who drops onto her knees and lays her head

in Miss Florida's low-valley lap. Everybody in Browntown's probably running for cover, 'cause when that girl lets loose with her
wailing, it cuts through the still of the night like an air-raid siren.

I report, "I don't know *why* she didn't tell you, but I suspect
the *who* is Willard and the *what* is his highness, Lord Sparky."

"Willard?" Miss Florida asks with a screwed face. "He that
hippie boy livin' up next to ya for the summer?"

I nod my head the same way she always does, slow and with
deepness.

"Who's this Lord Sparky?" she asks.

"Lord Sparky is what Willard calls his . . . ah . . ." I bring my
finger down to the front of my shorts, waggle it, hoping she gets
the idea.

"Oh, man alive, man alive!" She lifts Clever's slippery face up
in her hands. "He the father?" Clever does not answer right off
'cause she's heaving pretty bad, so Miss Florida tempers herself
some. "Ya should know by now, tears don' help none." Drawing
a hankie outta the sleeve of her polka-dot house dress, she dabs
at Clever's blotchy cheeks. "That Willard boy . . . he the baby's
daddy?"

Clever stutters out, "Can't . . . can't . . . say."

"Ya can't say? How many men you done had, for godssakes?"
Miss Florida thunders, which gets Clever air-raid sirening again.

"Stand up, girl. Let me see that stomach a yours." Miss Florida hikes up the flowing skirt past Clever's underpanties. Goodness. I can still see her ribs, but right in her middle section it
looks like she swallowed a world globe. And something *real* bad
has happened to her belly button. It's sticking out like a doorbell.

"You 'bout eight months?" Miss Florida asks.

Clever whimpers.

"Yer not all that big, but see how that baby's come down low? It's gettin' ready."

I ask, "Gettin' ready to do what?"

"To get on out of there and start bein' more trouble than you can ever imagine," Miss Florida says. Then the oven bell goes off—oh, that simply delicious smell. Maybe cherry? And with a shake of her head and a few *tsks . . . tsks*, Miss Florida braces her dimpled arms against the sides of her chair, pushing up hard on her way into the kitchen, and Clever is left to stew in her juices.

"Why'd ya tell her?" Clever snarls, shoving me down onto the sofa.

"Hush the hell up," I say, bouncing back up, ready to shove her to kingdom come 'fore I remember her condition. If she wasn't about to have a baby, I'd shove her back real good. She's so irritatin' when she acts like this. I'd much rather spend my time with that bubbly fruit smell than put up with her crab appleness. "I'm goin' to get me a piece of that pie now. Do NOT get any bright ideas," I warn her as I head that way. "I expect you to be here when I come back."

(It wouldn't be ladylike to repeat what Clever sasses back to me. Suffice it to say, when she gets a bee in her bonnet, her mouth gets *mighty* waspish.)

Coming into the small kitchen, I can see that Miss Florida is bent over at the waist in front of her old black stove. Her rump being so big, I cannot see past it into the oven.

"What will happen when the baby comes out and will be more trouble than I can ever imagine?" I ask her. "May I have some lemonade?" Uh-oh. That makes me remember Grampa. (If he should wake up and come to check on me out on the porch like

he does sometimes, well, I leave it to your imagination what kind
of tangled-ass trouble I'll be in.)

When Miss Florida straightens, she's got a beaut of a pie in
her hand. Browned just right. About the same color as she is.
"Hep yourself," she says, nodding over to the Amana. "That girl
is gonna have to give that baby up, is what's gonna happen. She's
not much more'n a child herself and gots no money. How she
gonna buy it food and diapers and such?"

"No, I meant . . . how will I know when it's time to take her
to the hospital?" I am pouring the lemonade into my favorite jelly
jar that's been mine since I was tiny. "That's what you're supposed
to do, right?"

Miss Florida stands back, appraises me like she does one of
her pies. "You's been a good friend to that gal all these years, ya
know that?"

"Like my mama was to Miss Lydia?" Folks around here still
talk about how Addy Murphy and Lydia Malloy were glued together practically from birth. And how if you pinched one of them
girls, the other would cry. Miss Lydia was in almost every old
picture I have of Mama. Until Grampa cut her out. "And the kind
of good friend you are to her now?"

"*Just* like your mama was to Lydia back then, and I am to her
now." When she isn't working at the diner washing up or rolling
out dough, Miss Florida helps out Miss Lydia, who has pet named
her the Tender. Miss Florida has mentioned to me that she's not
sure if that means she's good with the bees, or that she's got skill
with the growing of things, but that's not unusual. Because Miss
Lydia? She is so, so meaningful in her ways that sometimes we
all have to think for days to figure out what she's really saying to
us. Like in some of those Bible stories. Ya know how you got to

ponder them some to figure out what the hell the Lord is really trying to tell you? Like when He uses that word *smote* and you're not exactly sure what He means by that, but you get a sense that he's madder than a sprayed roach? Well, same with Miss Lydia.

"Please tell me what happened to Miss Lydia's boy," I say, rubbing up and down Miss Florida's arm.

"Oh, Gib. How many times we got to go over this, ya think?" I guess this is not the first time I have asked her about this subject because she adds, so put out, "Georgie drowned a few years back."

"How'd that happen? Whenever Clever tells me tales about him, she never fails to mention what a strong and wonderful swimmer he was." And that he was well known for his practical jokes. Like setting a grocery sack of dog duty on Miss Lilith Montague's front porch, taking a match to it and yelling, "Fire . . . Fire!" (Georgie Malloy's the reason Clever just about laughs her head off every single time she comes across an A&P bag.)

"Let's not go on 'bout Georgie," Miss Florida says, wiping her damp hands on the towel attached to her frilly apron. "We got ourselves enough trouble in the here and now. Like how we gonna get ya home. No ways you goin' back in that boat."

After I follow Miss Florida back into the parlor, somewhat disappointed she has not offered me a slice of that cherry pie, but nicely revived from the lemonade, Clever is nowhere to be seen. I was afraid of that.

"Now we got another one missin'," Miss Florida grumbles, sticking her head into her bedroom, where I have taken many a lie-down on her dried-in-the-sun sheets when Grampa got tied up with one thing or another.

"I like the new one a lot." I have stopped to admire her

paintings on velvet that hang off the parlor walls and am pointing to a curly-haired puppy wearing a coonskin hat. Like me, Miss Florida's an art lover. She's got two other framed ones of Jesus and the King—Dr. Martin Luther. And Darnelle, there are loads of pictures of the lovely Darnelle, who was Miss Florida's girl, and the mama of Cooter until she went missing some years ago when she was selling peanuts up roadside. There's also lots of photos of Cooter doing all sorts of things, like being sloppy in the mud when he was a kid, and swinging off the Geronimo rope down at the lake with his best friend, Georgie Malloy, but mostly he's playing basketball. Miss Florida and Grampa were so proud when he got a scholarship to college a few years back, but after his knee got jammed up, he had to come home to Cray Ridge and work at the dump. (Even though Grampa has asked Cooter time and time again to come back to cook up at the diner like he used to when he was a boy, he won't. I perceive Cooter can't stand the heat in the kitchen. Because he's gotten rowdy these days, mostly gambling. Grampa does not approve of that sort of thing.)

"What did ya mean when you said now we got another one missin'? Who else is missin' besides Clever?" I ask.

Miss Florida takes a look-see in her bathroom, pulling her head back out with a shake. "We jus' done went over this. Buster Malloy is missin'. 'Member?"

" 'Course I 'member," I fib.

"Miss Caroool Lever! Come out from wherever it is you is," Miss Florida shouts with her hands on her hips. "You ain't too big to feel my hand on your backside."

All's quiet 'cept for the *tick tick* of her Bulova clock and the soul music seeping through the open window.

"Maybe she went out for a breath of fresh air," I say, heading out to the porch and praying Clever hasn't deserted me. When she gets mad or caught doing something she shouldn't (exactly as often as you'd think), she's bound to cut and run. Everybody knows you can't catch that Lever girl once she makes up her mind to scoot. The bug light isn't doing its job, but it's strong enough that I can see my best friend snoozing on the swing. Vern and Teddy are lippin' their cigarettes, lettin' the smoke hang.

Upon seeing Clever, Miss Florida throws her arms up with a wouldn'tcha-know-it look and eases herself down into her rocking chair with a, "My, oh, my. Life sure is unrelentin', ain't it? Ya get one problem taken care of and 'fore ya can get an ounce of satisfaction, another one rears its head." She crooks her finger over to the swing. "I do believe this time that wild child got herself into somethin' she cain't outrun."

I'm afraid she's right. Picking up my best friend's tootsies, I set myself down beside her, letting her feet fall back into my lap. How funny that the creak of the rope swing is matching her snores. Vern and Teddy aren't paying us a bit of mind, too busy slapping down their tiles.

"Now what's that you were sayin' before 'bout Buster bein' missin'?" Miss Florida half wonders.

Buster Malloy. Buster Malloy. The next governor. Oh, my, yes. "I was sayin' that Mr. Buster is not actually missin'." (I figure I owe Miss Florida an explanation of sorts based on no other reason than me and Clever agitating the hell out of her on this loveliest of evenings.) "I saw him."

"Oh, yeah? Where?" she says, happy to pass the time like we do in the kitchen every morning when we form sausage patties.

"He was over at Browntown Beach."

"*Mmm....*" Miss Florida's begun drifting off after her hard day at the diner. Her ankles are swollen almost out of her shoes. "And when was that at?"

I can picture Mr. Buster splayed on the sand. Four holes in his chest. Neck all catawampus. But the details aren't filled in. "Can't say as I remember the day exactly."

"Buster be the first to tell ya he don't know how to swim," Miss Florida mutters with a lot of contempt. "So what'd he be doin' down at the beach?"

"Bein' dead."

Hoochie-coochie laughing is coming down the road from Mamie's Leisure Lounge. Clever and I spy in the window over there whenever we get a chance. There's a fantastic silver ball hangs from the ceiling that shoots sparkly squares on bodies swaying so close. I would very much like to work up at Mamie's when I get **QR** again. You know, temporary-like, until I find my apartment in Cairo.

"Gettin' late," Miss Florida says, not bothering to hide her yawn. She's acting like she didn't even hear me tell her that Mr. Buster Malloy is not missing but deceased. Maybe she didn't, and that's probably for the best, considering she can keep a secret just about as well as Clever can. "Vern, Teddy, finish up now. Ya gotta take Gib home."

"But what about Clever?" I ask, tugging Miss Florida out of the rocker with both of my hands.

"She'll be fine here for tonight. Ain't like she'll be missed," she says. "Ya know that."

I do, and so does everybody else in Cray Ridge, but I'm shocked straight down my spine that Miss Florida says this. Usually colored people do not say mean things about white people to another white person. It is considered untraditional.

Vern pulls up on his trouser knees and says to me, "Don't get her goin' on 'bout Janice Lever's poor motherin'. We be here 'til sunup."

Then no way in hell am I going to tell Miss Florida that Clever no longer *has* a home to go to. That her selfish, selfish mama kicked her out. Again. I CANNOT stay here 'til sunup. I got a murder to solve.

"All right then," I say, glancing back one more time at Clever, thumb in her mouth, looking not much older than the day she came scratching at Top O' the Mornin's back door asking for a handout when she was seven. Miss Florida took to Clever right off. Set her up next to the kitchen sink, dabbed at the dirt on her cheeks, and cut her a slice of chiffon pie, which is still Clever's all-time favorite.

Looking back down at her on that swing, I must have a hesitating look on my face 'cause Miss Florida says kinder, "G'wan, baby. She'll be fine with me."

"I know." I bend to deliver a kiss to Clever's forehead, and then straighten to give a wrap-around hug to Miss Florida. Vern and Teddy are already waiting on me roadside with Keeper in the bed of the truck. Backing that way, I say to her, "Thank you awfully much for not callin' Grampa."

"You ain't safe here no more, Gib. It ain't like it used to be," she says, and I can't perceive if Miss Florida's happy about that or not. "I'll have the boys sneak his boat back 'fore dawn."

"I got proof, ya know, 'bout Mr. Malloy bein' dead and if you want . . . ," I try, thinking that might give her sweet dreams, but that screen door is already closing on her big behind.

Vern and Teddy Smith. I've adored them since the day I met them. Besides taking such good care of Miz Tanner's farm, Teddy, who is the brawn of the outfit, is a help to Miss Lydia out at Land of a Hundred Wonders. She calls *him* the Caretaker. Teddy is slow on the uptake. Vern is a lot smarter, and does most of the talking for the two of them because his younger brother also has a high C voice that really doesn't suit him. I'd say I adore Teddy a little more than I adore Vern. There's just something about him I find so sympathetic.

A singing group calling itself The Temptations is on the truck radio harmonizing about how they wish it would rain and it looks like they might get what they want. Vern is behind the wheel, his arm out the window catching a breeze. I'm smushed between the two of 'em like an ice-cream sandwich.

"Why am I not safe anymore in Browntown, Vern?" I ask.

He looks over at Teddy, who looks back at him. Rakes his fingers down his stalky neck. Vern's stalling for time, trying to decide what to tell me because I'm **NQR**. Everybody does that.

"There's folks in Browntown who is mad at white folk," Vern says, not removing his eyes off the road.

"Why?"

Teddy is rolling a cigarette by the light of the glove box.

Vern says, "Times a changin'."

"Hey, that's a Bob Dylan song," I say. "Willard loves Bob Dylan."

"Who's Bob Dylan? Who's Willard?" Vern asks.

"Bob Dylan is a popular singer and Willard lives next door to us. He smokes hemp."

"That a fact?"

"Yes, it is. Did ya know if ya smoke hemp it relaxes ya?" I ask, picturing Willard's deboned-looking body when he's done inhaling the stuff. Hemp grows like weeds around here, in the ditches.

"Hemp smokin' is relaxin', huh? Maybe we should look into that, Teddy."

The golden light from the radio bounces off his brother's teeth as he runs his startling pink tongue across his white rolling paper.

I say, "Miss Florida says people do not like me anymore in Browntown. Why?"

"You's the wrong color," Vern says.

"Colored folks are mad at white folks?" Even though I may sound surprised, I'm really not. I can understand them being mad at people who treat them rude. "But I'm a nice white folk."

When Teddy lights up his cigarette, the glow of the tip warms up his face. He's got a scar on his chin that matches the lightning bolt that just flashed above the lake.

"Yeah, you's a nice white folk," Vern answers. "But some of the coloreds, they's not lookin' on the inside of a body no more, they's only interested in the outside."

"But then, aren't those colored folks actin' just as ignorant as those white folks? Decidin' if somebody is good or bad because of what shade they are?"

Vern gives me a strong nod of approval. "Ya know, for a girl wit a messed-up brain, ya say some very reasonable things."

"Appreciate you sayin' that, Vern. I've been working real hard at gettin' more reasonable."

"Well, ya can work your brain 'til it's blistered, but ya ain't never gonna be able to reason out hate."

Him saying that breaks my heart, for I've found hating doesn't make you feel too good. Well, maybe it makes you feel good for a little while. Sort of powerful and all, thinking up ways to have at a certain somebody. (Sneaky Tim Ray.) To get back at him for making you feel less right than you already do.

Just as we come upon Buster Malloy's farm, the rain lets loose. I can't see his place through the trees, but I know his mansion is made of bricks and has a four-car garage.

Over my head, Vern says to Teddy, "Haskell says nobody's been paid this week for pickin'. Buster better get hisself back soon or—"

"He won't be back," I blurt. "Mr. Buster is dead."

Next to me on the seat, Teddy Smith stiffens like a Sunday shirt.

For godssakes, Gibby. Why don't ya just head over to WJOY and have Sweet Talkin' Stan announce Mr. Buster's demise to the whole county?

"Buster dead?" Vern says. "No, he ain't."

"Would you like to see his body?" pops out before I realize I can't really do that. That'd blow my plan to kingdom come.

"Where it at?" Vern asks with a lot of suspicion.

"I . . . I . . . can't remember right at this moment but when I do, I will call you on the telephone."

Vern says, "Ya do that," crooking his eyebrow up at Teddy, who is still awfully starched.

We're quiet, listening to the radio and the rain 'til we make the last turn toward home. Pulling up to the cottage, the truck's headlights spotlight Grampa. Like he's the star of a magic show, the windshield wipers are making him appear and disappear. He's perched on a pail, his legs planked out, not even trying to keep his shotgun dry.

Vern says soft, "Ya in for it now, Gibber."

Reverend Jack

Cray Ridge is perched on the shores of Lake Mary, which is a good-size body of water. Not so large that you can't see across it, but when the sun is out, you do need to squint. I can see how the smallness of the town might get on some folks' nerves, but I find it quite enchanting. It's only six blocks long with trees running along Main Street. And the brick buildings have ivy twisting up their sides. Since you gotta pass through it on your way to the big cave down south, most of the shops and attractions do okay during the hot months selling trinkets and such.

Reverend Jack and me are sitting on the steps of his front porch that's right next door to the Cumberland United Methodist. He's a handsome fellow with brown hair trimmed into a crew cut so short that you can see summer beading all over his skull. Besides being a pastor, he's got a doctoring degree from the University of Mississippi in psychology, which he has explained to me is the study of a person's **Psyche: A human's soul, spirit or mind.** What this means is that he tries to unravel the reasons for why folks do and feel things.

"Do I understand the situation correctly?" the reverend asks.

"S'pose so," I say, watching Keeper give his paws a going-over.

"An elaboration would be most helpful."

"Grampa's upset 'cause I went to Browntown last night. He

told me that if he was a hide-tannin' man, both Clever's and my bottoms'd look like his cowboy saddle right about now."

When I first started coming to see the reverend, we spoke mostly about how wretched it feels to be an orphan. And how it's all right to feel sad about that and it isn't at all like feeling sorry for yourself, even though Grampa says it is. But now that some time has passed, whenever *anything* comes up in my life that Grampa doesn't feel "equipped" to cover, he brings me to Reverend Jack, who along with supplying Christian guidance has been teaching me exactly what's—and what is not—an "appropriate" way for an **NQR** girl to conduct herself. Like kissing tourists on the hand when they ask directions? Turns out, that isn't appropriate. Neither is offering to wash the windshields of the truck drivers who pull over when they see me strolling down the highway. (I tried to explain to the reverend that there is a perfectly appropriate reason for this behavior. After all, if Dixie Oil trucker Mr. Hank Simmons hadn't seen me balled up next to that creek after the crash—well, you get the picture.)

"Gibby?"

A heavenly smell is wiggling our way out of Loretta's Candy World—Home of the Best Chocolate-Covered Cherries in the Universe and Beyond. Miss Loretta gets out of bed before the rooster crows to melt these hunks of chocolate in silver bins that are warm and shiny and—

"Do you understand why your grampa is upset with you?" Reverend Jack asks.

"I have friends in Browntown."

He twiddles his thumbs. Round and round and round. "Do you know what the word *racism* means?"

If I had my leather-like with me, I could look it up in my *Webster's*.

"Gib?" He taps my shoulder. "Racism?"

"Spell it, please."

"R-a-c-i-s-m."

"Does it . . . does it have something to do with running?"

"No," he says, rubbing his palm cross the top of his bristly head, which I perceive he does when he's searching for the right words. "Racism means that some people do not care for people who are of a different color than they are."

"The sheriff hates the coloreds," I say.

"That's racism," he says with a nod. "The sheriff would be considered a racist. And that's a very wrong thing to be."

The reverend smells of caramel with just a little bit of ah . . . peanuts? Wonder what he's gotten himself into that would cause him to smell so sweet and crunchy?

"But only white people hate brown people. There are no brown people hatin' white people. That is not what happens," I say, no matter what Vern said and Teddy Smith nodded in agreement with. The both of them are awfully nice men, but they drink quite a bit of rotgut, and now that I've had some time to mull it over, maybe they're not complete strangers to hemp smoking.

Reverend Jack lets out a green apple breath. "People change."

I want to tell him how bad I wish that was true, but I'm a mite irritated with him today, so instead I stare across the street at Grampa's truck. I'm in no hurry to head home, his mad just about suffocating me when he's in one of his wet-blanket moods. He already kept me up most of the night giving me a tongue-lashing. I finally broke down and began to tell him about my plan to solve the murder of Mr. Buster and write an awfully good story so his beloved daughter could stop worrying about my **NQR**ness, that's how desperate I got. But Grampa was on one of his rips. Wouldn't listen. Which is fine by me. All he woulda told me was, "Forget about investigatin'. Forget about writin' that story. Forget about gettin' **QR**." I can't do that. Last night in my dreams, Mama was crying into her hands, and when I woke up drenched and shaky, me and Keeper dragged our pillow out to the pier, hoping it would rock us back to sleep, but it didn't.

"Your grampa's just tryin' to keep you safe," Reverend Jack says.

"He's bein' overprotective, as usual. No one would hurt me in Browntown. They're my friends. Like Miss Florida and Vern and Teddy and—"

"Not everybody in Browntown, or the rest of Cray Ridge, for that matter, is your friend."

"I already know that, for godssake." We've gone over this maybe nine hundred times. I have a tendency to think that all people have hearts of gold. Reverend Jack has suggested that maybe some of them hearts might be a little on the tin side. "Sneaky Tim Ray is not my friend."

"Has Holloway been botherin' you?" he asks, tensing.

The reverend promises he'll not tell anybody else what I confess to him during our talks. Like in **The Importance of Perception in Meticulous Investigation: Confidentiality:** *Reporters NEVER reveal their sources.* Still. He might "accidentally" tell Grampa about my dealings with Sneaky Tim Ray, and then that wretch would "accidentally" kill Keeper. I can't take that chance.

"I got a new necklace. Ya wanna see it?" I ask, looking down my blouse. "It's from Billy. He left it in our secret stump and it's got some nice pictures inside and it's . . ." *Where did my locket go?*

"You're wanderin'," the reverend says. "Again."

"Just tryin' to keep things rollin'. I can't stay too much longer.

I left my briefcase up at Miz Tanner's and I have to go get it. It has an important piece of evidence in it."

"Has Holloway been botherin' you?" he asks, not letting me off the hook. More than once he's told me that I should quit thinking of Sneaky Tim Ray as a regular type of person. How the reverend actually expressed it was, "Ya know how in those western movies you like so much there's almost always a drunkard sprayin' bullets at an Indian's feet, brayin' out, 'Dance, you dirty Injun, dance'?" And I answered, "Yes. That's right. That happens a lot in those shoot-'em-ups." And then he said, "You'd want to steer clear of somebody like that, wouldn't you?"

Not like I don't try.

"Have you seen this one?" I fold my fingers in, making my indexes into a point, and bringing my thumbs forward. "Here's the church, here's the steeple." I spread my thumbs, and wiggle my fingers. "Open the doors and see all the people."

"Gibby."

"Yeah?" I say, glancing over at Billy, who's pacing in front of Candy World like he's on sentry duty. (Sometimes he joins me at the counter for a brown cow when I'm done with my reverend visits.) I wonder why Billy never tries to rub my double D ninnies like Sneaky Tim Ray does. Maybe I don't make Billy pant fast and hard because I'm **NQR**.

"Your grampa does not want you goin' to Browntown anymore," the reverend repeats.

"Would ya mind if we talk about somethin' else for a few minutes? This subject is givin' me a chewed up and spit out feelin'. Are you and Loretta Boyd havin' hot sex?"

His mouth falls open and he fuschias clean up to his roots. "Why . . . why would ya think *that*?"

"You smell like her specialty," I say, showing off my perceptive investigative skills. "Green apple, caramel, and salty peanuts."

He thinks I won't notice that he's begun sniffing himself a little.

"I'm not being a nosy Parker," I explain. "I'm just trying to figure out why it's so damn important to everybody that they get some of this hot sex. A course I've seen animals . . . but is it the same with humans or does it have something to do with love?"

I don't think it does. But it could. I've heard hot sex referred to as "making love." On the other hand, I've also heard it referred to as "pounding the snow possum."

The reverend, even more fuschiated, asks, "Who exactly would ya be thinkin' about in regards to this topic?"

Well, I could go on and on, couldn't I, but settle on, "Well, Willard, for one."

"Who's Willard?"

"Our next-door neighbor this summer. He thinks about hot sex quite a bit and tells Clever he loves her, but he's makin' her give her baby away to a social."

Reverend Jack's mouth does not circle into a surprised O when he hears that Clever's having a baby. Not much of what she does surprises anybody anymore. "Hot sex, I mean, sex, I mean sexual relations, that's an awfully complicated subject." He checks his Timex. "How about we continue this discussion next time?"

I don't say it out loud, 'cause I don't want the pastor to feel like he's falling down on the job, but I think to myself, if Sneaky Tim Ray keeps on pace—well, next time might be too late.

A Not So Hot Mama

The next morning, same as every morning, I'm working at my bussing job out at Top O' the Mornin'. It's slow right now, so I'm using the time to get caught up on my reporting duties. My legs are sticking to the plastic on the booth that sits directly across from the COWGIRLS bathroom, where I recently checked those bruises on my legs. They're turning a sunflower color. Even though Billy thinks I do, I don't believe I fell down at the 57 Outdoor. No. Something else happened. I don't have time right now to figure that mystery out, but make no mistake about it, like a Ridgeback-Russell mix, I *will* stay on that scent.

The smell of half a can of Aqua Net gets to me long before Janice Lever does. I've seen pictures of her all done up in her twirling costume before she got pregnant with Clever in high school. Janice was rosy-cheeked and red-lipped back then and was planning to pursue an acting career. She's faded now. Her hips got a nice relaxation to them, though. She's worked at the diner for years, but before Grampa hired her, Janice was a bar girl at Mr. Bailey's place.

"Ya seen Carol lately?" Janice asks me in that snippy tone she's ALWAYS got.

"Last night."

"Oh yeah, where?" She's holding coffees in one hand, Morse

coding her pointy nails against the tray bottom with the other. *Tap . . . tap . . . tap.*

"Don't remember," I tell her, back to my writing.

"Well, the next time ya see her, tell her I put her belongin's in a sack on Rudy's back porch." *Tap . . . tap . . . tap.*

Oh boy, looks like Janice and Rudy Beaumont, who owns the bait shop, are an item.

"Ya hear me?" *Tap . . . tap . . . tap.*

I slap my pencil down. "I am **NQR**, not deaf, Janice. I hear you loud and clear," I shout. "Ya kicked your only child out and put her belongin's in a sack on Rudy's back porch. I'm proud of ya."

"Ya know, it ain't easy being a mother, so you can just get off your high horse," she yells back.

"For cryin' out loud, I am not on a high horse or any other kind of horse. I'm sittin' in my usual booth at the diner!"

Hell. On top of everything else, Janice musta started up drinking again. She's had a bushel of trouble with this in the past. Well, not the actual drinking part, she does that way above average. But the part where she shows up half naked with her sparkling baton in front of the post office singing "Return to Sender" at the top of her lungs? That's the part she's got the trouble with.

"Table three is waitin' on these specials," Grampa calls out the kitchen peek window.

"I'm on it," Janice calls back to him, giving me one of her scalding looks, which I'm returning with my steely cold investigative eyes that I hope are portraying how rotten I think it is of her to kick Clever out again, especially since she's knocked up. But that's Janice Marie Lever for you. I'm pretty sure nobody would ever accuse this gal of being **Selfless: Showing unselfish concern for the welfare of others.**

"Sometime this week would be good," Grampa hollers.

"How come ya want Clever to give away her baby like a free sample of fudge?" I ask her.

I'm sure she's about to tell me to keep my nose out of her business, like she always does when the subject of Clever comes up, when sudden-like her shoulders dip, and her lips draw up, and gosh, is Janice about to start crying? Well, that'd be a first. Mad is usually what she carries around. "Next time ya see her . . . tell her . . . tell Carol I'm sorry for bein' such a bad mama and that I promise to make it up to her someday, all right?" she says, heading off to the booth near the front door 'fore Grampa can yell at her again to get her butt in gear.

What I *don't* do is call after her, "Sure thing. I'll go find Clever and tell her that straight off, Janice," because her saying that? Making that promise? That might mean something if it wasn't what Janice has been promising since the beginning of time. That someday she'll make it up to Clever for her running around and drinking and treating her daughter like she's a hundred-pound weight been hangin' off her neck since the day she was born. Most heartbreaking thing about all this, even though she doesn't let on, I believe at the bottom of her heart, Clever holds out some hope for her mama's eventual redemption. Not me.

I go back to my writing on the Miss Cheryl and Miss DeeDee story.

"Our visits to Land of a Hundred Wonders have been the high point of our lives," says Miss Cheryl. "Who would have ever thought that . . ."

"Mornin', sunshine," Willard says, plunking down in the booth in front of me with the foxiest of looks. He's got on a tie-dyed T-shirt and pink granny glasses that're perched down on his nose like a canary on a stick.

"Hey," I say, borrowing some of Janice's pissiness. Ever since I learned about Willard wanting Clever to give her baby to that social, my bad feelings for him have multiplied faster than loaves. Why, he's even worse than Sneaky Tim Ray. Not so obvious, if ya know what I mean, more like an on-the-way-to-going-rancid piece of meat. As an investigative reporter, I've developed a smell for this sort of thing.

"Have you seen Carol lately?" Willard asks.

Before I can tell him that I don't have time to play Twenty Questions right now, that I got a deadline, Janice Lever shows up at Willard's booth with a sigh so long it flaps the paper napkins. "Top O' the Mornin'. What can I get for ya?" she drones.

Willard eyes her up and down, strokes his dark mustache. I wonder if he knows that he's making eyes at Clever's mama. Probably not. Can't see Clever introducing Willard to her over Sunday pot roast. 'Specially since there never *is* a Sunday pot roast.

"I'll start out with the biggest, chocolatiest piece of cake you have," Willard tells Janice with a lick of his lips. "And a scoop of . . ."

Where was I? . . . *in such a short time. It's nothing but* . . .

"Come on in here, Gib." Miss Florida beckons to me through the cracked kitchen door.

Damnation! It's like the whole world is in cahoots, not wanting me to finish this story so I can get going investigating the murder of Mr. Buster Malloy and Yes! Yes! Yes! That's the important thing I've been trying to remember all morning. Where's my No. 2 gone off to?

Miss Florida shouts again in that voice of hers that could raise the dead, "Right this minute."

Damnation times two!

When I shove open the kitchen swing door, there's Grampa bent over the deep fryers across the kitchen, his back to me. Miss Florida's hunched over the double sink, up to her elbows in bubbles.

"I'm tryin' to get the paper done. What the hell ya want?" I say to her, fuming.

"Mind your cursin'," she says, following it up with a swat on my arm with her warm, wet hand.

"I was in a car crash that hurt my brain so now it's got a blue streak runs through it. Please accept my deepest of apologies. I'm workin' on it. It's just that Willard's got my goat and Janice is doin' that nail tappin' and ya know how that irritates my brain and if I don't get—"

Miss Florida leans into me. "Ya shoulda told me las' night that Carol's mama kicked her out."

"Sorry . . . I just didn't . . ."

"I'm gonna keep her with me 'til the baby comes," she says, back to rinsing coffee cups clean. "So she's gonna need some a her things."

"Janice just told me she left a belongin's sack for Clever over at Rudy's. I gotta go up to Tanner Farm right now, but I could pick it up afterward."

With one eye, she throws off a withering look through the peek window at Janice. "Sack shouldn't be too heavy, knowin' her." While I wouldn't say the two of them were enemies, I *would* say they got cold shoulderin' down to an art form. Miss Florida's other eye is watching Grampa move from the fryers to the flat grill and back again. "Maybe we better keep this baby business on the QT for a while," she says. "We don' want him gettin' even worse upset, do we?"

No, we do not. He's called me Gibson all morning. And been bossy as hell. That's how ticked off he still is that me and Clever went AWOL the other night over in Browntown. And if he finds out that Clever's gonna have a baby, there's no telling how he'd react. Besides *loco*, I mean.

"Charlie?" I call over to him. "I gotta go get my briefcase. Be back quick as I can." Gonna have to get my scissors out tonight. His hair is curly round the collar. "Charles Michael Murphy?" Not even a shrug.

Well, the heck with him if that's the way he's going to be.

"On the QT," Miss Florida whispers at me when I rush past her on my way outta the kitchen.

The slam of the back screen door jolts Keeper awake. He can't come into the diner because there's a law, so when I'm bussing or writing, he spreads out back here beneath the pin oak with a mixing bowl of water and his beloved fetching stick. Grampa took that white bandage off Keep's head last night and smeared Vaseline across the wound to keep it dry, so this morning, the top of my dog's head looks a little like Elvis's. Swept up like that.

Debonair: Carefree and jaunty.

Bending down to give him a lively scratch behind his ears, I tell him, "Look sharp, you ain't nuthin' but a newshound dog. We're on assignment."

The Odd and the Otter

There's a shortcut to Tanner Farm through the woods behind the diner that empties out into Cubby's Curios and Cool Drinks. Like I previously mentioned, Mr. Cubby St. James is well known as a taxidermist. That's a person who plumps critters' insides up once they are dead. He told me once he'd be happy to do that to Keeper after he moved on to that great kennel in the sky, no charge. "Ya know, like Roy Rogers done with Trigger." I, of course, thanked him for his kind offer despite the fact that I was having a hard time not losing my peanut butter and honey all over him.

Scattered about Mr. Cubby's backyard showroom, in no particular order, there's all sorts of stuffed stuff, including a grizzly bear lying down on a webbed recliner and reading a newspaper. (Mine.) A wide assortment of writhing snakes. An otter with a trout in his paws. Interest in taxidermy must run in families because Mr. Cubby's brother, Mr. Owen St. James? He's the proprietor of Owen's Oddities out near the highway. Mr. Cubby's business runs a tad on the slow side, but his brother's place is thriving. That's 'cause along with *his* stuffed animals, Mr. Owen's got a pettin' zoo with a five-legged pig that is a real crowd pleaser.

Keeper, who normally goes pretty nuts for shortcuts, has not followed me through the trees into the showroom, but instead has chosen to take the long way around. (Don't think he cares much for the way Mr. Cubby eyes him.)

Weaving fast through the attractions, I am already waiting for Keeper next to the stuffed squirrel Mr. Cubby's got sitting on top of his mailbox. "We don't have all day," I shout out to the part of the road that I know my dog'll be coming down. "Ya better get on it, son. Looks like the weather's turnin'."

That'll get his attention. Keeper doesn't care much for storms, and sure enough, here he comes, whipping down Tanner Road, neck and neck with a black VW bus.

"Why did you run off?" Willard asks, when he slows at my side. He's slouched up against the van door, chocolate frosting dotting the corners of his mouth and a cloud of hemp smoke riding shotgun. "Can I give you a ride?"

"No, thank you."

"You never answered me back at the diner," he says. "Have you or have you not seen Carol lately?"

"Ready-set?" I say, acting like it takes all my concentration to throw Keeper's fetching stick for him.

"She's got something of mine that she needs to return immediately."

Could he mean the baby? Has he changed his mind about giving it up to the social? "What's she got that you need so bad?"

Leaves are juddering. Branches vibrating. There's another storm coming and it ain't dawdling. "You remember that map I showed the two of you a few nights ago?" he asks, so reasonable.

"N-o."

"Well, I showed it to you."

"What was it a map of?"

"It's a . . . treasure map."

I hadn't realized how far we'd come on account of us conversating, but here we are already on the edge of Miz Tanner's property. The Smith brothers are jogging horses back up to the barn from the paddocks. Teddy sees me, points up to the whirling dervish clouds. "Hurry on up here," Vern hollers.

"Be right there," I yell back, attempting to cross to the other side of the road.

Willard guns his engine, cuts me off. "How about if you and I make a deal? I'll give you part of the treasure if you get that map from Carol and bring it to me."

I think real fast, much faster than I thought I was able. If there really *is* a treasure, then Clever and me could find it and then she'd have some money to buy diapers for her baby and some food. Everything could go back to the way it was before. Even better maybe, because I've always liked babies' toes a whole lot. "Okay, it's a deal. If I see Clever, I'll get her to give me that treasure map and bring it to you straightaway. Swear on a stack."

(Boy, when I get my briefcase back, I'm giving myself two, no, three gold stars. I'm becoming a crackerjack liar!)

"You find that map and bring it to me or else I'll have to report Carol to the authorities for stealing and she'd have to go to jail," Willard says, not sounding so reasonable anymore.

The kind of thunder that turns tonsils into a tuning fork rumbles overhead and with a look of apology, Keeper takes off, butt scraping up Miz Tanner's drive. (Lightning's the only real thing that seizes him up.)

"Already swore I'd bring ya the map, didn't I?" I say, scooting behind the bus so he can't run over me. I wouldn't put anything past him at this point. He's got a look of desperateness about him.

"I'm warning you," Willard yells. "Bring me the map tonight or there'll be hell to pay."

Standing there, watching him take off down the road under the threatening sky, I'm left to thinking that man's got an even darker side to him than I'd previously perceived. In fact, it's clear as can be that Mr. Willard DuPree of New York City has got a whole lot more sympathy for the devil than he does for my Clever.

By the time I stagger through Miz Tanner's barn doors, the storm has shared half of itself with me. "Keeper?" I call out, swiping the wet off. Popping his head out of the tack room, he gives me a nod, but slinks back fast under a saddle rack. (I'd go and comfort him, but he doesn't go in for that sort of thing.) "I'm gonna get the leather-like, be right back." Because no way am I waitin' until the sky has finished throwing its hissy fit. I need my briefcase back NOW. I've been feeling as unbalanced as a tightrope walker without a pole. Inching out beneath the barn overhang, when I get to the bushes where I left it, I steady myself against the soaked barn wood, reach in and grope for the worn handle, but it's nowhere there.

"Gib? What . . . rain . . . doin'?" Miss Jessie yells. I didn't notice her on my way up, but I shoulda known she'd be out on the porch in her bentwood rocker since she and I have more than once enjoyed watching a good gully washer together.

I wave, but go right back to searching. Where the heck is it? With slipping feet, I try further down the side of the barn, around the evergreen bushes. Oh my God of heaven and earth. Did I put it somewhere else and don't remember?

Next I look up, here comes Miss Jessie jogging across the yard with a red umbrella. Adjusting it over both our heads, she says, "Well, this was sure unexpected."

I'm not sure if she means me or the rain.

"What *are* you doin'?" she asks.

"I'm lookin' for my briefcase. I set it in these bushes when I came for the egg order and went home without it. My blue spiral's in it and some film that I need to get right over to Bob's Drug Emporium for developin'."

"I guess you and me are in the same boat. I can't find Tim Ray and I need him to do some fence mendin' once this storm passes. A couple of the herd broke through that back pasture this mornin'. Ya haven't seen him, have ya?"

I slide toward the hedge closest to the barn door and hatchet my arm straight down, but my hand comes back with nothing but scratches. "Can't recall exactly," I say, worried sick.

"Be best if we come back and look for our lost items once this lets up." It really is coming down almost biblical. "Let's make a dash for the house," Miss Jessie says, tugging on my arm.

I don't want to go with her. I need to keep looking for my leather-like, but I also don't want her telling Grampa that I don't have enough sense to get out of the rain. So given no choice, I call, "C'mon outta there, Keep," and the three of us take off.

"Have you by any chance seen my briefcase? It's black. Leather-like," I huff out when Miss Jessie tosses me a tan towel from outta the mudroom off the porch. "I put it in those bushes outside the barn when I came to pick up the egg order and now I can't find it."

"Ya already asked me that, hon," she says, easing into the back of her rocker in sort of a pooped-out way. "Ya sure it was *those* bushes you left it in? Tim Ray trimmed that side of the barn yesterday and didn't say a thing about findin' your briefcase."

Lord.

Of course you understand by now how deadly important that briefcase is to me at this point in my investigation. Looks like my next order of business will be locating that scannel Sneaky Tim Ray to negotiate a ransom. I feel like I ate a whole loaf of greasy bread.

"Blot your hair," Miss Jessie tells me, demonstrating on Keeper.

What a sweet and helpful woman. I can't hardly spend any time with her without thinking what a nice wedded couple she and Grampa would make. Besides all the other things they enjoy doin' together, like their bird-watching and square dancing, Charles Michael Murphy, hailing from Abilene, Texas, knows the front end from the back end of a horse so would be a real help around the farm. Sadly, I believe I know exactly why he doesn't go full bore on romancing her. He yearns for Gramma Kitty some. "Do you ever miss your dead husband?" I ask her.

"Whatever brought that up?" she says, frowning.

Tilting forward in my chair to run the towel down my dripping legs, I get a view of the hayloft. Up against the crackling sky, Sneaky Tim Ray is leaning against the half-open doors, dangling my briefcase from his putrid fingertips.

"Look! There he is," I yell, pointing.

Miss Jessie rocks forward, but by the time she gets the right angle, Sneaky Tim Ray's already backed up into the shadows. On her rock back, she shoots me one of those looks she gives a horse when she's checking its trot for lameness. "You all right, Gib?"

I pounce to my feet. "No, I am not! Tim Ray's up in the loft with my briefcase." (I never call him *Sneaky* to her face. Even though she's not fond of him, he's still her kin.) "I'm goin' up there."

"You can forget that. You'll get soaked worse than you already are. Catch your death of cold. Your grampa wouldn't like that," she says, nurse-like 'cause she used to be a practical one up in Louisville before she got married to her dead husband.

"We really oughta close those loft doors. Ya don't want your hay to get wet," I urge, still raring to go.

"The rain's not comin' from that direction. The hay'll be fine." When she pats my chair, I reluctantly sit down on the edge because I *also* don't want her telling Grampa I forgot my manners. I'll bide my time, my eyes locked on the loft. According to **The Importance of Perception in Meticulous Investigation: The Stakeout:** *Patience is a virtue when an operative is observing a suspect. One must remain alert and ready.*

When he shows himself again, I'll be quick.

"What was your husband's name again?" I ask, refusing to blink.

"Har—"

Sneaky Tim Ray scutters back into view.

"There!"

By the time she's tilted up next to me, he's vanished again. That tricky butthole.

Miss Jessie gives me another diagnosing look and says, "That reminds me, speaking of the dearly departed, I was pickin' up some pies this mornin' down at the diner and Miss Florida told me that you told her that ya found Buster Malloy dead. Is that right?"

"No, ma'am. Why would I tell her that?"

"Look at me, Gib."

This reporter does *not* take her eyes off the loft.

"You tellin' me the truth?" Miss Jessie asks, getting me by the chin.

"Cross my heart," I say, even though I *am* lying. I don't want her to know about dead Mr. Buster Malloy because she could tell Grampa, who would immediately put the kibosh on my investigation, and where would that leave my mama? I'll tell ya where. Knowing for all eternity that I might never get **R**ight again. I'd rather be planning my own funeral than let that happen.

"Ya *positive* ya didn't tell Florida you found Buster dead?" Miss Jessie asks.

"A hundred percent," I say, pulling out of her grasp. Sneaky Tim Ray has not reappeared. I know what he wants. He wants me to lie down in the hay with him and lift up my shirt and won't give me back my briefcase until I do.

"His name was Harry," she says, settling back again.

"Whose name was Harry?"

"My husband's. You remember him, don't you? He and your grampa were the ones that taught ya to ride when you were just a bit of a thing."

Harry? Doesn't ring a bell, but I say, "He was such a nice man, Miss Jessie. A real nice Harry." I spring outta my chair even though I can tell it's important to her that we sit and remember him together. I don't want to hurt her feelings, but, well, the rain is letting up some and I got a fish to fry.

"Life sure is peculiar, ain't it," she says. "The way a warm body is keepin' you close, takin' care of you and then just like that." She snaps her fingers. "You're one instead of two."

Or one instead of three.

Memories are washing across Miss Jessie's face. What a comfort that must be, to recollect whatever you want, whenever you want. To wade right into those good old days. When there was a mama and daddy. And a me that is no more. When . . . for crissakes. What a complete dope I am. Why in the world did I bring up her dead husband when the purpose of this whole conversation was to glue Grampa and her together in a love collage?

"Ya know how ya been askin' me to help you move some of that hay from the loft down to the feed room?" I switch subjects, hoping she'll do the same. "Now would be a real good time for me to do that for ya."

"What?" she answers.

"I said, I'll move that hay outta the loft for you today."

"Oh. Well, thanks for the offer, but that's a job for two and I gotta get into town. I'm on the food committee for Cray Ridge Days and we got our final meetin' this afternoon," she says, setting Keeper down. "C'mon, I'll give you a ride back to the diner."

Crap on a cracker. I can't say, Don't trouble yourself, I'm looking forward to walking back through this hellacious storm. No. Miss Jessie's a sharp cookie. That would make her suspicious as hell. I look back up at the loft. There he is. Giving me one of those movie-star smiles of his. Those pictures of Miss Cheryl and Miss DeeDee sitting in their car in front of the pumps are in that briefcase. And, more important, the ones of Buster Malloy dead on the beach are in there, too. The leather-like is locked so Sneaky Tim Ray can't get at them unless he breaks it open. But I'm pretty certain that's not what he wants to get into.

"Gosh, I just remembered something," I say, walking beside Miss Jessie on the way to her truck. "I told Peaches I'd give her a bath."

"Ya sure you wanna do that today?"

"Ya know how I get when I set a plan, Miss Jessie. Ya know what a goddamn terrier I can be."

"Matter of fact, I do," she says, giving me a caring look that ends by her hooking my bangs over my ear. "All right, I guess that donkey could use a rinse off. She's one of 'em that broke through that fencin' today and she's caked up good. Use the soap in my trunk." Once she gets herself situated behind the wheel, she turns to me and says in her most full-hearted way, "Life has a short wick, Gib. Burn bright whenever you can, hear?"

"I will, Miss Jessie. I promise." I am struggling to hold myself back from smothering that adorable face of hers in kisses. She's so nice. Sorta innocent. I don't believe there's any point to snuffing out all that goodness by telling her that I don't believe anything that I'm about to do with her rotten cousin by marriage would be considered enlightening, here, there, or anywhere.

An Eye for an Eye

Yesterday after we left Tanner Farm, Keeper and me took a stroll over to Candy World. Loretta wasn't there. Probably busy rolling around in salted peanuts and sticky caramel with Reverend Jack. But Sue Pie, her help, sold me a bag. I think my mama musta been fond of chocolate-covered cherries, too, since almost every time I eat one, that picture of her and me down at the lake catching pollywogs drifts into my mind. Reverend Jack has told me that when things like that happen, when a smell or a sound or a taste makes something rise up familiar in your head, that is called—a cents memory. He says that's a good sign. I have to agree with him. My brain feels as shiny as a brand-new silver dollar.

I also dropped my roll of film at Bob's Drug Emporium and told Bob that it was a RUSH job. He said that he wasn't so busy and that I could have the pictures back today because he develops them himself in a closet at the back of the store. I sure am glad to have my black leather-like back.

After making our usual morning stop at Land of a Hundred Wonders to help Miss Lydia with her hives (honey is an important ingredient in many of her miraculous potions, particularly the one she makes to treat shingles), I'm back doing my job at Top O' the Mornin', lapping that creamy cherry center out of the waxy dark chocolate and gloating like crazy over the new headline I've just written in my blue spiral:

Buster Malloy Found Dead on Browntown Beach!

My ears are still ringing from the row Janice and Clever had out back of the diner just moments ago. It went something like this:

"Goddamn it, Carol. When ya gonna learn life ain't *always* about you. I got needs too, ya know," Janice yowled.

Clever catted back, "What ya mean, life ain't always about me? When has it *ever* been about me?" and her hair was all crazy-looking, too. "It's been 'bout you, Mama. Ya don't care a whit 'bout me. All ya care about is gettin' a bottle and a man to keep ya—"

That's when Janice hauled back her ropey arm and slapped Clever straight across the face so hard that the yellow rose flew outta her hair smack dab into a puddle. And Janice probably woulda hit her like that again if I hadn't yelled, "Charlie, come quick," and he hadn't come running through the back door, and seeing what was going on, said, "That's about enough of that." Clever waited 'til Grampa got a good hold of her mama and then she hawked and spit at Janice's white waitress shoes, picked up the rose and stuck it back into her hair, mud and all, and went running off into the woods with one of Miss Florida's chiffon pies tucked under her arm.

So, that's what's been going on around here. Sorry. Nothing else much new to report.

HA! HA! HA!

You think I've forgotten that I left you hanging in suspense after Miss Jessie left for her Cray Ridge Days meeting and I slunk over to the barn to negotiate the return of my briefcase with Sneaky Tim Ray, don't you?

Well, I haven't. Not by a long shot!

(I'm proud to report that my sense of humor may be reassembling itself. To quote the *Jokes-A-Million* book: *Doing the unexpected is important in the funny business.*)

Sooo . . . let me get ya caught up.

This is what happened yesterday right after I waved goodbye to Miss Jessie, who was on her way to the Cray Ridge Days refreshment meeting.

Keeper and me hurried up to the barn, and without further ado headed toward the narrow stairs to the hayloft with a lot of **Trepidation: Trembling fright.**

Teddy Smith was sweeping the barn aisle at the time, moving a piece of straw from one corner of his mouth to the other, concentrating with all he had. I am in general much more acquainted with him than I am with his brother since Teddy is over at the Land of a Hundred Wonders so much of the time helping out Miss Lydia with this and that. He was there this morning, in fact, same time I was.

Vern called over from the work sink, "Hep you with something, Gibber?"

I was about about to say, No, thank you, but then from outta nowhere this plan came to me . . . just about blinded me, that's how bright it was.

"Ya need somethin' outta the loft?" Vern asked, as I was placing my foot on the bottom step.

I most certainly did. Because nobody, I mean NOT ONE BODY, is gonna stop me from writing that story about Mr. Buster. And that includes Sneaky Tim Ray Holloway. So I arranged my brilliant plan in my mind and a bothered look on my face when I answered him, "Sneaky Tim Ray's up top. He had some real bad things to say about Miss Florida yesterday and I'm fixin' to have a few words with him to set him straight."

Vern stopped rinsing the bucket he was holding and said, "What 'zactly that uselessness Holloway have to say?"

Winging it, I said, "Ah . . . he told me with a lot of digust in his voice that Miss Florida smelled like . . . like . . . a chicken coop."

On hearing that, Teddy leaned his broom against a stall door, brushed his hands down the front of his work pants, and headed up the loft staircase with jackhammer feet. I could smell his mad comin' off him. Almost see it in waves.

"Don't kill him," Vern warned, because his brother is the classic example of still waters run . . . waters still run . . . Teddy's the strong, silent type.

"Long as you're up there, would you mind terribly retrievin' my briefcase?" I called after him. "Sneaky Tim Ray stole it off me."

Even though he didn't say, I sure will, Gibber, I knew Teddy heard me by the way the muscles in his back got even bulgier.

"All right then," I said, pleased as punch with my little plan. "Need some help, Vern?"

Turning the water back on full force, he said, "A body could always use a little help."

"I'd have to agree with you," I said, and picked up a rough brush from the shelf above the work sink.

That's right about when the storm, not entirely satisfied with the job it'd done earlier, decided to give it another shot. Hard rain on a tin roof makes Billy ascared because it reminds him of gunfire, but to me, that *tat . . . tat . . . tat . . .* was real soothing, especially since it was harmonizing with the *shud . . . shud . . . shud* from above that could only mean one thing. Teddy Smith had gone back to his sweeping. Only this time it was the hayloft floor and he was using Sneaky Tim Ray Holloway instead of a broom.

Don't think a girl could ask for sweeter sounds.

After it got all still up top, Teddy sauntered down the steps looking refreshed and swinging my briefcase like he just got back from a job in a Louisville office. Normally, if a colored man beat up on a white man, there would be quite a to-do around here. But when it came to Holloway, thank goodness, nobody seemed to care who whacked him around. (Since Teddy only uses his high C voice once in a blue moon, I knew I could count on him NOT to inform Sneaky Tim Ray it was me who told him that Miss Florida was coop-smelling.)

When all was said and done, the Smiths were kind enough to drop me off back in town.

"Thanks for the ride," I told 'em, slamming the Chevy door behind me.

And they musta really liked the gold stars I gave them because they gifted me something in return. Teddy tossed it to me through the truck window, and Vern said, "Think of it as a souvenir," and tuba-laughed. "An *eye*-catchin' one."

Other than forgetting to pick up Clever's belongin's bag, which I promised Miss Florida I would do today, I consider it one heck of a successful afternoon.

So here we are back at the diner, in case you've forgotten. (Awful feelin', ain't it?)

"Gibby?" Grampa calls from behind the cash register. Top O' the Mornin' is closing-time empty 'cept for me and him and Miss Florida, who is done folding her apron square.

"Charlie?" How relieved I am that he's called me Gibby instead of Gibson. His mad at me from going to Browntown the other night must be wearing down some.

"Frank Bailey told me the perch are bitin' off Witch Point," he says, counting coin.

"That right?" I say, not looking up from my blue spiral. I don't want to break the mood.

Miss Florida calls from the back hall, "See y'all tomorrow. God willin' and the creek don' rise."

"Stay dry," I shout.

"So?" Grampa says, emptying the till into his bucket.

"I'd love to go fishin' with you, but I can't today. I gotta get busy investigating the death of . . ." *That was a close call.* ". . . the death of . . . ah . . . Miz Titwilliger's cat."

He's coming to sit down in the booth across from me. Uncapping his black pen so he can jot down the egg order. "What happened to Miz Titwilliger's cat?"

(Damn, he's cagey.)

"Ahhh . . . not sure. That's why I gotta get over there to interview her ASAP."

Sliding over the napkin that he wrote 3 doz on, he says, "First things first," and tips his cowboy fishing hat back hard enough to make the lures jangle. "I believe we have a paper to look over."

Grampa never lets the *Gazette* get typed up and run off by Miss Ruth over at the library until he checks it over. To make sure I haven't spelled something incorrectly or written about a subject that might get me in a heap of trouble, like it did with that picture I printed of bare-butted Janice Lever doing something she shouldn'ta with Gus the handyman last year.

Grampa reads aloud from the ***Love, Love Me Do*** column:

"There's word in town that Reverend Jack, the Lord's help, and Loretta Boyd, owner of Candy World, are *sweet* on each other." Giving me an almost apple-puckerin' smile, he says, "Good," and flips to the front of the paper to read the lead story, the Miss Cheryl and Miss DeeDee one. All of a sudden Grampa doesn't look so amused.

"Ya gotta stop describin' Hundred Wonders like it's some sorta miracle place. Folks are gonna get the wrong idea," he says, testy.

"I've seen things up there that you wouldn't believe," I protest. My feelings get hurt that he never takes me at my word. Miss Lydia tells me it's because Grampa got wore down after Gramma died, and when a short while later my mama died, and then when *I* almost died, his faith just eroded away. "Land of a Hundred Wonders *is* a miracle place. Miss Lydia does all sorts of heavenly things for folks who—"

"Lydia is nuttier than one of Loretta's caramel apples and Hundred Wonders is nuthin' but a third-rate—"

"But I heard you tell Miss Jessie once that if I ever get quite right again, that'd be a miracle."

"I meant a different kind of miracle. Not like what Lydia is up to. What she call them things? Actuations? Visitations? All she's doin' is salving her guilty conscience. Enough is enough. I'm headin' out there this afternoon and havin' some strong words with her."

"Is havin' words all you'll be doin' with her? Maybe *you're* the one's got a guilty conscience. I heard that you and Miss Lydia were an item at one time."

"Why, that's . . . that's nuthin' but hog swallow! True, I loved that girl, but not in *that* way." He looks like he might blow a gasket. "Where'd you hear that?"

Gathering up my reporting supplies and jamming them into my leather-like, I reply tart, "A reporter never reveals her sources." (Clever.)

Grampa is stubborn as a new bottle of ketchup, but I can hold my own, too. Smacking his palms down hard, he slides out of the booth. I chase after him, even though I'm feeling toward him a way I can't ever remember feeling. Hollerin' from the diner's back steps as he stomps toward the truck, "Ya gotta stop coddlin' me. How am I ever goin' to get quite right if you keep ridin' roughshod all over me, every minute of the day? Let me do my own thinkin'."

"Sharper than a serpent's tooth ungrateful is what you are," he shouts, slamming the truck door hard behind him.

I could spit, that's how infuriating he's being. "What's wrong with me spreadin' my wings a little?"

He's staring straight ahead through the windshield, mouth straight and white as a highway line. "You comin'?" he yells, gassing the engine.

"No, I am not," I yell back.

Without so much as a see ya later alligator, he charges out of the parking lot, tires spinning and exhaust smoke spewing.

"The hell with you," I shout, shaking my fist. "I can do just fine all by myself. You'll see . . . you . . . you . . . goddamn peg-legged-fishin'-cowboy-whittlin'-bird-watcher."

Hiding and Seeking

Completely peeved at Grampa, I dropped the paper off at the library myself, then swung by Rudy's Bait Shop to pick up Clever's things. Now I'm sprinting down Lake Mary Road like I'm gettin' chased by a wet hen. I mean it, the hell with him. Bossing me day and night, giving me those disappointed looks of his. I've had him clear up to here, I tell ya. I even threw away the egg order. Let the customers eat scrambled dirt tomorrow, for all I care.

I've got my briefcase in one hand, Clever's belongin's bag in the other. Maybe I shouldn't, but I take a peek inside and see a once red, now pink sweatshirt, Cray R dge Bul rogs peeling across the front. Ratty jeans. Two pairs of stretched-out socks that don't match at the heel. But there is also something so extraordinary, something so thoughtful that I'd never believe that selfish, selfish Janice Lever would be capable of sending it along. It's Clever's prized possession. The movie poster she got at the county fair of Paul Newman and Robert Redford in *Butch Cassidy and the Sundance Kid* that used to hang above her mattress in the apartment. (Like I mighta mentioned earlier, that is our most *absolutely* favorite movie of all times. None other even comes close. We got to watch it every single night for the weeks it was up at the Outdoor 'cause Clever was allowing pimply Dennis Franklin to touch her heinie around that time and he ran the ticket booth out near the road, so all we had to pay for was popcorn.)

We can say almost all the words by heart. For me, who can't recall the day of the week without checking my underwear, that's quite the accomplishment, wouldn't ya say? That movie means something **Profound: Penetrating into the depths of one's being** to the two of us. Might be Butch and the Kid's fine friendship. Maybe it's the strong cowboy atmosphere. I've thought about it and thought about it, and I'm still not entirely sure what it is that stirs us so. All I know is that movie makes Clever and me feel like a double anchor resting secure on a sandy bottom, so I put the poster back into the belongin's bag with a lotta careful.

I'll show Grampa. Keeper and me are on our way to the beach. Mr. Buster Malloy will be lying there in the sand, more'n likely a little riper. Being at the scene of the crime should help me set the tone for my story once I solve who done him in.

The Importance of Perception in Meticulous Investigation says: *Journalists must make sure their readers feel as if they are witnessing a reported event firsthand. Your article must have the right tone.* What that means is you wouldn't want to sound too cheerful when you write Sugar Jenkins's obituary. Telling your faithful readers how unusually clean he looked in his white Sunday suit and wasn't that creamy coffin the most interesting of choices? No. You'd want that obituary to be sorrowful as can be, and not have the same tone as the story you wrote on the 4-H fashion show.

Squiggly heat is coming up off the road and the cicada noise is pecking alongside my mad. When I gear down to get my breath, I can hear him. No, not hear him. Feel him. I don't recall if I had Billy radar in the old days like I do now. He was there waiting for us at the cottage the day Grampa brought me back from the hospital. That memory comes to mind 'specially easy 'cause when I spotted Billy sitting on our picnic table, a bouquet of wildflowers in one hand, a WELCOME HOME sign in the other, I remarked, "Well, isn't that as thoughtful as can be. Who is that boy?" and Grampa's eyes brimmed up, and that hardly never happens.

Keeper looks up at me for permission to go track Billy down in the woods, and when I nod, he takes off. Ya know, I think that might be one of that dog's best qualities. No matter how many times he searches for Billy, never mind that he has *not once* found him—Keeper has hope, and like me, a short memory, which I have come to believe might be the most important aspect of hopefulness. Ya start remembering all the times hope has left you holding the bag, and ya still keep up with it, hell, that's just plain ignorant.

"Hey," Billy hollers out from the trees.

"Where you been?" I answer belligerently, because I'm not only ticked at Grampa, I'm ticked at Billy, come to think about it. I depend on him, and he woulda been a real help when Sneaky Tim Ray jumped out of those Browntown bushes the other night, showing me how the south has risen again.

"I hadda go see Doc Sam yesterday for more tranquilizin' medicine," Billy says, still flitting around in the woods. "Ya been okay?"

"Fine," I answer in a clipped-off way. Don't feel like reporting everything that has happened since I saw him last. He doesn't deserve to know. Besides, it's too hot to talk.

"Where you headed?" he asks.

"Browntown Beach."

"Why?" he asks, sounding alarmed.

I say, so ornery, "I got my reasons." But what are they? I can't remember *what* the heck I'm doing out on Lake Mary Road.

"If ya got the time, I was hopin' you'd come up to the cave with me."

He's *always* bothering me to go up to Blackstone with him. Back before everything happened that's happened—before the crash, before Billy went off to war, before Clever knew about hot sex, before Cooter knew how to play craps, even before Georgie died—Blackstone Cave was our hideout. Clever and Billy reminisce about those days all the time, leaving me to feel like I'm the only one not invited to a family reunion.

"Why ya always buggin' me about goin' up to Blackstone anyways?" I call.

"There's something I need ya to see up there." Billy steps out of the brush with Keeper in his arms. "Something that might jar your memory."

Goodness gracious. With his stomach muscles below his cut-off shirt rippling in the heat, this boy looks ripe and good enough to eat. I take a step toward him. He steps back. He smells like a slice of just-cut watermelon. I take another step toward him. He takes another step back.

"William Brown Junior . . . S-T-A-Y, goddamn it," I command, breathy. I swear, I don't know what's come over me, but it's something real powerful. "I . . . I believe I am havin' the desire to run my tongue down your juicy neck."

I check to see if his pants are pooching out the way Sneaky Tim Ray's do at moments like these, but that camouflage material is doing its job.

"No," Billy takes his time saying, staring up at the sky, the bushes, anywhere but at me.

"Why the hell not?"

He cannot speak. Or won't. Just like Grampa, he's giving me the silent treatment.

"Don't you like my fine young body with titties that taste like milk and honey? Yum-yum?" I ask, repeating what Holloway says when he catches up to me.

Billy's breathing is gettin' sorta raggedy, too. Just like me, he's feeling *something*. Why won't he touch me and let me touch him? What's wrong with him?

Uh-oh.

"You're not like the Carmodys' coon hound, are ya? Ya don't like boy dogs more than girl dogs, do ya?" I ask.

Nothing comes back but the cicadas.

"Answer me right this minute," I demand, inching closer.

"I love you," Billy says, inching farther.

"Well, I love you, too. Now we got that settled, c'mere to me." I reach out for him, but just like that, Billy retreats into the trees and I'm left standing sweaty by the side of the road with not the slightest idea what to do about this starving feeling that's come over me.

By the time Keeper and me get to Browntown Beach, I recall why I've come here in the first place. Yes, to set the tone for my story. So I head straight over to where Mr. Buster Malloy should be lying out with quite the tan. Keep's got other interests. At a gallop, he sails through the air, landing in the lake with a raucous splash.

I musta mixed up the spots. There's the Geronimo rope. The lake. The sand. Dang it! First Grampa. Then Billy. Now dead Mr. Buster has up and went! Men. Bah. The lot of 'em got better disappearing acts than Mr. Harry Houdini.

White Sheets

picked some flowers on my way home through Wally's Woods. Grampa's favorite bluebells. I have plans to apologize for my earlier outburst at the diner, eat a crispy-skinned perch, soap up the dishes, and let him beat the pants off me in Scrabble. Then spend the rest of the night trying to figure out the mystery. Never mind my corpse has up and left. The film I dropped off at Bob's Drug Emporium should be ready any minute and I'll have proof that I found Buster on Browntown Beach deader than dead.

When me and Keeper come through the cottage's picket gate, we raise our noses, expecting to inhale the odor of the catch of the day crackling over the coals, but nothing yummy is wafting our way. Matter of fact, the air has a peculiar odor to it. Unstirred.

"Charlie?" I shout out, coming round to the front. "Charles Michael Murphy?"

For some reason I cannot fathom, Sheriff Johnson is sitting on the lawn in Grampa's chair. Miss Jessie is there, too, hunched over the picnic table. What are they doing here? Oh, of course! Grampa musta invited them for supper, which is extremely good-hearted of him considering how much LeRoy turns his stomach.

"Hey, Miss Jessie, Sheriff," I say, setting down the bluebells on top of my briefcase. "Sorry, but it looks like chow is gonna be a little late tonight. Grampa probably lost track of the time. The fish were bitin' off Witch Point." His boat's gone. And his other knife, the one he uses to scrape scale, is missing from where he keeps it next to his whittlin' knife. "He should be back any minute. Can I get y'all a glass of lemonade and crackers to start things off?"

The sheriff isn't paying me any mind, arms twined behind his head, sweat stains running like stalactites down the sides of his sandy shirt. But Miss Jessie raises her head and rimmed rose eyes. "No, thank you, Gib."

"Would you prefer water?"

A tiny peep escapes from her lips. "Honey . . . your grampa." She takes my hand into hers, clamps it shut. "There's been a . . . a kind of accident."

"Really?" I say, excited. "What kind?" Accidents, like folks slipping in the bathtub or getting kicked by a horse, always make GREAT news. Grampa calls it there-but-for-the-grace-of-God thinking. That dear, dear man, he musta motored over to the accident site. I bet he's taking notes for me 'til I can get there. That was so sweet of him to send the sheriff and Miss Jessie to come fetch me so I wouldn't miss out on the story. I feel doubly bad about losing my temper with him this afternoon. "We gotta hurry. Don't wanna get scooped."

Guess they don't get it. They aren't budging.

"Sorry," I say, picking up my leather-like, "y'all are gonna have to come back tomorrow. There's no supper tonight. Grampa does all the cookin' and he's at that accident, waitin' on me."

Sheriff Johnson, fingering the whittled Peaches statue Grampa has been working on, says, "Fact is, Charlie *is* the accident."

"LeRoy!" Miss Jessie reprimands.

"She's old enough to know the truth," he says to her, and then, turning to me, "Frank Bailey found your grampa out on the lake, lying on the bottom of his boat, barely breathin'."

"What?" My brain is diving down to its bottom. When it comes back up to the surface, there he'll be, flipping over a fish and humming a Johnny Cash tune and Keeper will be sneaking up next to him, vying for an eyeball.

I look over to Miss Jessie. The sheriff would lie. She wouldn't.

She nods.

"Is he . . . is he gonna die?"

"Doc Sam says it was a heart attack," Miss Jessie says. "Ya know what that is, hon?"

"His heart is real sick," the sheriff throws in.

Lying again. My grampa's heart is healthy and bursting with love.

"He was alone out on the lake and nobody knows for how long," Miss Jessie murmurs.

"Coulda been most of the afternoon," the sheriff says, offhand.

And that's all it takes, the sound of his not caring about my grampa and his hurt heart, for me to fling myself at him. Start beating on him, screaming, "You goddamn liar, you bad bully, ya aren't worth—"

"Gib!" Miss Jessie shouts, pulling me off him and enveloping me in her arms.

This is all my fault. I shoulda gone fishing with Grampa like I always did when he asked. He woulda been okay if I had. Because I attended that Red Cross class Miss Jessie taught at the library, I know what causes a person to have a heart attack. Their blood begins to boil. And one of the reasons their blood can get to boiling is if they get *real mad* at somebody. Somebody they sacrificed their life to take care of. Somebody who just this afternoon acted sharper than a serpent's tooth ungrateful.

I used to close my eyes and hold my breath whenever Grampa drove past St. Mary's. My mama and daddy died in a hospital and I spent months in one recovering from the crash. They shouldn'ta named it after our lake. A hospital is nothing like a lake.

Miss Jessie is by my side. "You gonna be all right?" she asks.

"I doubt that very much." I am leaning my shoulder against the glaring wall outside room 123. I snuck Keeper in beneath my shirt and he's making a whimpering noise I never heard him make before and never want to hear again.

"They've given him something to make him sleep," Miss Jessie says, placing her hand on my back and pressing me through the doorway.

Up against the far wall, next to a shaded window, there's a silver bed. Tubes on a pole are emptying something clear into his arm. It's dim in here, so I edge closer. "Praise you, Mighty Lord," I moan after gettin' a good look at him. Someone has made a tragic mistake. This cannot be *my* grampa. This grampa's face is slack, lips shiny with drool. And his hair is mussed up. There's-a-place-for-everything-and-everything-has-its-place Charles Michael Murphy would never stand for that.

I whisper to Miss Jessie, "What we're experiencing here is a classic case of mistaken identity." Mr. Howard Redmond in **The Importance of Perception in Meticulous Investigation** in his chapter entitled **Mistaken Identity** writes: *Be sure you have* *the right subject. Many people bear a remarkable resemblance to each other.*

"Gib," Miss Jessie says, "don't."

I study the old gentleman again to make sure. How pale his skin. My grampa is as brown as a nutberry. (I knew the sheriff was lying like a no-legged dog. Just knew it.)

"I bet Grampa's over at the Tap chatting with Mr. Bailey about the army days," I say, backing away. "C'mon, let's go find him. I need to tell him a couple of urgent-type things 'fore I forget." On the drive over, I decided to let him in on me finding that dead body on the beach. It's the least I can do.

As Miss Jessie bends down to adjust the sheet, Keeper shoves off my chest, landing in the empty space right below his knee, and I cannot bear to look. Over in the corner shadows . . . there it is. The fake leg with the shiny black shoe and blue diamond sock that never needs washing. His cowboy fishing hat sitting on top.

Miss Jessie reaches for me, reels me to her side. "I know he doesn't always come right out and say it 'cause that's not his way, but you . . . you mean the world to him. I'll give you two some time alone," she says, kissing the top of my head.

The door to the room sighs shut behind her, slow enough that I can hear her suffering start up.

Patting his hair into place, I slip onto the bed next to him, stretch my body up close to his and pick up his hardworkin' hand in mine, whispering into his ear, "Charlie? Ya in there?" He seems so delicate, like something that clumsy me has no business touching. Pressing my cheek against his, I breathe him in and he doesn't smell sick. More like the sun, and the sky, and the lake at dawn. He wouldn't like it if I cried, which I'm fighting so hard against, 'cause I just remembered with no problem at all what I yelled at him this afternoon, when we fought at the diner. *Ah, the hell with you . . . you goddamn peg-legged-fishin'-cowboy-whittlin'-bird-watcher. I can do just fine all by myself.*

I was lying.

On My Ownish

After I held Grampa's hand tight two days straight, Miz Tay Lewis, the nurse who was minding him in the hospital, told me he was in good hands and that I should get some rest. Miss Jessie suggested I stay at her farmhouse. I told her—"No, thank you." Though being around the horses'd be comforting, I didn't need to be keeping an eye out for Sneaky Ray. No. I needed to be back at the cottage with my mama's paintings, Grampa's Lucky Strike–smelling shirts. The lapping of the lake.

Don't much feel like it, but I know what I really should do, what is of #1 importance, is to put all my concentration on solving this murder case and then writing my awfully good story. Not only for Mama, but for when Grampa comes home from the hospital. So he'll see that I'm getting **Q**uite **R**ight enough that I can take care of him the way he's been taking care of me all these years. "While you're recuperating, take a nap out on the porch and I'll catch us a bass," is what I'll tell him.

Not being able to stand the stillness of the cottage, I've come out to the pier. The water is slick with gas, but the minnows don't care, they're darting around my toes. All that's left of the day is a lemon slice of sun. It's bad enough to be without Grampa in the day hours, but in the night?

Just a bit ago, Mr. Frank Bailey came by. 'Cept for me, he's Grampa's best friend. "What're you doin' with his boat?" I asked him when he got done tying up at our pier. "When's he comin' home?"

He went over the whole damn heart attack story, finishing up with, "Ya know that you're always welcome to come stay with me and the missus."

I told him, "Thank you for the kind offer, but roses need quite a bit of water if they're to bloom to their fullest." Grampa's been crisscrossing them since I was a little girl. Mixing a bit of this rose with a bit of that rose until he came up with three original peachy pink types he calls the Gibby, the Addy (after Mama), and the Kitty (after Gramma). "These flowers remind me of my girls," he boasts. "Nice smellin' and pretty as hell, but mind where you grab on to 'em. They can be a tad prickly."

Mr. Bailey nodded over at the gardens. "Charlie always did have one hell of a green thumb. Shout out, ya need anything," he said, peeling off bills from the wad he's always got in his pocket, because when he's not fishing, he owns the Tap—Home of Two Beers for a Buck.

"I got coin in the cookie jar, and in case I get hungry, there's cans of soup and crackers in the cupboard," I said, even though I can't imagine ever eating without Grampa.

He said, "God bless," and looked sad clean down to his rubber boots. A minute later, all that was left of the visit was a foamy green trail and Grampa's boat bobbing gently in the wake.

It wasn't until after Mr. Bailey had gone that I thought of something I *did* need. Not me, really, but Top O' the Mornin'. Who's going to wrassle up the chow? Who's going to turn on the pumps?

"Hey," Clever calls. She's right on time, coming toward me in a tan T-shirt and too-short skirt that used to fit her just fine.

Picking up a flat rock, I side-arm it. After I watered the roses and tossed the birdseed, I moved my collection of skimmers down here to the pier. I'm not going to sit in my matching chair on the lawn 'til Grampa gets back.

"Ya left the hose on," Clever says, plopping down next to me.

I draw my knees up outta the water.

"It's all right. I closed it up for ya." She presses up against me, letting her bare feet dangle in the water next to mine. The sky looks like a baby present. Pale blue with ribbons of pink wrapping it up. "Miss Florida told me ya went and got my belongin's offa Rudy's porch."

She's acting a little cocky, like she doesn't care that her mama kicked her out, and I don't know, maybe she really *doesn't*. That apartment they lived in above the Tap wasn't so nice. Dirty clothes balled up in the corners. Empty beer cans sitting on the windowsills like feeding troughs for flies. And when you tried to drift off to sleep, the shouts coming up from the bar below always reminded me of those religious pictures of lost souls calling for help from hell.

"Mama promised that she and Miss Florida will keep takin' care of the diner until Charlie . . ." This is hard on her, too. Clever loves Grampa and he her.

If Janice and Miss Florida have been tending to Top O' the Mornin', it's probably the second coming of World War Two up there by now. And that's a big IF. I know I can count on Miss Florida, but Janice Lever's promises aren't worth a plug nickel.

"I picked up the *Gazette* from the library and dropped it off at all the regular places for ya," Clever says, picking up one of my flat rocks and letting it rip. "Ya ever gonna talk again?"

"Your belongin's sack is next to his chair."

I side-arm two nice ones. My dog should be divin' for these rocks.

Clever returns with her bag of things and sets it down between us. "Where's Keep at?"

"I . . . I was just wonderin' the same thing."

Sometime back, we discovered if somebody lays their hands on me, I can recall things better. Clever says it works 'cause another person's energy sinks into my skin, flows up to my brain and gives it a jump-start. Pressing her sticky palms to my cheeks, she says, "Ready?"

I close my eyes the way she likes me to and wait for something to come into my scrambled-up mind, but all that appears is the realization that Grampa's gone and he might not be back. "I can't . . . nuthin's happenin'," I say, giving up. My memory feels matted. Worse than usual.

"Grampa had a heart attack," Clever says. "He's in the hospital."

Miss Lydia is always telling me that having trouble with my memory might be more a blessing than a curse. Maybe she's right, because unlike a breath ago, I can picture him now in the cold metal bed, breathing so slow.

"That's where Keeper is, too." Dr. Sam Cooper, knowing that dog like he does, he told me it'd be fine for me to leave him at the hospital. When Grampa wakes up and feels my dog curled up next to him, maybe his heart'll get happier, the same way it does when he spots a red-wing blackbird, his most favorite feathered friend of all. *Oak-a-lee . . . oak-a-lee . . . oak-a-lee.*

"Mama says he's bad." Clever dabs at my tears with the bottoms of her T-shirt. "Ya gotta prepare yourself."

"And just how am I supposed to prepare myself for . . . I don't want to talk about it anymore," I say, kicking up a spray.

She hunches her shoulders and looks over at Willard's place. "Wait a minute . . . I might got somethin' to cheer you up." She takes a box of Top O' the Mornin' matches out of her skirt pocket. On her third try, the lantern that hangs off the dock flames up. Opening the top of her belongin's sack, Clever spreads out what's inside. Those stretched-out socks. That used-up sweatshirt. She gives a yelp when she sees her rolled-up *Butch Cassidy and the Sundance Kid* poster. "Well, I'll be damned," she says, hugging it close. "That was real thoughtful of Janice to send it along, don'tcha think?"

I guarantee you, her mama didn't give it one thought 'bout how happy that poster'd make her girl.

"What's that?" I ask, poking at the tip of a piece of paper that I hadn't perceived earlier. It's jutting out the back pocket of the raggedy jeans.

"*That's* the somethin' I thought might cheer ya up." She knocks my hand away, slips out the folded piece of paper and irons it straight on the dock. "I stole it off Willard. It's his precious map."

A map? Willard? Where have I heard . . . "He was askin' me about a map this afternoon. But he told me he was lookin' for a *treasure* map." *And that I should get it off Clever and return it to him right away tonight or there will be hell to pay.* "This doesn't look at all like a treasure map," I say. "Shouldn't there be a big X that marks the spot and a coupla skulls?"

Clever asks eager-beaverly, "It's a *treasure* map?"

"That's what Willard said." The wobbly dock lantern is sending darting shadows across the paper. "Wait a minute," I say, pointing. "Isn't that the Malloy place?" Me and Clever, Billy and Georgie and Cooter used to play hide-and-go-seek in those rows of tobacco when we were kids.

"That figures. Willard's got something clandestine going on out there with Bishop Malloy. I heard 'em talkin'."

I wheel toward her, shocked from my nose to my toes. "You know what *clandestine* means?"

"Got a book outta the library when I picked up the *Gazette*. Been workin' all afternoon learnin' some new words. Figured you and me . . . well, with Grampa . . . maybe we could start playin' some Scrabble." Clever clears her throat twice and announces, "Clandestine relates back to the Ku Klux boys."

Really, I don't have the heart to tell her.

But just like this investigative reporter suspected, Willard *is* up to no good. And not by his lonesome. Sounds like he's joined up with rotten Bishop Malloy, who is deceased Mr. Buster's only child with his wife, Suellen, who is also dead from something I don't recall. Never have been able to tolerate Bishop, who is NOT religious even though his name makes him sound like he is. He does bad things to stray cats. And I've seen him pull the pants offa kids to humiliate 'em. What could those two troublemakers be up to out at the Malloy place?

Clever's stomach grumbles.

"Sounds like ya need some chicken noodle soup," I say, swinging my legs outta the lake. "Straight from the can, just the way you like it."

"That sounds real good," she says, stuffin' the rest of her belongin's back into the sack, but folding the map up neat and sliding it into the top of her swirly skirt. "And then what say you and me go firefly catchin' like we used to. When we got a jar full, we'll take 'em up to Miss Lydia and she can make a feel-better potion for Grampa. You'd like that, right?"

When I don't answer, when the tears come again, she gathers me into the kind of fierce hug that Clever's well known for. The kind where she's not so much hugging as holding on to ya like you're a life preserver. "He'd expect you to saddle up and ride hard, and here ya are feelin' all sorrowful," she says. "Ya gotta be strong for him, Butch. C'mon." She takes her bag up in one hand, my hand in the other. "I'm starvin'."

When we pass his Adirondack, I run my fingers down the wood. Give it a smooch right where his head falls against the grain. Clever's right. I *am* feeling sorry for myself, and like Grampa always says, feeling sorry for yourself never gets nobody nowhere quick.

"Maybe instead of takin' the fireflies to Miss Lydia, we can take 'em straight to Grampa and they could be his night-light?" I say.

Clever gives me a playful shove. "Now there's the rootin'-tootin' cowgirl I been lookin' for."

We're almost to the cottage when a reedy voice says outta the shadows, "Good evening, ladies." A few steps closer and I can see it's none other than Willard DuPree, sitting cross-legged in the thatched chair to the side of the screened-in. Bare-chested and twirling one of Grampa's roses between his fingers. A yellow one.

I'm not sure how Clever's feeling about him now, but I don't want to take any chances. "If ya stopped by to find out if we wanted to play strip poker, we don't," I say, tugging on her.

Getting up, Willard breaks the rose off its stem. "Actually, I stopped by to beg your forgiveness, Carol." When he's done setting the flower in her hair, he circle pets her globe tummy. "After a thorough examination of my conscience, I've changed my mind about giving up the baby and wanted to rush right over and tell you."

Clever says, swooning, "Oh, Willard, I knew you'd change your mind."

"Can't you see he's jukin' ya?" I say, choking her wrist. "He doesn't even *have* a conscience, for crissakes." (I'm pretty sure I know what Willard's after and it isn't Clever or the baby. Or even hot sex.)

"I . . . I miss you," Willard tells her, crocodile tears watering his whiskers.

Clever wrenches out of my grip and rushes to wrap him up in her arms. She can't see it 'cause she's got her face buried in his scrawny chest, but even if she *could* see his trickery smile, she'd be helpless to fight off those love feelings. It's in her blood to surrender to men. "Ya sure?" she asks him. " 'Bout the baby, I mean."

Pointing to her belongin's bag, he answers, "Do you have my map in there, sweetie?"

(Just as I thought.)

"No. I got it right . . ." Clever fidgets in the top of her skirt.

"She's not your sweetie and she doesn't have the map." I don't want to say it, but I have to. It's for her own good. "She gave it to me for safekeepin'."

Faster than I've ever seen him move, Willard shoves Clever off to the side and takes a giant step toward me. "Hand it over."

"Why, I'd love to, Willard, but for the life of me I can't remember what the hell I did with it. I'm **NQR**, ya know," I say, not looking at him, but eyeing Clever, waiting for the realization of his two-faced phoniness to dawn across her face. It's out of the corner of my eye that I see him whipping his arm back, his palm wing-flat.

Clever springs into action, wedging herself between us. "That's all ya really want, ain't it? The map? Well, then take it, you . . . mealy-assed liar," she cries, flinging it at his feet along with the yellow rose.

Willard tells her with a winning smile, "Once again, I'd like to apologize. I completely misjudged you, Carol."

"Really?" she says, hope bobbing back up into her watery eyes.

"Really." Willard bends down to retrieve the map. "It turns out you're only about half as dumb as I thought you were."

Hearing him laugh wicked like that, before I know it, I'm yelling, "AHA!" and my hand is coming down hard across the back of his spindly neck with one of Billy's Oriental choppers that lays him out flat.

Nobody talks to the Kid that way.

Nobody.

"I'm so sor—" I try to tell Clever.

"Shut your trap," she hisses at me as she snatches the map outta Willard's fingertips.

Now, I know she could use a hug, no matter how bad she's behavin', but I dare not touch her until the sorrow is done sweeping through her. She'll beat the snot outta me if I try something pitiful like that.

Boy, what a stimulating idea!

Willard's already struggling to his hands and knees, so I put my arm around Clever tight, and aim her like a weapon. Just like I knew she would, she gets hot as hell, spinning and lashing out dervishly, eventually landing a solid kick in Willard's stomach that deflates him like a day-after-the-party balloon.

Once Clever's got her breath back, I ask, "You all right?" even though I *know* she's fine. (She's blessed with high recuperative powers.) I also *know* exactly what she's about to say. That's the way it is with sidekicks.

Sure enuf, she hawks and spits, landing a goober square in the middle of Willard's forehead, then goes ahead and quotes the BEST movie line of all time: "For a moment there, I thought we were in trouble."

Baby Talk

Raindrops keep falling on my head. Pouring down, really. What *have* I gotten myself into? Besides all the churning worries about Grampa, now there's this treasure map situation. And I haven't even started investigating who murderd Mr. Buster. Jesus alive, Miss Florida is right. You get one problem solved, and another rears its head. (The head belonging to Willard this go-round.) I confess, this is one of those times I thank heaven for my **NQR**ness, since I'll probably disremember these troubles in the bat of an eye. Fifteen at the most.

Clever is sitting at the kitchen table feeling somewhat **Discombobulated: Confused.** At first she wanted to beat Willard some more, but two seconds later, she wanted to kiss on him. I wouldn't let her do either, so she's acting mopey, but asking for seconds, a good sign. Now it's my turn to chase the sad out of her heart, the same way she did for me. And I believe I've come up with a pretty good plan to do just that.

"Under no circumstances are you to give Willard that map," I say, setting the soup down in front of her. I gave her most of the noodles since she's eating for two. "You and me and Billy are gonna go up to the Malloy Farm and find that treasure, and when we do, you'll be rich beyond belief and won't have to give the baby up to the social."

Clever slurps, sighs, says in her most dramatic of all voices, "Don't think I'll be feelin' up to a treasure hunt anytime soon."

(Don't be fooled. She's inherited a bit of her mama's theatrical baton-twirling nature. Alongside that, while the good book tells us not to judge lest we want to be judged, truth is, Clever doesn't resemble her name all that much. She needs some time to let the plan sink in.)

I didn't want to turn on the lights, in case Willard could see us once he came to, so the cottage candles are flickering in the night breeze that's coming off the lake, the parlor curtains floating inward like spooks.

"You wanna play a game when you're done?" I ask.

Picking open another cracker pack with her gnawed-to-the-moon nails, she says, "Don't feel much like that either."

That's fine, because the second after I asked her, I realized that seeing the Scrabble board, smelling the score pad, they'll only twist up my heart worse than it already is. Memories are already waving hello to me out of every nook and cranny. His whittling knife is sitting out on the side table alongside the Peaches carving he's been working on for me. I put on one of his Johnny Cash records, so he's singing a love song as I head toward my briefcase. Wouldn't do me a bit of harm to start writing some on that Mr. Buster is dead story. Background, at least.

"Baby's makin' a fuss tonight," Clever says. "Come over here and feel it."

"I already did down on the pier, didn't I?" I say, reaching for my leather-like offa the sofa.

Lifiting up her shirt, she says, "Not on skin, ya didn't. C'mon. Ya gotta get friendly with it."

I kneel down in front of her, and she shows me where to place my hands on her hard tummy. "It doesn't like me," I say, feeling the kicks.

"It don't even know you," Clever chuckles. "That's just what it does. 'Specially up against my ribs."

"Goodness. That's really something, isn't it? A miracle."

Clever radiates proud. "I'm not givin' this baby up no matter what anybody says. Already got a name picked out and everything." She weaves her fingers through mine. "I changed my mind. We gotta go after that treasure. Ya still game?"

"A course I am, Kid. First off, what we gotta do is—" I start up, but am so crudely interrupted by a hell of a ruckus at the cottage door.

Bang-bang. Bang-bang.

"Y'all in there? It's Sheriff Johnson checkin' up on ya, Miss Gibby."

Bang-bang. Bang-bang.

I lay my fingers across Clever's lips. She shakes them off, and yells out, "Nobody's home."

The brass knob on the cottage door circles back and forth, forth and back. Followed by a jumpy jiggle.

"Keep quiet, goddamn it," I tell her, heading toward my bedroom window that looks out on the porch. My neighbor is standing out there next to the sheriff with a shit-eating grin on his face. I tiptoe back into the kitchen. "LeRoy's got Willard with him. They've come for the map."

Clever shoves back her chair and starts to get up. "I'm gonna open that door and turn Willard in to the sheriff."

"No, you are n-o-t," I say, pushing her back down.

"But smokin' hemp is against the law," she says, struggling against me. "He'll have to take Willard down to the jail."

Bless her heart. Having a baby must make you get amnesia because Clever knows damn well the law around here can't be trusted. She's had plenty of run-ins with the sheriff that have ended with less than favorable results. I so wish Grampa was home. He'd sock LeRoy Johnson clear off our porch with a one-two punch.

"Open up in there," the sheriff yells, louder and meaner.

"No matter what, they ain't gettin' the map," Clever says, tough. "Just like you said, I *need* that treasure for the baby." It's either candlelight or desire flickering in her eyes, can't tell which. "Hey, I know what we gotta do! We gotta go on the lam to Bolivia! Just like Butch and the Kid did."

"I believe there's a large body of water between here and there. Don't ya think a boat'd be more appropriate?"

"No, goin' on the lam doesn't mean . . . ya, ya, a boat would be fine," Clever says.

Recalling the language problems Mr. Cassidy and Mr. Kid encountered in the movie, I say carefully, "Maybe runnin' off to Bolivia is not that smart 'cause neither one of us knows how to speak much *Espanol*."

"But . . . but . . . ," she sputters.

"Maybe we could invite *Senor* Bender to join us."

"*Siiii*," she says, grinning. (Clever has always considered the *Senor* one hot *tamale*.)

Bang-bang. Bang-bang.

The knock this time is no joking matter. Those two are not going to give up on their idea about getting in here.

"Then again," I say, "Grampa's in the hospital and I need to keep track of him and I don't recall there bein' any telephones in Bolivia."

"But . . . but . . ."

"I didn't say we can't run off. We just need to run off someplace closer. Someplace that's got pay phones, all right?"

"I got a good idea! We could go over to Browntown. They got a phone at Mamie's."

"No, that's *not* a good idea." Browntown woulda seemed like a fine place to lay low before Vern Smith warned me about the coloreds not liking us whites so much anymore. "Give me the map," I say, not at all trusting Clever when it comes to matters of the heart. If Willard starts in again on how sorry he is, and how much he wants her, I know her, she'll hand over the map faster than Secretariat does the quarter mile.

Clever slides the paper out of her skirt and into my hand, not complaining at all when I lock it up in my briefcase. "If we're *not* going to Bolivia, and we're *not* goin' to Browntown, then where in the hell *are* we goin'?" Clever asks, hands-on-hips belligerent.

"Let us in or I'm gonna knock this goddamn door down," the sheriff shouts. I can picture him out there huffing and puffing.

"Well?" Clever asks.

"I believe Land of a Hundred Wonders would do us just fine, Kid." I haul her up out of the chair, push her toward my bedroom. *"Vamanos!"*

On the Lamb

After I kiss good-bye the picture of Mama above my bed, Clever and me squirm out my bedroom window, sneaking around the sheriff and Willard like a couple of tenderfooted Apaches. Of course I have my Eveready flashlight in my briefcase, but I dare not switch it on until we are farther down the path. On account of Clever's tummy being so protruding, we can't belly-crawl, even though that's what Billy woulda suggested. All we can do to stay hidden from the two of them is to crouch over like a coupla old crones and make our way steady toward Hundred Wonders.

When a *who . . . whoo . . . whoo* comes from somewhere behind us, Clever lets loose with a squeal. "They're comin'. Run, Butch!"

"It's just the horned owl," I say, grabbing for her. "Hush, they'll hear us." You never got to light a fire and breathe on it hard to convince Clever Lever to haul ass, but she's especially jittery this evening. Must be 'cause she's about to become a mother. Mothers can become quite alarmed when their children are in peril. My mama came looking for me in the gully after we crashed. Miss Lydia told me she called my name over and over, arms outstretched and smoking. It took all the fireman's muscles to get her into the ambulance.

"Ya think we're far enough away to slow down?" Clever pants out when we come up to the fork in the path.

Glancing back, I say, "Seems like they lost our scent for now, but I wouldn't count on that being a permanent situation. You know what an excellent tracker the sheriff is." (He's not the best in the county, that would be an honor taken by the Brandish Boys. But ole LeRoy, he's pretty damn good.)

"Oh, the hell with the sheriff and Willard. I gotta pee," Clever says, hopping from foot to foot and eyeing the bushes.

"Careful," I say, sorta laughing when I remember the day she got her driver's license and somehow talked Grampa into borrowing his truck so she could take us to the drive-in to celebrate. Halfway through *The Appaloosa*, she had to tinkle, but you know Clever, she wouldn't miss a chase scene if her life depended on it, so she ended up squatting in the scrub that rims the 57 and came back howling with stinging nettles in a most inconvenient place and . . .

Oh, Jesus.

"You okay?" Clever asks. "You're tremblin'."

"I . . . I . . . don't know. I'm not sure, but I think I just remembered something from . . ."

"Well, good," she says, disappearing behind a leafy bush.

I collapse against the oh-so-familiar sugar maple that lets you know you're halfway to Hundred Wonders. I haven't been able to do that since the crash. Recall something so clear from so long ago, like that stinging nettle memory. I'm shocked. This remembering doesn't feel good like I thought it would. Like getting to sleep between your own cool sheets after coming home from a long, hot trip. No, it doesn't feel that way at all. It feels scary and sorta foreign. Like I'm paying a visit to a strange place and that strange place is me. I rub my cheek against the maple bark. *Focus, Gib, focus. You're all right. Probably just recalling a dream. You're just worn down, is all.* I open up my leather-like and remove my blue spiral. Shine the flashlight on my **VERY IMPORTANT THINGS TO DO** list, which always gets me back on track.

1. Solve the murder of Mr. Buster Malloy and write an awfully good story so Mama can rest in peace eternal and I can get **Q**uite **R**ight.

2. Check out apartment listings in Cairo.

Yes! That's exactly what I should be doing instead of running around these woods with Clever, trying to stay two steps ahead of that obnoxious sheriff and that scheming Yankee, thinking my memory's coming back. I should be looking for clues to solve the murder and starting up my search for Egyptian housing.

But I can't do that without proof. **The Importance of Perception in Meticulous Investigation; Proof:** *A reporter cannot state facts unequivocally unless he or she has proof of said crime. Proof is similar to evidence, but not the same. Proof is what is obtained once a reporter sifts through the evidence.*

I don't recall picking up the pictures from Bob's Drug Emporium, but here they are in a still-sealed envelope with RUSH stamped across the top.

Clever whispers loud from outta the bushes, "Ya got a tissue or something?"

Am I remembering? Or is my brain playing fever tricks like it did in the hospital? I check my forehead. Warm, but not sickly so.

"Gib!"

"Drip dry, for crissakes!"

I got to focus. I got to. Forget about the remembering. Get to the pictures.

First off in the stack, there's a real nice shot of Grampa in his lake chair, Keeper at his side, also snoozing. Just like in the hospital. I need him so badly to be here with me. To say, "I'd call this an interesting turn of events, wouldn't you?" That's what he *always* tells me when something unexpected springs up. But what would he say to me right this minute? *Nose to the grindstone, Gibby girl.* Yes, yes, that's what he'd say.

Maybe something'll turn up in the pictures that I took of dead Mr. Buster. Maybe the murderer left an item behind that'd right off let me know who he is, like . . . I don't know . . . something that I'd recognize as belonging to that person. Like if Grampa murdered him for instance, I'd see a fishing lure half buried in the sand, or if Willard did it, I'd see a Mallomar wrapper stuck in the Geronimo tree branches. Ya know, something real telling like that.

There are a lot of snapshots of the lake in the envelope. Five bird pictures. Two of crows, which happen to be my favorite. Two cardinals, who have the same crappy disposition as Clever's mama. A redbreast. The one of Miss Cheryl and Miss DeeDee at the pump. Every hair on my body is rearing up. Where ARE they? I rifle through the packet. Where are the shots I took of Mr. Buster lying on the beach, dead as can be?

"What ya got there? Pictures?" Clever says, coming out of the bushes. She kneels down next to me, yanks them out of my hand. "This is a nice one of Grampa and Keep."

Feels like a beehive got into my head. My brain's buzzing. I have to know, so I ask, "Do you recall the day ya got your driver's license and . . ." Suddenly, I feel too ascared for her to say—Why, yes, that's exactly what happened, or what if she says, Why, no, that never did. Damn, Gib, looks like your **NQR**ness is spreading faster than Miss Florida's behind—so I chicken out and go instead with, "Ya know how everybody is searchin' for Mr. Buster?"

"Hmmm." Clever's not really paying attention, too busy sniffing the photos, which she's always loved the vinegary smell of.

"Well, I found him."

"Ya already told me and Miss Florida that," she says, so damn uppity that I'm real relieved that I didn't mention that 57 Outdoor nettles memory to her.

"Did I also tell ya that he was dead when I found him?"

"Ya did," she says, STILL not believing me.

"Jesus in a jumpsuit, Clever!" I say, knocking the pictures outta her hand.

"What?" she says, indignant.

"Listen to me good. Mr. Buster IS dead. I found him lyin' over on Browntown Beach stabbed in the heart four times with his head about twisted off."

Maybe it's how testy I say it, I can tell Clever *finally* believes me by the look of pure excitement on her face. "Mr. Butter is gonna be planted in the marble orchard? Oooeee! Let's get over there and take a look at him."

"We can't."

"Why not?"

" 'Cause his body's disappeared."

"No kiddin'. Well, knowin' you, ya took a picture, right?" she asks, gathering the photos off the ground and searching frantically for Mr. Buster's parting shot.

"That's the thing. I *did* take pictures, I *know* I did, but now I can't find 'em and nobody's gonna believe **NQR** me without—"

We both hear it at the same time. Branches stirring, birds

shushing. I cover the flashlight beam with my shirt, clamp my hand over Clever's mouth.

Rustle . . . snap . . . rustle . . . snap . . . snap.

Damn. It's gotta be the sheriff and Willard. We got to stay still, not even breathe. I take a sip of air. I gesture for Clever to do the same.

Nuthin' but night for a bit, but then out of the blackness comes, "Gibby?"

Clever and me let out our breaths in a great *haaa*, and I say into the trees, "Well, for godsakes, Billy. You 'bout scared the skin right off us!" I didn't even consider it was him. He's usually so sneaky-footed. "Where the hell ya been?"

Swooping down from a thick branch, he lands in a squat in front of us.

"Little Billy!" Clever rushes to give him a hug and almost bowls him over. "You're a sight for sore eyes."

Clever's certainly acting **Exuberant: Extremely joyful and vigorous**, forgetting how Billy doesn't much go in for touching. If I could see his face, I know it'd be the color of ripe raspberries.

Me? I'm not feeling so joyful *or* vigorous. Where's he been all day? He's supposed to be guardian angeling me and this is the first I've seen of him since I told him I wanted to run my tongue down his juicy neck the other afternoon. What the heck got into me? Musta been this devil heat seeping into my pores and making me all hot sexish because yes, that's what those hungry feelings were, all right. Not sure how I know that, but I do.

"We heard you," I scold Billy. "You should be ashamed of yourself." In the military, he was a sniper, which meant his life depended on him being wily until he could get a bead on somebody with the intention of shooting them dead.

"I got some new boots," he apologizes down to the creaking leather.

"Good for you," I say, giving him a disappointed look, which is not at all like me since I got firsthand knowledge of how bad that kind of look can wound. And so does Billy. It's the same look his daddy's always got papered on his face.

"You all right?" he asks, toeing the dirt.

"No thanks to you," I tell him with a *huff.*

"I meant, are you handling Grampa being in the hospital?"

I must have a confused look on my face 'cause Clever says, "He got that heart attack?"

It comes back to me in a sorrowful *swoosh.* What if he doesn't get better? What if . . .

"Soon as I heard, I went up to check on him," Billy says. He's got a nice voice. Deep, but not scarily so. Sorta like Grampa's. "Miz Tanner told me he's doin' as well as can be expected."

Feeling awfully bad about my previous wretched tone, I reach into the special slot in the briefcase where I keep them and peel off four well-deserved gold stars. "You are a good Sumerian," I say, pressing them onto his shirt pocket. Up close like this, he smells of sweat and a certain dog. "How's Keeper holdin' up?"

"Don't waste your time worrying about *him,*" Billy says with a foxy grin. "Got all the nurses eatin' outta his hand."

Oh, poor, poor Billy. I worry about him so. Besides his overall jumpiness, he's afflicted with **Flashbacks: An intensely vivid mental image of a past traumatic experience** that make him think he's someplace he's not, and that these people called the gooks are coming for him with bayonets and jungle thread, and off he runs like a panicked animal. Or sometimes he sobs hard. Or gets awfully mixed up, like he is now. He should know by now that Keeper has paws, not hands.

"Guess what, Billy?" Clever trills. "I'm gonna have a baby."

"I can see that." Not being of a judgmental nature, Billy smiles and says, "That's nice," like she just told him she's gonna have a haircut, which wouldn't be a half-bad idea. She's starting to look kinda witchy, if ya ask me.

"And we're on the lam," Clever adds.

Just as I start to explain it all to Billy, the horned owl, with the kind of well-timed interrogation technique that I can only dream of musterin', jumps in with, *"Whoo."*

"The sheriff is chasin' us down. Willard, too," I say, suddenly wanting Billy to pet me. A lot. All over the place. What the heck? *Focus, Gibby, focus.*

I tick off on my fingers:

"*The What:* The treasure map. *The Where:* In my briefcase. *The When:* Right this minute. *The Why:* Must be valuable as hell."

Billy scrunches his face up, which is mighty adorable. "A treasure map? What kind of treasure?"

We've gotten comfortable in a powwow circle. When me and Clever were escaping out the bedroom window, I slipped one of the squat candles into my shorts pocket. I've lit it up and the shadows are two-stepping under our chins. This reminds me of something. I can't recall what, but I can feel the edges of a memory forming. Billy sure looks appealing with those cheekbones that remind me of a sheer cliff and popped cherry lips and . . .

"I don't know what the treasure is. Willard never said. But I think Gibby is right," Clever says, in a juiced-up way. "It's buried someplace on the Malloy land, and you and me and her are going to go dig it up and use it to buy diapers and food for the baby so I don't have to give it up to a social. Show 'em, Butch."

Between the candle, the full moon, and the flashlight, we're doing okay vision-wise. I remove the map from my briefcase and spread it out on the ground. Billy's hair is lovely in the firelight. I would adore caressing it, I know I would. Just wrap those ringlets right around my fingers.

"Oh, man," Billy says.

"What?" Clever nudges closer, like she owns him or something.

"See that? These rows are a different color ink. They're red and all the other rows"—Billy runs his hand over the map—"they're black."

What the heck is wrong with me? I'm about to write the story that'll go down in the anus of Cray Ridge history and all I can seem to think about is touching Billy's tummy to see if it's as hard as it looks. "What do you think those red rows are?" I ask, struggling to get involved the way a trained reporter *should*. "Prime burley tobacco? Do you think that's what the treasure could be?"

Maybe this all has something to do with Mr. Frank Reynolds from New York City since that's where Willard is from. Even though he finally ended up telling me, it woulda been just a matter of time before I perceived where he hailed from on account of his accent, which resembles that Streisand gal's in the movie *Funny Girl*, which was not at all funny, by the way.

Holy smokes. I bet Bishop Malloy, Mr. Buster's son, who Willard is being clandestine with, is going to steal that tobacco off the farm and take it to Mr. Frank Reynolds in New York City for a reward, on account of Mr. Reynolds's concern about cigarettes causing cancer. Just like one of those rattler roundups that Grampa told me they have down in Texas. Bring in a sack of sidewinders—ya get ten bucks reward. That has to be Willard's plan. Rustle up the tobacco and haul it north for cash money. Yes, I'm absolutely certain that's what he's up to.

Wait just a cotton-pickin' minute.

Am I jumping to conclusions AGAIN?

What if Willard doesn't work for Mr. Frank Reynolds at all? What if . . . what if . . . he works as an operative for Mr. Howard Redmond, also from New York City, who has sent him to Cray Ridge to check up on my investigative techniques?

I grab my camera out of my briefcase, ready to snap a picture of the treasure map. Just to make sure. In case Willard *is* reporting back to Mr. Howard Redmond, I want to be extra thorough.

But when the flash cube pops, I see more than I bargained for. Peering through the trees at us is Sneaky Tim Ray Holloway. An up-to-no-good grin on his greasy lips.

The No Good, the Bad and the Ugly

"Well, my oh my. Who *do* we have here?" Sneaky Tim Ray says, coming out in the open and dropping to his feet a burlap sack he's got slung over his shoulder. He's been doing some hunting and has come up with a coon. Maybe a possum. It's the first time I've seen him since Teddy Smith gave him that hayloft whuppin'. An oily rag is barely concealing the black socket that should be filled up by his glass eye. His nose looks farther east than it used to. And some confused soul's been kissin' on his neck, leaving strawberry-colored lip prints behind. Dang. If Grampa was here, he'd exclaim right about now, "Boy looks like somethin' the dog's been keeping' under the porch."

"What ya got in the sack, Holloway? Your brain?" Clever taunts. (She is not at all afraid of him, or anything else for that matter, because, really, what does she have to lose?) "What the hell ya want?"

"Ain't 'bout what I want." Sneaky Tim Ray tugs on the rope that's holding the bag closed. After rootin' around some, he yanks my Keeper out by his front legs. " 'Bout what y'all want."

"Jesus," I yell. Billy's gotta hold me back when Sneaky Tim Ray circles his hands around Keep's throat.

Clever shouts, "Hand over the dog, ya one-eyed fool."

Keeper doesn't seem right. He's logy looking. Isn't he s'posed to be at St. Mary's guarding over Grampa? "How'd you get ahold a him?" I ask, completely confused.

"Well, the Lord do work in mysterious ways, don't He, darlin'? There I was over to the hospital payin' a visit to a lady friend of mine," he says, puffin' up. "And who should I find sittin' outside one of them rooms but this here mutt."

When Billy pounces off the ground toward him, Sneaky Tim Ray pliers his hand around Keeper's neck tight enough to make his legs go rigid. "One step closer, soldier boy, and this dog'll be headin' off to the happy huntin' ground."

"Wwwhat do you wwwant?" Billy says, gripping and ungripping his fists. He wants to get at this louse so bad, but he can't, and it's causing his stutter to flare up.

"Wwwhat I wwwant is that mmmap," Holloway mocks.

"Give it to him," I command to Clever.

"But . . . but . . . what about the treasure and the baby and—"

"He's got Keeper!" I holler.

"A course," she says, popping open my briefcase and removing the map. "Don' know what I was thinkin'."

"Leave it there on the ground," Sneaky Tim Ray instructs, smug.

Keep hasn't moved for the longest time.

"Whatcha do to the dog?" Billy is not tripping over his words anymore. I knew it'd be just a matter of time before his torrential temper poured into his head and swept away his fear.

"Back off, Brown," Sneaky Tim Ray warns, sensing the shift in Billy.

"You ready-set?" I call, hoping Keeper can hear me.

His right ear cocks. Then his left. His tail gives a feeble tock.

All right then.

"What's gonna happen next is," Sneaky Tim Ray announces, "y'all are gonna turn around and head down that path. Once I have procured that map, I'll set the dog free."

(He's lying. I know him. He'll break my dog's neck just for the fun of it.)

Getting an idea, I tell Holloway in the sweetest voice I got, "Wait a minute."

As usual, he's on a slant. Sweatin' hooch.

"I might have something ya want more than that map." I step closer and point to his oily patch.

Holloway checks me out from stem to stern, loitering on my double D deck. "Hand it over."

He's referring to the "*eye*-catching souvenir" Teddy Smith tossed me out the truck window the day he beat the hell out of Holloway. I've been carrying it around in my brassiere, anticipating a moment like this. I may be **NQR**, but I'm no fool. I got him now. **The Importance of Perception in Meticulous Investigation** thoroughly covers: **The Art of Distraction**. Slipping my shirt up over my head, I say, "Come and get it."

When it comes to my yum-yum ripe melons, Holloway's as helpless as a crayfish to a mealy worm. Add on the promise of getting his precious eyeball back, well, just like I hoped, he loses what little concentration he's been able to muster. He's shuffling toward me like he's in a trance. So when I yell, "Now!" and Keeper chomps down hard with his needle teeth onto Sneaky Tim Ray's thumb, it takes him time to react and he loses his grip. Seeing his chance, Billy rushes forward with outstretched arms. The two of them are rolling around on the ground, tugging on my dog like he's a piece of taffy, when from out of the dark comes, "Back off, Brown," alongside that unmistakable rifle-cocking sound.

When he steps into the candlelight, we can see that Cooter Smith's the one aiming a shotgun at Billy's chest. "Ya dumb-ass cracker," he says, booting Sneaky Tim Ray in the butt. "Quit hollerin' like a stuck pig and get that map."

I am stunned! I have never heard a colored talk that way. Not even to a cracker. Cooter better watch his step. The sheriff hears him mouth off like that, he'll cook his goose well-done.

"Hey, Cooter," Clever sings out, eyelashes flapping like sheets on a line. Here we are in the depths of despair and . . . I swear. The girl's got a fire in her drawers and she doesn't care one bit whose hose puts it out.

Cooter says, "Carol?"

Sneaky Tim Ray's one-armed crawling toward the map, sucking on his bleeding thumb. "Ya could show a bit more grateful that I found the goddamn map," he whines.

"I'll give ya a gold star later," Cooter says, pulling his eyes off of Clever to glance down at me.

They're all watching Sneaky Tim Ray grab for the folded-up treasure paper. Not me. I'm watching Keeper, who's lying on the ground between us, not moving one bit.

"See what I mean about her titties? Look at 'em," Sneaky Tim Ray gurgles as he hands the map over to Cooter, who isn't looking at my titties. He's giving a jaw-dropping look at Clever's globe belly.

"Le's take the girl and the dog with us. We can sack drown the mutt and get some money for her if this other thing don' work out," Sneaky Tim Ray tells Cooter as he reaches over and picks Keep up by the scruff. "She got cash from the crash that made her a dummy. Jessie tol' me."

Billy's doing not much of anything but being stone petrified.

He gets like that when somebody's got a gun pointing at him on account of the war.

"Just fer a bit?" Sneaky Tim Ray begs.

Cooter says, "That's kidnappin'. Ya want the law after us, ya fool?"

Like on cue, from outta the woods comes a shout. "Gibby McGraw? This is the sheriff orderin' you to show yourself."

And then Willard chimes in with, "Carol, baby? Please come back to your daddy."

Dumber than a stick of chew gum, is what he is. *Everybody* knows that *nobody* knows who Clever's daddy is. No matter. She's not even paying attention to him. Too busy licking her lips for Cooter.

"We got what we came for," Cooter says, yanking Sneaky Tim Ray up by the shirt collar and dragging him back off into the woods.

"Carol, hoooney?" Willard sings out. "I bought you a diamond riiing."

I'm trying to pick up Keep but get a good hold of Clever, too. She's looking like she'd like to chase after Cooter, but then again, she might relent if Willard keeps up this repent.

Billy whisks my dog up into his arms and whispers frantic, "They're comin', Gib. They're comin'."

"Who's comin'?" For the life of me, I can't recall what the hell we're doing in these woods in the pitch of the night.

"Ain't you ever tracked before? Shut the hell up," the sheriff squawks. "You're lettin' 'em know our position."

Billy pulls us back behind the trunk of the sugar maple. "That's who's comin'. 'Member?"

No, I don't. And I don't care neither. I nuzzle my lips down on Keeper's chocolate milk stain. Besides being the best dog there ever was, he'll be all the family I've got left if I lose Grampa. "Is he gonna die?" I ask.

Billy peers around the tree bark, trying to get a fix on the exact whereabouts of the sheriff and Willard. "He's gonna be okay. Smell his breath."

I lower my nose to his snout.

"Holloway got him drunk, is all," Billy says. "I need my hands free if we run into the enemy." He passes me Keep. "Get out your flashlight and keep it aimed to the ground."

My Eveready is not. "I can't. It rolled under a bush."

"Then follow close as ya can," he says, proceeding with purpose down the skinny lake path.

"Stay close," I say over my shoulder to Clever, who is looking off to where Cooter disappeared.

Billy is stepping lightly, carefully. (In the Oriental jungle they got wires that can trip you and blow you up so you have to be mighty careful where you place your feet if you wanna hang on to them.) "Remember back in the woods when Clever told me you two were on the lam?" he asks, holding a branch back for me.

"I do," I say, proud.

"Where were ya headed?"

"Hundred Wonders."

Keeper's nose is quivering. He's not so sloshed that he can't get enthused about paying a visit to our most favorite place of all. He can smell the miracles.

Billy says, "It's probably not safe over there right now."

"Why?" Like Keeper, I'm yearning something bad to see Miss Lydia. I am craving a VISITATION with my mama.

Clever yanks on my shirttail to get my attention. "Billy's right, ya know. Didn't occur to me back at the cottage, but anybody with half a brain could figure out that Wonders is the first place we'd head."

"Thanks, Kid. That was a real thoughtful thing to say."

"Shoot. Ya know I didn't mean it like that."

We're all quiet for a bit while trying to negotiate the place in the path that'll let ya slip into the lake before ya know it.

"Would Browntown be an appropriate place to hide?" I ask Billy.

"Probably not with the way they're so worked up."

"But *where* then?" I ask, feeling like a desperado without a horse.

Keeper sneezes in threes. We smell it then, too. Winding its way through the woods. Smoke.

When we get farther down the trail, we can see flaming fingers tickling at the belly of the sky.

"Oh, my sweet Jesus," Clever says. When I turn, she's bent over at the waist, steadying herself against a coffee tree.

"What is it?" Billy asks, coming up next to her.

"Don't know. I'm feelin' puny." Clever reaches for my hand. Hers feels like a chicken gizzard.

For my ears only, Billy says, "She needs to rest. If we don't lay her down for a bit, her baby might come 'fore it's ready."

We can't go forward on account of the fire and we can't go back to the cottage because of the sheriff and Willard. "We're surrounded," I whisper.

By the trapped look on his face, I can tell Billy has pieced that together, too.

"Caroool," Willard starts up again.

"The only reason they're huntin' us down is they think we still got the map, right?" I ask Billy. "Let's just tell them what happened. That we got ambushed by Sneaky Tim Ray and Cooter, and that they're the ones they oughta be chasin', not us."

"Ya sure you wanna take that chance? Ya know how the sheriff can get," Billy cautions.

He's right. LeRoy Johnson gets a heap of pleasure from hurting others. 'Specially brown-skinned ones, but not limited to.

I cup my hand over Clever's mouth, too late. A groan escapes her lips.

"Ya hear that?" LeRoy says off to our right.

"What?" Willard says.

They're statue-still. We're statue-still.

Until the sheriff cracks the silence wide open. "Sumbitch! You smell that? Somethin's burning in Browntown. I gotta get over there right quick."

"But what about the map?" Willard keens. "If we don't get it back, they're gonna figure out what we're up to."

By how far off they sound, I can tell they've already turned back toward town, the sheriff's voice trailing off with, ". . . ya damn carpetbagger."

Sweeping Clever up in his arms, Billy says, "The best place for us would be up at the cave."

"All right," I say, giving Keep a kiss on his noggin. "Ya know a lot more about hidin' out than me."

I'm sorry I said that the minute it comes outta my mouth, because that made Billy remember Vietnam even more than he was, so he shrinks a bit. But then, I don't know, he seems to get a little straighter, bolder, after he makes the turn down the path that'll take us to Blackstone Cave. The smoke is billowing and smelling of . . . burnin' rubber? Clever has gone quiet, which is not at all like her.

"Are you sure we shouldn't take her to the hospital?" I ask him, getting so ascared as we draw closer to the flames. Billy doesn't answer me, just keeps missioning his way, not giving me much choice but to follow, and think while I'm doing so, the coloreds don't like white people anymore and here we are.

We could almost reach out and touch Browntown.

The Hideout

Billy's just the opposite of me. A person who DOES NOT need stimulation of any kind. When he's far off from the hustle and bustle of life, hugged up secure by Mother Nature, he feels less perturbed. He's done a nice job of housekeeping Blackstone Cave. Even though he won't move outta his tent down at the creek and back up here 'til first frost, his larder is ordered and well stocked. The floor swept clean like you'd expect from an army man. This was a good choice as a hideout, sitting like it does at the top of a hill where you can see down to both Browntown and Land of a Hundred Wonders. Which is probably one of the reasons he chose it as his winter home in the first place. Nothing can sneak up on him here.

Clever's snores are bouncing off the cave walls. She curled up on a sleeping bag right after we filled our bellies with cowboy beans. I rubbed her back and sang that "Hush Little Baby" lullaby while Billy went and scouted what's goin' on in Browntown. That was so brave of him. When he came back up the hill, lookin' sooty, he told me, "You can quit your worryin'. It's not Miss Florida's house or Mamie's or any of your other favorite places that's burnin'. It's the dump. That's why it smells so bad and the smoke's so thick. It's all them tires."

"The dump's on fire?" I asked, picturing that swell of trash that welcomes ya to Browntown.

"And a couple of those shacks sit next to it."

"Are they workin' on puttin' it out?"

Billy sets his head to shakin'. "It's the damnedest thing, Gib. The coloreds . . . they're all dancin' and drinkin' round that fire. Like they're celebratin'."

"WHAT?"

"I think they set the fire themselves."

"Oh, Billy, that's silly!" He must be havin' another one of his confused spells. "Why would they do somethin' like that?"

He didn't have an answer.

Now I'm locked on what's looming behind him. Our names slashed across the big black boulder that sits outside the mouth of the cave. GIBBY and BILLY are lassoed by a heart of red paint. We're lying side by side, but not touching, on a blanket in front of the campfire.

Noticing my gaze, Billy says softly, "The rock's the reason I kept askin' ya to come up here with me. I heard that if a person who's lost their memory is shown something familiar, something real important to them, that sometimes it *jars* their brain."

Tossing a kindling stick into the campfire, I ask him, "We used to be more than just friends?"

If he had a hat, it'd be in his hands. "Ya could say that."

I look back up at the boulder. CLEVER is painted off to one side, opposite GEORGIE. Down at the bottom is COOTER. It's funny how our names still shine so bright, the moonlight glancing off them. You'd think life woulda worn them down some. Like it did us. None of us are what we were back then. Most of all—Georgie.

Billy's so desperate for me to remember. He's running the tip of his tongue over his lush lips.

"I'm sorry," I say. "Nuthin' seems to be comin' back."

"It's all right," he says with a downhearted smile. "Maybe it takes a little time, is all."

I feel so horribly bad for him. Doesn't seem like a person should be able to forget that they loved someone even if they are **NQR**. Important information like that should be stored in more than one place. Why hasn't Clever told me about this romance between me and Billy? Golly, maybe she has.

There's an explosion at the bottom of the hill that makes me think of the crash. The both of us startle. Billy says, "Rrreminds me of . . ."

"I know, I know." Even though those gooks were America's enemies, and he was just doing his job to keep the rest of us safe, he felt so bad about that bloodshedding that he came apart at the seams. That's why the army sent him home early. Billy wears his heart on his sleeve now. "Ya did what you thought was right for your Uncle Sam," I remind him.

"It was a bbbad thing to do . . . all that kkkillin'."

What sad sacks we are. Him wishing I could remember and me wishing he could forget.

Be real nice if Grampa was here right now, he'd say something so meaningful. Smart words that would make a direct hit to Billy's heart. Because they both got damaged by war—Grampa on the outside, Billy on the inside—those two got something to talk about on nights like this. When certain things mean more than others. I bet Billy has not been taking his calming medicine. He can get extra weepy like this when he doesn't.

Pointing to the western sky, I exclaim, "There's a shootin' star! That's a sign, plain as day, that the Lord is forgivin' you from the bottom of His heart."

He won't even look.

"Ya know what I learned in the army?" he asks.

"How to bounce a quarter off a bed and sneak through the woods silent as a vine?"

"Yeah," he says, like those skills aren't nuthin' to be proud of. "But I also learned that when it comes to people, we're pretty much all the same. No matter what the color of our skin or the slantiness of our eyes. We were *all* scared over there the same amount."

"I would have to agree with you," I say, thinking mostly of the color of skin since I don't know anybody with slanted eyes 'cept for a cat of Miss Lydia's she calls the King of Siam. What difference does it make what somebody looks like on the outside? The same things make life worth living for all of us, don't they? A crunchy walk in the woods, your dog by your side. An afternoon on the lake, when all you got to do is think trout and one hops on your line. I guess some white folks believe the coloreds are different feeling on the inside 'cause they're so different looking on the outside. That's just not true. Coloreds got a whole lot of heart and a whole lot of soul. And they make the best damn pork barbecue.

"What ya thinkin' about?" Billy asks, so full of hope.

"About the coloreds and how if what you said is true, 'bout them settin' that fire on purpose, what bad trouble they're gonna be in."

The silky hair under Billy's arms is twirling in the breeze. His bare chest is brown and smooth as a pine table. Swiveling his head back toward our names in the heart, he says with such yearning, "Anything at all comin' to mind?"

"Not yet," I tell him, but the campfire, the rock, it all seems so familiar. *Something* is jiggling my cents memory . . . something I can't quite . . . and then suddenly, it's like I'm watching the movie screen out at the 57. Oh, look . . . there's Billy and me. We're riding through a summer hay field, laughing, touching. Sweet-smelling clover is coating the air. And then the scene changes and we're swinging off the Geronimo rope down at the beach . . . and then we're lying around a campfire just like this one and I can feel the crackling heat on my cheeks. Yes. Here at Blackstone. His arms around me. In more than a friendly way. Our names entwined. Rock solid.

Sweet, sweet Jesus. I really *am* remembering after all. Only this time it isn't about Clever getting her driver's license.

Billy turns back to me, not seeing what I just saw in my mind. Us. "Ya given any thought to what you'd do if Grampa . . . if he . . . ?" He shakes his head. "All I want ya to know, to remember is . . . he's not the only one cares for ya," he says in a tore-down way.

"Please . . . please don't cry . . . 'cause I think it's . . . I be-lieve something *is* coming back to me. Not in a jar like you said, but . . ."

Raising those lovely eyes of his to mine, he must see true love radiating outta me because he doesn't hesitate at all when he reaches out for me. Wraps me in his arms like a long-hoped-for gift. How could I have *ever* forgotten his warm cheek pressed against mine. These satin kisses. The home sweet homecomin' feeling of Little Billy and me.

The leftover smoke from Browntown is mixing in with my side-kick's musky scent. My man, who's curled close, musta woke up to stoke the fire and add some wood 'cause it's still flickering. "You asleep?" Clever whispers.

"No, I was just checkin' for holes in my eyelids." (That's what I always say when she asks me that.) Rolling outta Billy's arms and into hers, I ask, "What?"

"It's about time," she says.

"Now? You're havin' the birthin' pains *now*?"

Clever raises her eyes toward Billy. "I meant it's about time you remembered him. He's still got the engagement ring, ya know."

"I do indeed," I say, showing her the sparkly band I got on my finger. That's why Billy kept leaving me all those rings in our secret stump in the woods at Miz Tanner's. And that *jar* of rice? That was a good hint. (Just in case you're not familiar, that's what ya throw at people after they get hitched.) "You knew all along we were plannin' to get married, didn't ya? Did ya tell me?"

Clever's breath is hitching when she answers, "I . . . we . . . when you never said nuthin' after the crash, when you didn't even recognize Billy, me and him and Grampa and Miss Jessie, we got just everybody to go along with not tellin' ya about the wedding plans 'cause we thought the shock . . . it might be too much for your **NQR** brain to handle. We didn't want to make ya worse, ya know? Did we do wrong?"

"No, no, y'all did just fine. Please don't cry," I tell her, catching one of her tears with the tips of my fingers.

Billy stirs. Sets his hand on my hip.

"Sure you ain't mad?" Clever asks, shivering some.

Like Grampa always says, secrets bear down hard on a person's foundation, and she's kept this one for so long. Even though I really do wish she woulda told me, I cannot stand to see her crumbling. "I'm sure, Kid."

She draws her eyes close to mine. To see if I'm telling her the truth. "All right, then," she says, satisfied. "Now we got all that past business put to bed, we need to talk about the future." Clever places the palm of my hand on her tummy. On her baby. "I don't believe the two of ya have been formally introduced. Butch, if you would be so kind," she says in her asking-a-favor voice. "Please say hey to the newest member of our gang. Miss Rose . . . Rosie Adelaide."

"Rose? 'Cause of Grampa's flowers?"

Clever gives me her chipped-tooth grin.

"And Adelaide . . . after my mama?"

When she says, "Ya know how I always favored that name," I try to answer with a lot of joyfulness, "Nice to meet ya, Rosie Adelaide. Charmed, I'm sure," but memories come sneaking up on me—one of my grampa in that hospital bed, maybe dying, and another of Mama, already gone—and like a thief in the night, sorrow steals away all my words.

Back Home

Morning light is reflecting off the well-deserved gold stars on Billy's shirt pocket. (His hair smells of wild lavender, by the way.) "Gonna go look around some," he tells me, slinking off with a bashful smile. Thanks to that idiot Holloway, Keeper's nursin' a horrible hangover. Wouldn't even suck a raw egg, and he's listing to port. Clever teases him, saying, "Ya know what ya need? What ya need is the hair of the dog, son." (Since her mother is the town drunk, she is quite knowledgeable in these day-after-a-hoedown remedies.)

When he gets done doing his **Reconnaissance: The act of reconnoitering, especially to gain information about an enemy or a potential enemy**, Billy comes back into the cave and tells Clever and me, "It looks bad down in Browntown. A couple of the shacks burned to the ground and the dump is rubble. But there's no sign of Willard or the sheriff. Now'd be a good time to hightail it back to the cottage."

I would have to agree with him, as would Mr. Howard Redmond, who writes in **The Importance of Perception in Meticulous Investigation:** *Time is of the essence.*

So's my loved ones.

After I make sure all's well in the cottage, after I breathe in Grampa's smoky smell and say hello to Mama's paintings, I head out to the lake 'cause I've discovered that for some reason, my brain works better the closer it gets to water. Right off, I open my leather-like up on the picnic table and remove the information card the nurse, Miss Tay Lewis, gave me the last time I was at the hospital. It's got the afternoon visiting hours noon to two printed on the front. From where the sun's in the sky, I can tell it's around ten o' clock, so that leaves me plenty of time. Whistling Billy's gone looking for a box to pack Grampa's things in and Clever's humming like she doesn't have a care in the world while she's watering the roses. Even Keeper, who's sleeping his hangover off out on the pier, is doing so with a smile on his snout.

But me? Guess you could say I'm only semi-gleeful. Of course, I'm feeling thrilled about Billy and me reuniting. And his believing me. Last night, after a million and one satin kisses, we had bedroll talk. He's the only one so far that didn't *pshaw* me when I told him about finding Mr. Buster dead on Browntown Beach. But there's another part of me that's experiencing stomach-churning worry. And it's not only about Grampa that I'm so worked up. What with all that's come barreling at me the last coupla days, I haven't had a bit of time to do any investigating of Mr. Buster's murder. *Sorry, Mama. I can't write the* awfully good *story 'fore I solve the crime. And without the story and the resulting admiration beams jetting to heaven, you're in the exact same position you were in when this all started. Restless.*

Done with her chore, Clever hikes herself up on top of the picnic table, a yellow rosebud pinning up her hair. "Whatcha got that weird look on your face for?"

"I'm deep thinkin'."

"What for?"

When the cottage phone starts clanging, I swing my legs off the bench and say, "Gotta get that. It's probably Miss Jessie calling from the hospital."

I'm already halfway up the lawn when Clever yells something excited. I spin around to see what she's so fired up about at the exact same moment Sheriff LeRoy Johnson steps out from behind a big elm not more'n a yard away from me. "Looks like the lost sheep have finally found their way home," he says, put out. (One thing I gotta say for the citizenry of Cray Ridge—even though pound for pound most of 'em are what you'd consider fat as hell, they're light on their feet. Must be from all the hunting they do.)

"Be right back, Sheriff," I say, trying to scoot around him. "The phone's ringing off its hook."

"It'll wait." He latches on to my elbow and practically drags me back down to the picnic table. Depositing me next to Clever, he says, "I got a few questions to ask the two of you."

Oh, I just bet he does. But actually? I don't have time to mess with him. Taking care of Grampa and Mama are #1 and #2 on my **VERY IMPORTANT THINGS TO DO** list for the day, so I'm gonna take my chances and tell the sheriff the truth. That we don't have that stupid treasure map. That Cooter Smith and Sneaky Tim Ray stole it from us, so he should go hunt them down and leave us be. He can't beat up all of us. Can he?

"Sheriff, about the . . . ," I try.

"Why'd ya take off into the woods last night?" he asks Clever, ignoring me like I'm part of the landscape. (The reason he's chosen to give *her* the third degree instead of *me* is because he thinks she's the weakest link. Not finishing high school and all.)

"Ya hear me?" the sheriff asks, bending not more'n four

inches from her face, and I'm staggered. Though a lout, LeRoy's not dumb, and should know by now that getting Clever Lever to cooperate with the law gives new meaning to the word **Futile: Useless.** The girl's got the will of a mustang.

I tug on his sleeve. "Sheriff, about . . ."

"The coloreds burned the dump down last night," he says, still not taking his hog eyes offa Clever, who's braiding the ends of her hair and acting all la de da. "And this morning when the smoke cleared, guess who we found in the ashes, burned alive."

"Who?" I ask, searching around in my briefcase for my blue spiral. This sounds like breaking news!

"Buster Malloy," the sheriff says.

"WHAT?" I shout. "Why, that's just—"

"We already got somebody under arrest for that murder." LeRoy reaches into his pocket and draws out a pouch of Red Man chewing tobacco. "Thought ya might like to know who that somebody is, Carol."

"Why'd I care who killed Buster? He was nuthin' but *another* fat old fart who—"

"Clever!" I scream out before she can say something she's going to have to pay dearly for.

Hearing my call of distress, Billy barrels out of the cottage, whoaing at my side. And I'm just gettin' ready to explain what this prevaricatin' bully just told us, about Mr. Buster Malloy being found dead at the dump, when LeRoy bends back down toward Clever and says in his most taunting voice, "The reason I thought ya'd be interested in who killed Buster is . . . well." He pauses to smirk. "It's a friend of yours we got locked up good and tight."

"Ya don't say." Clever's returning smirk could win a blue ribbon, because, really, when it gets down to it, me and Billy and Miss Florida and Grampa are the only friends she's got, and not one of us is sitting down at the sheriff station behind those black bars. "And who might that friend be?" she asks, so sure of herself.

The sheriff slips the chaw behind his lip and says, "Why, that'd be Cooter Smith."

(Damn it. I forgot about Cooter.)

Clever gasps, and Billy's struggling to keep his breathing regular and not doing that good a job.

"But that's not right, that's not . . . ," I yell before Billy shakes his head at me ever so slightly, letting me know now's not the time.

The sheriff says, "We got that uppity boy dead to rights this time. Even got an eyewitness."

Clearly shaken, but refusing to back down, Clever sasses, "And who'd that be?"

The sheriff looks as smug as a bug in a rug. "Tim Ray Holloway will testify in a court of law that him and Cooter and Buster were playin' a game of craps over in back of Mamie's and when the dice didn't go his way, Cooter lost this temper and beat on Buster 'til he was dead. And threatened he'd do the same to Tim Ray if'n he didn't help him drag Buster's body onto the dump so he could set it afire."

It takes mighty *focus* for me not to shout out, Why, you lyin' red-faced baboons! Even though everybody knows that Mr. Buster Malloy had a love of craps, he's been dead for days already over at Browntown Beach!

Nuts. I bet I know what he did. When I went back to look for Mr. Buster the other afternoon? And I found that he had up and disappeared like Mr. Harry Houdini? The sheriff musta stole him right out from under my nose! And then he dragged that dead body over to the dump for the sole purpose of trying to pin this crime on Cooter Smith because he hates him with his whole heart.

(I believe this would be considered a perfect example of what Mr. Howard Redmond calls in his excellent book: *A frame-up: A fraudulent incrimination of an innocent person.*)

But ha! on you, sheriff. I got *proof* Mr. Buster was murdered on that Browntown sand and NOT the dump. I got pictures!

Uh-oh.

Just remembered those shots of Mr. Buster are missing from my stack. Maybe somebody from down at Bob's Drug Emporium put them in the wrong envelope? Right after my visit to Grampa at the hospital, I'm gonna make a beeline over there.

"Well, been real nice visitin' with y'all, but I got a prisoner to tend to." Turning to leave, the sheriff stops with a chuckle. "Just recalled the main reason I came up here in the first place." Pointing back and forth between me and Clever, he says, "I believe the two of you got something that belongs to that gentleman who lives next door." He takes out a pad from his back pocket and flips a few pages. "Mr. Willard called down to the station last night to report that he's missin' a map of some sort. Said y'all stole it from him." LeRoy takes a giant step back toward the picnic table, saying, "Ya don't mind I have a look in your briefcase for it, do ya, Miss Gibby?" Before I can answer, I certainly do, Sheriff, I mind a whole lot, he's already plucking at one of the leather-like's compartments with his porky fingers. Then another. Rustling around the bottom, and not finding what he's looking for, he slams it shut with a lotta show and says to Clever, "Maybe you's the one hiding that map, Carol."

"Map? What map?" she says in her most innocent-of-all-wrongdoin's voice. "I have no idea what you're talkin' about."

"Ya weren't over at Browntown last night, were ya? Spendin' the night with the Smith boy? Maybe ya even helped him murder Buster. I know how ya favor the coloreds." He comes in close enough to sniff Clever, maybe for dump smoke. Or barbecue sauce.

Clever hawks and spits to the side, says, "Why, no I wasn't, and no I didn't, LeRoy. Ya know, I could swear I already tol' you that. Seems to me"—she bobs her eyebrows at me—"what we got here is a failure to communicate."

Oh, my cool-handed Clever!

"But thanks ever so much for worryin' about my whereabouts," she says so realistically, even *I* believe her.

Shifting his weight toward me, LeRoy asks, "How about you, Miss Gibby? Ya over to Browntown las' night?" I can tell he'd love to add on, "You who are dumber than anthracite coal."

"She was with me," Billy says, trying to maintain a hold of Keeper, whose appetite must be returning 'cause he's eyeing the sheriff like he's a chicken-fried steak.

"And just exactly where was *you*?" he asks, politing his voice some since Billy's daddy, Big Bill Brown of High Hopes Farm, is the richest man in Grant County. It's not likely the sheriff is ready to belly flop into that kind of hot water. Not with an election coming.

Billy says, "I was with Gibby."

"Sheriff, ya hear anything new about my grampa?" I ask, suddenly remembering. If anybody knows what's happening over at the hospital, it'd be busybody him.

LeRoy gives us the once-over one more time, and then with a turn of his heel heads back up the lawn.

"Sheriff Johnson?" I call, chasing after him. "Grampa?"

"Gibby?" Billy calls after me, worried.

"I'm fine," I yell back at him, and then to Clever, "Stay put," 'cause I can tell she's just itching to skedaddle.

Hustling, I catch up with LeRoy just as he's pulling open his cruiser door out back near the road. I'm about to ask him again about Grampa's condition when he warns, "Keep your trap shut about findin' Buster on the beach or else."

OH MY GOODNESS! HE KNOWS I KNOW!

Or is he just warning me about spreading gossip that can't be proved? **Slander: A malicious false statement.**

"I'm givin' you fair warnin'." He grabs on to a handful of my hair hard enough to wrench my head to my shoulder. "Ya hear?"

"I'll . . . I'll write a story in my newspaper. Everybody in Cray Ridge will know that you're trying to blame Cooter for something he didn't do."

"Be my guest," LeRoy scoffs. "Who ya think they're gonna believe? The man who's been the law of this county for eight years or some . . . imbecile."

Seconds after he backs out, siren blaring, Keeper whips past me. He musta been eavesdropping and no longer able to contain himself, 'cause he full-out chases that squad car down Lake Mary Road. "Careful," I shout after him, even though I know he won't heed me. That's the thing with that dog. He's brave, almost reck-lessly so, and doesn't EVER give up. No. Keeper will take it on himself like a sworn duty not to let the sheriff outta his sight. I read the whole book out loud to him, placing special emphasis on chapter 16: **Tracking.** *A good hunting dog can be indispensable. And tenacious.* So I'm not worrying about the sheriff's threats as I turn back to the cottage.

But ya know who should be worried, don'tcha? Cooter Smith, that's who. Because no matter how rascally he's been acting lately, we'd all feel real bad if he was found twisting on the end of a rope in Wally's Woods, the sheriff not bothering to hide a revolting grin when he announces to the town, "He up and escaped. I have no idea who strung the boy up like that. What a goddamn shame."

Yes, indeed. Cooter Smith should be worryin' his fool head off.

Cheating

While Billy and Clever are in the kitchen stirring us up some lunch, I'm picking through Grampa's dresser drawers. His worn-at-the-seat jeans. The bleached undershirts he wears no matter how hot. I run my finger across the pearl buttons of one of his Texas shirts. The kind you see on rodeo riders. I've never been in his room without him. Pressing my face into his pillow, there's a faint smell of trout twisting out of the lake. My salty tears aren't helping. They're only reminding me how the two of us had planned on doing some ocean fishing someday. "The Atlantic spreads out like a Texas prairie," Grampa told me, thrilled. "Fish the size of calves. Ya'd have to see it to believe it."

Above his cherrywood bed there's a portrait of him and Gramma Kitty. They don't look much older than me and Billy. I'd give up my favorite No. 2 if I could climb into that picture and feel all that love blanketing me and . . . *focus, Gib, focus*. What does he always tell me when I get to yearning like this? "What sense does it make cravin' something ya can never have? That's like a whippoorwill wishin' it were a sparrow."

Oh, Grampa.

What else is he gonna need in the hospital? His deerskin slipper? Yes, he's awfully fond of that slipper. I check under the bed for it, sending dust bunnies on high. There it is, next to what looks like a wooden hatbox. As I slide them both out and set them on top of his chenille spread, a voice in my head tells me to go ahead and open the box, and it isn't Grampa's. He'd raise holy hell if he knew I was going through his personals. I trace the smooth raised-up letters. A M. Addy Murphy. Bet he whittled this box for Mama when she was a little girl. Wonder why he never showed me this before. The top comes right off. There's a jumble of stuff inside, but what catches my eye right off is the pink ribbon tied around a curl of dusty brown hair. And a letter.

June 2, 1970
Dear Daddy,

Might as well get straight to the point. I caught Joe cheating with the art dealer who owns the shop where I exhibit my paintings. (Calm down. Remember your heart.) After we drop Gib off at your place, the two of us are heading to a cabin in the Cumberlands to try and work things out. Don't worry.

Love,
Addy girl

Well, goodness. Daddy was cheating an art dealer? So that's why Miss Lydia can never see him up in heaven when she does one of her ACTUATIONS. This also answers my pestering question as to why he's not buried with my mama. My grampa despises cheating of any kind.

"Soup's almost on." Clever sticks in her head, and seeing what I'm doing, gets herself comfy on his bed. "Whatcha got there?" Boy, she could stand a bath. She smells like giblet stuffing right after you scoop it out of the bird.

I hand over the letter from Mama I found in the box. Clever moves her lips when she reads, so it takes her some time. When she's done, she shakes her head. "Another man shows his good-for-nuthin' side," she says, mimicking her mama to a T, but then adds with some wistfulness, "Do ya think they're *all* like that?"

"*My* man doesn't have a good-for-nuthin' side," I say. "He wouldn't cheat an art dealer." (Billy doesn't even like art all that much. He's more the rugged outdoor type.)

"You gonna be all right?" Clever asks, eyeing some coins Grampa left on his bedside table. "'Bout your daddy, I mean."

"A course I am. If he wouldn'ta died in the crash, I'm sure he woulda paid that art dealer back." I set Grampa's red-striped pajamas into the packing box next to his whittling knife and records. "Bad timin' is all."

"But that's not what . . . ," Clever says, choked up some since *daddy* talk is generally considered **Verboten: A taboo subject** between us. (Her not knowing . . . you understand.)

"Yes, my daddy was *another* man who truly loved his woman." I'm back to gazing adoringly at the picture above the bed. By the blissful smiles on their faces, anybody can see that Grampa and Gramma were enraptured in love just like me and Billy and Mama and Daddy. "True love must run deep in our family, wouldn't ya say?"

"Deep as hell," Clever replies, *real* huffy.

(Jealous, is all she is.)

"Well, I'm gonna give Miss Jessie a jingle down at the hospital," I say, replacing Mama's letter in the hatbox and putting it back under the bed. "Put those coins back on the bedside table, hear?"

Out in the parlor, I dial up the numbers printed on the hospital card and say, "Charlie Murphy's room, please."

On the other end of the line, the phone's ringing and ringing. Miss Jessie finally picks up and says in a running-out-of-breath voice, "Hello?"

"Hey, Miss Jessie. I'm just about set to head over to the hos—"

She interrupts with, "Oh, Gib, where ya been? Ya better get down here quick. Time's runnin' out," and hangs up without even saying see ya later alligator.

Clever is plumb wore out. It musta been all that daddy talk drained her or maybe it's coming up with THE PLAN that made her get-up-and-go get up and go. I got her set up real nice on the flowered sofa on the screened-in porch. Two pillows. A packet of crackers sitting alongside her bowl of chicken noodle. Billy, him being such a long drink of water, managed to tape her beloved movie poster up on the ceiling so Mr. Paul Newman and Mr. Robert Redford can watch over her while she rests. Billy and Keeper've gone off to check on the mooring of Grampa's boat to the dock, so me and Clever are alone when she asks, "What'd Miss Jessie say?"

"She said time was runnin' out, but I could tell that she was in a hurry. She musta read the clock wrong."

I checked the hospital card AGAIN after speaking to her, just to be sure. Visiting hours are *definitely* 'til two o'clock. I got plenty of time to get done what I gotta get done and still get over there.

Clever asks, "We clear on the plan?"

"Maybe ya better go over it again."

She sets her spoon in her bowl, and says, "First off, don't you dare tell Billy what you're up to. He'll try to stop you, on account a him being so righteous."

"Check."

"Second off, go and break Cooter out of jail. Miss Florida will never forgive us if he's found hung, and 'sides that, we owe him. From the old days."

"Check."

"Last off, you're gonna take Grampa's things to the hospital and have a real nice visit." Fingering the rose she's got in her hair, Clever adds with a smile, "Tell him for me not to worry. The flowers are doin' mighty fine. 'Specially the Texas ones."

I'm sure Grampa won't mind being last off. In fact, he'd be disappointed as hell in me if I didn't take care of this Cooter problem first 'fore I go see him. It's the cowboy way to stand up for a body that cannot stand up for hisself. 'Specially one that is about to get his neck stretched in a permanent kind of way. 'Specially since that neck belongs to Cooter. Grampa's as fond of him as he is of Billy. All those years calling birds and cooking together up at the diner have bound those two together like biscuits and gravy and birds of a feather.

After I get Clever replumped, she hands me the still half-full soup bowl, saying in a barely-there voice, "Gib?"

"Yeah?"

"You're gonna stay focused and remember, ain't ya?" Her lids are heavy and her breath noodley when she takes a good hard look, first at the ceiling poster, and then back at me. "Don't think I could bear it if ya let me down, Butch."

Not Copacetic

"If it's all the same to you, I'll drive," I tell Billy, lifting the truck keys off the hook near the back door. He's been reteaching me behind Grampa's back. First time we went out, I was beyond ascared. (Considering what happened to me and my mama and daddy, a vehicle of any sort can feel a lot like a murder weapon. You understand.) But I practiced and practiced on the back roads, and Billy has patience when it comes to me, so I'm not half-bad. The staying on my side of the road part could use a little more work, but my turns are nice and smooth.

Billy's next to me on the bench seat, holding a box full of Grampa's jammies, his whittling knife, his Johnny Cash albums, and the bird book with the glossy pictures. I also slapped together a couple of peanut butter and honeys for him.

"Tell me *exactly* what Miss Jessie said to you on the phone," Billy says as I back out of the cottage drive, careful to check BOTH mirrors like he taught me.

As much as I hate lying to a Vietnam veteran, the Kid is right. This outlaw business is between her and me. Billy'd never go along with a jailbreak. He's too law-abiding. I have to ditch him.

"Well," I say. "Let's see . . . oh, that's right. Miss Jessie asked if you could go over to her place and see if Vern and Teddy need any help with the horses since she's not sure when she'll be able to get home." We're running down the road next to the lake. Charles

Michael Murphy would adore being out on that sleek water today. Casting his rod and reel, spinning Texas tales. "So . . . ah . . . I'm gonna drop you at her farm and then I'm gonna run over to see Grampa at the hospital and when we're done visitin', I'll come back to get ya, all right?"

"But—" He cuts off as we pass by Top O' the Mornin'. A white bag is cartwheeling through the empty lot. The candy-cane window awnings are hanging lifeless. Even the lucky horseshoe looks more crooked. Am I remembering right? Didn't Clever tell me that Janice and Miss Florida would tend to things while Grampa was in the hospital? Well, if they are, they're doing a deplorable job.

Seeing the diner abandoned like that is spooking me, and maybe Billy feels that way, too, 'cause the both of us don't say much 'til I slow down in front of Miss Jessie's drive-up. Where normally I feel breathless at the sight of all this gorgeousness, the reason I can't catch air right this minute is because who should be sitting on a stump near the road like a wart on a beauty queen's face but evil's own **Emissary: Agent.** Sneaky Tim Ray Holloway.

"This here's private property," he gnarls, when I pull up next to him. "Go away."

Billy gets out of the truck and stands tall next to this runt. "Miss Jessie sent me to help with the horses."

"Where's Jessie at anyways?" Holloway winks up at me. "I'm hungry."

It's been bothering me and bothering me *why* Sneaky Tim Ray would go along with the sheriff's frame-up of Cooter. True, Holloway is walking the path of the wicked and could be lying about seeing Cooter choke Buster dead over a game of craps just for the kick of it, but . . . I don't know. Never known this belly crawler to do somethin' for nuthin'. Something seems off here. Something isn't **Copacetic: Okay**.

Wait just a cotton-pickin' minute.

I just recalled how Sneaky Tim Ray and Cooter ambushed us in the woods last night, stole that treasure map off us. With Cooter behind bars now for murdering Buster . . . yes . . . Sneaky Tim Ray can keep that treasure ALL FOR HIMSELF! Next time he comes hunting for me, he'll be dripping in sapphires and rubies. Because that's what the treasure's GOT to be, never mind the lack of an X on that map. Pirate booty. *Not* prime tobacco like I first thought.

Billy grinds down the smoking butt Sneaky Tim Ray tosses at his boot, and says syrup slow, the way he does right before he's about to explode, "Miss Jessie's keepin' vigil up at the hospital with Charlie Murphy. He's had a heart attack."

"Well, ain't that too bad," Sneaky Tim Ray's lips say, but his eyes say otherwise. "Ya gonna be on your own now, darlin'? Footloose and fancy free?" He laughs and laughs 'til he coughs and coughs.

When Billy bunches his fists, Sneaky Tim Ray, so used to getting pummeled, is alert and harefooted, and already 'bout half gone through the trees.

"Leave him be, Billy. I gotta get to the hospital and you gotta check those horses. Time's runnin' out," I remind him. (As you know, I'm lying. Right after I leave here, I'm heading for the sheriff station to bust out Cooter.)

When he doesn't respond, I shout, "Knock knock."

"Who's there?" Billy answers, finally dragging his feet back to me.

"Love," I say, taking hold of his hand when he passes it through the window.

"Love who?"

"You, Billy Brown. Y-O-U. And not the same way I love Grampa. That is not a joke, by the way, just in case you thought it was."

"I know the way you mean," he says with a lot of confidence. Boy, does he ever seem different! Usually after an encounter such as the one he just had with Sneaky Tim Ray, Billy's temper would be choking the reasonable outta him. But he seems hardly riled at all. Maybe it's the scoop after scoop of sweet lovin' I gave him last night. Maybe all that his Vietnam-bombed nerves needed was a little of that homegrown sugar. (We did NOT pound the snow possum, if that's what you're wondering. The both of us agreed that we wouldn't break out his wedding tackle 'til we're on our honeymoon.)

"Ya better git," Billy says, planting a kiss on my forehead with those extra-fine lips a his. "Give my love to Grampa. Drive slow and keep a good lookout. There's things happenin' around here that're makin' my stomach feel like it's tangled up in barbwire. Ya know what I mean?"

My stomach is feeling jumbled as well. And yes, I do know what that means. **The Importance of Perception in Meticulous Investigation: Gut Instincts:** *Follow that feeling in the pit of your stomach. Many mysteries are solved by a reporter who followed their gut hunches.*

Free at Last

After sliding into a spot in the sheriff station lot, I get to feeling so jumpy that I forget to put the truck in P and it hops halfway to the Methodist church. Sure as May follows June, Reverend Jack will tell me during our visit next week that breaking Cooter Smith out of jail was not an *appropriate* way for me to behave. (Sorry, Reverend. There's no two ways about it. I can't let Grampa or Clever down.) If I don't cut Cooter loose now, the sheriff is gonna settle this nastiness between them once and for all. Like *all* feuds, this one goes way back. "Niggas belong in their place, and that Smith boy is overreachin' his," is *exactly* what LeRoy says after he's had a few too many down at Frank's Tap. "Like Daddy Carl always said, ya get 'em educated and they'll turn into rabble-rousers."

What LeRoy's referring to is when Cooter went off to that college in North Carolina, but he doesn't have that right. Miss Florida told me that Cooter was a Blue Devil, not a Rabble-Rouser, which just goes to illustrate how messed up the sheriff's thinking can get when Cooter Smith is the subject of the conversation. You're probably thinking it's his color that makes the sheriff hate Cooter so, but you'd only be a little right. Mostly, it's *love*.

Cooter's mama, Darnell, the one who went missing selling peanuts up roadside years ago? Clever told *me* that Janice told *her* that back when the bunch of them were young, the sheriff was badly smitten and having bushels of hot sex with the lovely Darnell. But Darnell, not equally smitten, she up and dropped the sheriff and took up with Cooter's daddy, Willie. Who Cooter takes after EXACTLY. I mean, like an identical twin. I've seen pictures. So that's why I've always thought the sheriff has it out for Cooter. LeRoy was scorned. And he's still furious as hell.

Focus . . . Gib . . . focus. Keep your mind on THE PLAN. Pulling open the station's front door, I call out, "Anybody home?" The only greeting I get back is Skeeter Davis singing out from a radio, so I make my way toward the back room where I know they do all their important business. This is where me and Grampa get our fishing licenses. There's knotty wood paneling and file cabinets and telephones and Deputy Jimmy Lee Boyd. His head is lying flat on one of two metal desks next to a burger bag from Tee-ter's Drive-In. Boy, this is going to be A LOT easier than Clever and me figured on. Let's see . . . from what I remember from my western movies, the cell keys should be hanging on a hook right around this. . . .

"Hey," the deputy pops up saying, a paper clip stuck to his flushed cheek. "Didn't hear ya come in."

A few years older than me, with a button nose and the type of sandy hair that always looks like it could use a wash, the deputy is the only child of Miss Loretta, who owns Candy World. She accidentally dropped him into one of her steel melting-chocolate vats when he was a baby, so Jimmy Lee is well known for being sorta dumb. But good with a gun. Almost *always* wins the target-shooting contest during Cray Ridge Days.

"Well, hey, Jimmy Lee," I say. "How ya been?"

"Fine as a frog hair," he says, trying to hide a yawn. "What can I do ya for today, Gib?"

"I . . . ah . . ." (Clever and me hadn't planned this part out. Least I don't think we did.) "I . . . um . . ." There's a CRAY RIDGE DAYS AUGUST 16–23 FUN FOR EVERYONE poster sitting on the corner of his desk. "I . . . ah . . . stopped by to see if you or the sheriff wanted to buy some raffle tickets."

"Already got mine." Jimmy Lee squints toward the big black clock on the wall. "Almost one thirty, the sheriff should be back from lunch soon. Maybe he'd like a couple," he says, peeking into the top of the burger bag with a disappointed grunt. "Sorry to hear about your grampa's heart givin' out, by the way. How's he doin'?"

"On the mend," I say, my eyes scouring the room. I don't see a cell key hanging anywheres in plain sight and I don't have a bunch of time to go looking for it. I need to get over to the hospital to make sure Grampa really *is* on the mend.

Jimmy Lee says, "Been hot, ain't it?"

"Sure has."

"Ya hear 'bout the goin's-on in Browntown?"

"No, I haven't," I lie. The jail key must be in his desk or something. "What happened?"

"There was a fire," he says, getting all revved up.

"A fire? In Browntown? Why, Jimmy Lee, that's a front-page story! Would ya mind terribly if I interview you for the *Gazette*?" I ask, with no intention whatsoever of doing so.

"Why, an interview'd suit me just fine, sugar."

"Well then, let's get started." I sit down across from him, trying to look as professional as can be. "Oh, my goodness, ya know what I just remembered?"

"What?"

"Well, over the years of interviewing important subjects from all walks of life, I've found a bitty bite of something sweet helps my subjects to . . . well . . . maintain their liveliness. Would ya care for a coupla your mama's chocolate-covered cherries 'fore we begin? Just happen to have some right here," I say, gratefully recalling THE PLAN. Clever slipped the pills through a hole she made in the bottom of the candy with a pencil. They're a mite melty from being in my pocket too long, but Jimmy Lee won't mind. The boy loves his vittles no matter the form.

"Don't mind if I do," he says, lifting the chocolates outta my hand and disappearing them into his mouth.

I hope Clever was right. She figured if Billy has to take one tranquilizing pill to calm himself down, it'll take at least three of 'em to knock Jimmy Lee's "lard ass out." (The Kid's nimble fingers stole the pills right outta Billy's pocket.) "How about another?"

"And that fire ain't all that's been happenin' in Browntown," he says, plucking the chocolate outta my palm. "More goin' on over there last night than a Ringlin' Brothers show."

"Oh, Jimmy Lee," I chuckle. "You are the funny one." (Clever also instructed me to give any male I run across during the course of the jailbreak tons of compliments. High praise makes men putty in a girl's hands.) "Do go on."

Giving me a know-it-all grin, he says, "Guess who we found in the dump once we got the fire put out?"

"I'm sure little ole me has no idea."

"Buster Malloy."

"No!"

"Yup," he says, swiveling back in his chair, elbows akimbo. "There he was . . . the next governor of the fine state of Kentucky . . . lyin' in the rubble, his body burned blacker than Moses Washington at midnight." (Mr. Washington is the deacon at First

Ebenezer and is colored in a way that there is no mistaking which side of town he belongs on no matter what time of day.)

"Ya got any idea who murdered him?" I ask, fawning.

"Sure do. Cooter Smith done it. We already got him locked up." The deputy takes the keys out of his pocket, jangles them in my face, and shoves them back in.

This is NOT going so well. I told Clever we shoulda given him *four* pills, instead of *three*. Jimmy Lee doesn't seem tranquil at all. In fact, he seems darn right perky.

"Got any more of them cherries?" he asks.

"Sorry, I'm clean out." I got to stall until I can come up with another plan. "My, oh my, a thirst has snuck up on me something bad. Might I trouble you for a cup of that cool water?" I ask, pointing to the cooler over in the corner in a damsel-in-distress kind of way.

"Comin' right up." The deputy takes some time to pry himself outta the chair. "If'n this deputyin' don't work out, maybe I could get me a job at Top O' the Mornin.' *Hardy . . . har . . . har.*" Squatting down in front of the cooler, he says, "Shoot. Looks like we outta cups. Gotta get some from the supply room. Be right back." And off he goes, maybe . . . wobbling? Yes! He is definitely looking rubber-legged, but I don't know how long that'll last. I gotta hurry. I know where the key is now . . . but . . .

According to **The Importance of Perception in Meticulous Investigation: Searching the Premises:** *In the midst of a case, an operator must take **every** opportunity to uncover any and everything that might help solve the case. You never know when something useful might turn up.*

Sitting down behind the desk that's got a SHERIFF LEROY JOHNSON plaque on it, I pull open the top drawer. All it's got is some worn-down pictures of women in skimpy nighties, a couple of gnawed pencils, and a ballpoint from Chessy's Feed and Grain.

"Can't find the cups," Jimmy Lee yells from down there somewhere. "Thtill sirsty?"

"Parched," I shout back.

Desk drawer two is stuffed with envelopes and a .22. I relocate the gun to the small of my back. Just in case. My grampa taught me how to shoot. I do okay. (I'm showing off my humble here. Remember when I just told you that Jimmy Lee almost *always* wins the target-shooting contest at Cray Ridge Days? Guess who wins the *other* times. Yup. I can shoot the eye out of a squirrel from fifty yards off. Used to be able to anyway.)

"Gotch 'em," Jimmy Lee slurs out.

"Bless your heart," I call back, moving down to the last drawer of the sheriff's desk. Lo and behold! Lying right on top, it's my pictures of Mr. Buster Malloy! On Browntown Beach. Dead. How the hell did LeRoy get ahold of 'em?

"Gotta, just gotta get, this larder moved to here and . . . ," Jimmy Lee shouts, dragging something.

Oh, mother of pearl! I know who gave the sheriff my shots of dead Buster Malloy. Had to be Mr. Bob of Bob's Drug Emporium. I heard tell from Mr. Cubby, the taxidermist, that if you take in pictures to get developed, and if they're of things that Mr. Bob Johnson, the Christianist of Christians, doesn't think are the moral thing to be taking pictures of—for instance, a stuffed alligator and a stuffed bear positioned so it looks like they're having hot sex—well, when you come to pick up your pictures, he'll waggle his finger at ya in the name of the Lord, and turn them over to his baby brother, LeRoy. I shoulda remembered that. Next time I'll take my film over to Appleville to get developed.

Just as I'm shoving my pictures of dead Mr. Buster next to the .22, the awfulest *screech* echoes down the hall, chased by a crashing *thud*.

"Ya all right?" I yell, hurrying. "Jimmy Lee?" Peeking my head into the supply room, there he is, splayed out on the concrete floor, a box of Dixies his pillow.

Well . . . well . . . well. Didn't that work out nice. REAL NICE. Just the way the Kid planned it. I'm ashamed I doubted her. (As we all know, the girl is criminalistic by nature.)

I help myself to the keys in his pocket and jog the rest of the way down the hall. Using both hands on the heavy jail door, I wait for my eyes to adjust to the dim light. Behind the bars to my right, there's a body lying long, but it's shadowy, so I can't tell for sure if it's Cooter. Outta the other cell to my left, Aqua Net and whiskey are drifting my way, bringing to mind all the other times I been in this jail with Clever to retrieve her mama after one of her benders. So that's why Top O' the Mornin' was so haunted looking. Miss Florida can't run the place all by herself. And instead of helping her, taking care of the diner like she said she would, selfish, selfish Janice Lever got herself pie-eyed last night and here she is, sleeping it off. So tempted am I to shout at her through the bars, "When *exactly* are ya gonna start deliverin' on your promises? Especially the one to Clever to make up for all your bad motherin'?" but battling with Janice is not why I'm here.

"Cooter?" I call into the other cell. "It's me. I've come for ya."

"Gibber, that you?" comes off the bunk.

Remembering that LeRoy Johnson and his .38 Special are speeding their way back here on a full stomach is getting me cranky. "Well, I just said it was, didn't I?" I slip one of the keys

I got outta the deputy's pocket into the cell lock, but it doesn't budge.

"It's that one," Cooter says, getting up close to the bars and pointing to a key that's larger than the others. He looks only slightly worse than I thought he would. His right eye is swoll shut and his top lip has a jaggedy cut that looks fresh. On his forehead, a lump the size of a doorknob is sprinkled with blood.

This is NOT going smooth like it does in the movies. Cooter doesn't rush out when he hears the lock clank open, sayin', "Thank you from the bottom of my heart. I owe ya my life." He stands steady and says, "This some sorta trick?"

A gurgling groan comes from the supply room.

"No time to explain now," I say. "Sounds like Jimmy Lee is comin' to and the sheriff's gonna pull up any second."

Cooter glares at me with the eye that isn't closed up tight like a string purse and finally gives the cell door a push. He's gimping. "LeRoy piped my bad knee."

"Ya need help?" I ask, offering my arm to steady him.

On our way past the supply room, Cooter hops in and slides the deputy's gun free from his holster, saying, "Been my experience, the Lord helps those who help themselves."

"Amen to that, brother," I tell him, patting the .22 and my dead Mr. Buster pictures. "Now how's about we get the hell outta here."

Vengeance Is Mine

Cooter doesn't want me to stop at the hospital. Since he's almost always in trouble with the law, he knows that when you're on the lamb, it's best to skedaddle. But what he *doesn't* know about is Grampa's heart attack. After I fill him in best I can, he backs off, saying, "A course ya got to tend to him." He's still fond of Grampa. I can tell by the way his forehead is crinkling up like crepe paper.

After I get done parking us way back in St. Mary's lot, I instruct, "Visitin' hours are just about over. Stay low in the seat. When I come back, we'll go get Billy and he'll fix that leg up for ya."

Cooter is, I think, a year older than me, but looks a *lot* older than he should for a man his age. Goodness, I guess just like Billy, Cooter grew up when I wasn't looking. He's the most fantastic cake brown with eyes the color of toasted walnuts. I completely understand why Clever finds him so tasty.

"Why you doin' this, Gibber? Takin' a chance like this. It ain't like we're friends no more," he says, sleepy. The sheriff musta kept him up the whole night givin' him the third degree.

"Miss Lydia says sometimes old friends will loiter on the edge of your life, hopin' for a chance to get close again," I say, but I can tell right off that Cooter, being naturally on the tart side like his gramma Florida, ain't buying that sweet talk.

"What about me stealin' that map from y'all last night in the woods? Ya tellin' me ya ain't mad about that?"

"Maybe you're sufferin' from some sort of confusion from that hit on your head. Like me." I point to his noggin . . . then mine. "I have no idea what map you're talkin' about." I run my eyes down his body, looking for more serious injuries. "Ya know, when the sheriff comes huntin' for us, he'll spot that red shirt ya got on from a mile off." I rummage behind the driver's seat and take the plaid rodeo one outta Grampa's box. But instead of putting it on the way I meant him to, Cooter balls it and rests his head down. "All right. That's fine. Ya must be beat."

"Ya could say that."

"Didn't I?"

"No, I meant—"

"Cooter, I don't mean to be rude, but I don't have time for a visit right now. Go ahead and grab a little shut-eye, but whatever you do . . . stay outta sight," I say, rushing outta the truck. I simply can't wait to see Grampa. For once in his life, he won't be able to walk off when I tell him how much I love him.

At the welcomin' desk, Darlene Abernathy is doing what they pay her for, greeting and keeping track of who comes in and out the hospital doors. Up until a few months ago, she worked at the high school. Until she got caught making out in the boiler room with the janitor. With her egg white hair and lips the color of strawberry jam, I gotta admit, the girl stands out in this lobby like Top O' the Mornin's #6 special.

"Darlene?" I say, approaching on guard. (She and me don't exactly make beautiful music together.)

"Sign in," she says, not glancing up from her beauty magazine. (Like I figured, she's still harboring a grudge against me since I mighta mentioned that boiler room meeting of the mouths in *Gibby's Gazette*.)

Balancing Grampa's box of stuff on the ledge of the desk, I write my name into her reception book, barely able since that smell coming off her mouth is so sickeningly fruity. AND familiar-lookin'. Lordy. It's the same strawberry lip color I saw covering Sneaky Tim Ray's neck when he ambushed us in the woods! Darlene must be the "lady friend" Holloway was visiting the night he snatched up Keeper outside Grampa's room.

"Well, nice chattin' with you. Gotta get these things to him," I say, hurrying down the hospital hallway, feeling repulsed.

"Hold up," Darlene calls after me in that smoky voice of hers. She's got something in her stretched-out hand. Grampa's wedding ring, his gold watch. His rubbed-worn wallet. "You're too late," she says, when I come back to the desk. "Ya can take these things home with the rest of the stuff."

"Are visitin' hours over?" I ask, doubtful.

"They are, but even if they weren't . . . your grampa ain't gonna be needin' his things."

"*Why* isn't he gonna be needin' 'em?"

Darlene looks down. Hems and haws. Looks back up. "He's gone."

Oh my Lord . . . no . . . no . . . no.

"They took him off just a little while 'fore you got here." She pats my hand. "I'm sure sorry you didn't get to say good-bye.

Didn't I overhear Miss Jessie tell ya on the phone to hurry?" she says, unnaturally sweet.

What have I done? I shouldn'ta broke Cooter out . . . I shoulda come right over here . . . I shoulda. . . .

The overheads are haloing and the hallway tilting.

"When?" I ask, barely able.

"Just a little while ago."

Oh, Grampa. I'm so sorry . . . I didn't even . . . I . . .

Darlene stares at me with subzero eyes, then says, "The ambulance took him . . ."

"What?"

". . . out to the airport. They's flyin' him all the way to a hospital in Texas on Mr. Big Bill Brown's private airplane. Ya knew 'bout that, right?"

Her words aren't coming out at the same time her mouth moves. "What did ya just say?"

"And then they're gonna open his chest up with a saw and operate on his heart."

"Grampa's *not* dead?" I whimper.

"Now," she says, "I don't recall tellin' you he was *dead*. That's something your messed-up brain came to all by its lonesome." Darlene gives me a loathsome look that says—*That right there, missy? That's what you call tit for tat. For the smooching in the boiler room story you printed in your dumb newspaper that caused me to lose my secretary job up at the high school.* "What I *said* was, your grampa was *gone*."

"Darlene Judy Abernathy, I'm . . . I'm on an important case at the present time, but I'd like you to know, I'm intendin' to come back." Scooping up Grampa's valuables, I slip them into my back pocket, brushing up against the Mr. Buster pictures and the .22, one of which I am mightily tempted to avail myself of. "So might I suggest at your earliest convenience that you pay a visit to the Okins Funeral Salon to make arrangements?"

"Why'd I wanna do that?" she says so damn snippy.

"Because on my return visit you can count on me beatin' the ever-lovin' shit outta you with a rusty shovel. Twice."

Her vengeful self is practically vibrating in victory when she hisses back, "Miz Tanner left this note for ya," and spins an envelope across the desk at me that looks like it's already been opened and licked closed again by her been-all-around-town tongue.

Dear Gibby,

We're taking Charlie to Houston, Texas. Dr. Sam has arranged for him to see a special doctor who's going to perform heart surgery on him. Sorry we couldn't wait. Big Bill is piloting us. He's also promised to send some of his boys to help out at the farm.

Your grampa wants you to say your prayers to you know who and go stay with Mr. and Mrs. Bailey until he gets back. And keep away from Browntown.

Miss Jessie

"How long is this all s'posed to take?" I ask Darlene, trying like hell not to give her the satisfaction of seeing me sob in relief. "In other words, when's Grampa gonna be back home?"

"I'm sure I don't have the slightest idea. Take care now, ya hear?" she says, when her receptionist phone starts ringing. On my way out the sliding glass doors, I hear her yowl, "Cooter Smith murdered Buster Malloy? And he's 'scaped? A reward? How much?"

Outside in the parking lot, pausing to get my bearings, I look up to the western sky. Lightning's swimming through the black clouds like electric eels. As I hurry back to the truck, it's easy for this trained investigator to perceive two things.

Another storm is headed our way.

And that varmint Darlene Abernathy is one hard-hearted woman.

Like a Greased Pig

When I fired up the truck engine, Cooter was dead to the world and is only just now rejoining us living as I steer us out onto Route 12. "How was Grampa feelin'?" he asks, cranking down the window farther, not that it'll help. The air's hanging like velvet.

I pass him the letter Miss Jessie left for me.

When he's done reading, Cooter says, "He'll like bein' back in Texas, don't ya think?"

"He will. He'll like that a lot." I wish I coulda gotten his Johnny Cash records and whittling knife to him 'fore he left. I hope that Houston is near a lake. He needs a lake. And his peach schnapps.

Cooter asks, "Where we headed?"

"Browntown," I say, thinking we better get someplace safe ASAP.

"Tha's maybe not the best idea ya ever had. Tha's the first place they'll come lookin' for us. Didn't ya mention something earlier about goin' to get Billy?" he asks, rubbing on his leg. "Where's he at?"

"He's . . . ah . . . he's at . . ." *Where the heck did I leave him? Let's see . . . we were at the cottage and then we saw that wart Sneaky Tim Ray and then we were talking about love and how our tummies were feeling all balled up and . . . that's right.* "Billy's at Miss Jessie's,"

I say, making a quick turn onto Tanner Farm Road. "I know you didn't kill Mr. Buster, by the way. I got the proof."

"Ya do?" Cooter says, rousing himself.

"I do." But when I reach back to my waistband to retrieve the snapshots that I boosted from the sheriff's desk, the truck gets away from me and starts to drift and I slam on the brakes, but then forget about the steering part, and the next thing I know, we're stuck in a ditch on a tilt. "Damn it all!" I shout, but I'm also thanking the Lord in all His glory that we made it this close to Miss Jessie's place. If need be, I can fetch Billy to come help us. We landed soft, but I ask anyway, "Y' all right?"

"Fine," Cooter says, picking up the pictures that've slid across the seat. Even though Mr. Bob from Bob's Drug Emporium can be a stinky little tattletale, he knows his way around a darkroom. Anybody can see those gaping holes in Mr. Buster Malloy's heart. And the Geronimo rope dangling above the glistening sand. Clearly, the man is dead on Browntown Beach and NOT the dump. Cooter spends some time comparing the two shots I took. There is a close-up one. The other's from far off. Mr. Howard Redmond advises in his chapter **Using Your Tools:** *Two or more photographs are beneficial to lend perspective at any crime scene.*

"Well?" I ask, proud of my photo-taking skills. "What do ya think?"

Cooter *should* be showing some relief that he's holding proof of his innocence in his hands, but instead, he says with a lot of sadness, "Seein' that rope . . ."

"Now, now, don't start worryin'. We won't let the sheriff hang ya. Me and the Kid got a plan."

"It's not that. The rope . . . reminds me of Georgie. He sure did love swingin' into the lake. 'Member that, Gibber? 'Member how loud he'd shout Geronimo?"

Not exactly. What I do remember, though, is that those two boys? Cooter Smith and Georgie Malloy? No matter the color of their skins, they were blood brothers. Inseparable.

"Ya miss your Puddin' and Pie?" I ask, calling Georgie by his pet name.

"Things seemed a whole lot better when he was alive, don'tcha think? Been a patch of bad road since he left us."

Poor, poor Cooter. Maybe I should rub on his black fender hair. Or give his wide shoulders a deep massage. I got strong hands from riding every day.

"Not a day goes by I don't wish I woulda stopped Georgie from goin' out on the boat that day with Buster," he says, running his finger down the picture.

It was me who found Georgie's body washed up on Browntown Beach in almost the exact same spot where I found Mr. Buster's. Something like that is real hard to forget. The lake flowing outta his ears. Eyes like tarnished quarters. "Are ya talkin' about the day Georgie accidentally drowned?"

"That weren't no *accident*," Cooter spits out. "Everybody in town, they don't say it out loud, but they all know that Georgie was murdered. Buster *claimed* Georgie dove into the lake to cool off while they was fishin' and he got the cramps, and Buster, not being able to swim, couldn't save him, but that's nuthin' but a lie."

"WHAT?" Am I the only one hasn't heard this? Or maybe I have and just don't remember. "Why would Mr. Buster want Georgie dead? He was his own nephew!" I'm trying to recall and not having much luck what Mr. Howard Redmond says in his chapter entitled **Why People Kill**. Cooter's gotta be wrong. No-body could be so evil as to murder sweet Georgie. That boy sweat sugar. His death *had* to have been an accident. "Cooter? Answer me now."

He's quiet as a moose.

"I just broke you outta jail, I believe you owe me a little some-thing for that," I say, using what Clever would call a feminine wile. The laying upon of guilt. (Which I am not proud of, by the way, but a reporter has to do what a reporter has to do. I NEED to know this information for my awfully good story.) "I repeat, why do you think Mr. Buster killed Georgie?"

"Ya ain't squeezin' that outta me. I already said way more than I shoulda. 'Sides, we ain't got time now for storytellin'. We gotta git. The sheriff and his boy gonna come lookin' for us soon." It's the fourth time he's checked out the back window. "You's in as much trouble as I is, ya know?" he says, shouldering the truck door open.

"Wait for me," I bark out. "Ya can't barely walk."

"If I gotta crawl, I'm gettin' outta here."

Cooter's right. Deputy Jimmy Lee will've come to by now. Even dumb as he is, he more'n likely mentioned to the sheriff how I paid a visit to the station right before their prisoner went missing. I bet they've already started rounding up the dogs. Folks around here are always up for a good hunt. Throw in that reward money I heard Darlene squealing about on the hospital phone, they'll be thrilled to track us down.

Oh, how I wish Grampa was here to take care of this situa-tion. He'd call a town meeting, pass the pictures around of Mr. Buster dead on the beach. Explain everything in that easy-peasy voice of his. And when he was done, the men would smoke what they got and the women and children'd have shortbread and milk, and this whole mess would draw to a close. *This* Cooter mess anyway. There's still the treasure map mess. The sheriff threatening to come after me mess. The Clever giving birth mess. And Grampa's *not* here.

"Let's take the paddock path up to Miss Jessie's," I tell Cooter. "It's quicker." Pushing on the driver's-side door, I give it all I got, but it won't move an inch.

"It's gettin' caught up in the mud. Get out this way." Cooter reaches back through the passenger window for me. Our fingertips are barely touching when he gulps out, "Mercy," and slides down the side of the truck out of my reach.

"What's wrong?" I ask, scooting over the rest of the way. Leaning out the window, I can see him cowering in the ditch. "Your knee give out on ya? I'll go get Billy."

Cooter snivels, "Too late for that."

"Whatta ya mean?"

I turn my head back toward the road where he's pointing. Yes. It *is* too late. Those flashing red lights barreling our way can mean only one thing.

Sheriff LeRoy Johnson has come to do his job.

Surrounded

don't want the sheriff comin' over to the ditch side of the truck. He's sure to notice the upchucking Cooter's had. "Slide under the truck. Take the pictures with ya, just in case LeRoy gets it in his mind to search me." (Which he will.) "And for crissakes, hush up," I warn Cooter as I move toward the front bumper. "You're pantin'."

Spinning halfway up Tanner Farm Road, the county car makes a turn back and glides to a stop not two feet from me. "Afternoon, Miss Gibby. Didn't think that was you at first," Sheriff Johnson says, using his most mannerly voice. (He doesn't mean it. LeRoy's been eating at the diner for years. I know how much he enjoys playing with his food 'fore he eats it.) "When'd ya start drivin' again?"

"Well, let's see . . . just today, yeah, today is when I tried drivin' again. Wanted to go to St. Mary's to see Grampa. Guess I could use a little more practice, huh."

"Yeah, the hospital's where I figured you'd head," he says, prying a bit of lunch outta his teeth with a toothpick. "And Darlene Abernathy was kind enough to confirm your visit."

(That varmint.)

I ask firm, making sure LeRoy knows Grampa WILL be coming back so he better watch his step, "Did Darlene also tell you about how Big Bill Brown, the richest man in Grant County, is flyin' Miss Jessie and Grampa to Texas so he can have an operation on his heart to make it all better?"

The sheriff puts on a face of such stupid sorrowfulness and says, "That don't sound too promisin', does it now?"

(What a ball of grease. That'd suit him just fine, wouldn't it? Grampa being dead AND having Miss Jessie all to himself?)

"Well, thanks a lot for stoppin', but I best be goin'," I say, backing up toward the trail that runs through the woods. Billy's waiting on me right up at Miz Tanner's. I got to get to him. He'll know what to do 'cause all of a sudden, I feel real ascared and tiny. Even though I'm not letting on, LeRoy bringing up the operation like that has set the contents of my heart scattering every which way. What if he's right? What if Grampa *doesn't* recover?

"Hold on," he says, heftin' himself out the squad's door. "Got a few questions for ya."

"Isn't that kind of a waste of your precious time, Sheriff? You know me. Dumb as anthracite coal," I answer, suddenly feeling a whole lot more sure of myself. Because there he is. This girl's best friend.

"My deputy tells me you paid a visit this afternoon down to the station." LeRoy comes close enough that I can smell his sweat mixing in with his Vitalis. "Now it seems I'm missin' a few things."

His heart is set on framing Cooter for Mr. Buster's murder, but if somebody gets ahold of those pictures of Mr. Buster dead on the beach and not on the dump—I know, and he knows, he won't get that chance. What's more, this beast'll lose his star for attempting to perpetrate that nasty deed.

"Haven't ya heard?" He's got me jammed up against the truck's grille. The gun I took outta his desk is pressing into my sacroiliac. "Your deputy fell into a chocolate vat when he was a baby," I say, focusing my eyes back on the tree line. (Just like I told you he would, he tracked the sheriff down and now he's drawing back into the lime green of the undergrowth, concealing himself just like Billy taught him. Won't take him long to assess the situation.)

Jerking his head this way and that, the sheriff asks, "What ya lookin' at?"

Keeper.

"I asked you a question." The sheriff brings his eyes back to mine. Rain clouds are somersaulting across his mirrored glasses.

"Looks like another bad storm is comin'," I say with a knowin' smile.

" 'Nuf of this foolishness. Where's Cooter at?"

"Who?"

"You're aware that what ya done, breakin' that boy outta jail, is called aidin' and abettin' and is punishable by law, correct?"

Between getting chased after and pawed on and Grampa's heart attack and remembering my love for Billy and well, just the whole kit 'n' kaboodle, you'd think my **NQR** head would be feeling tromped on, wouldn't ya? But watered like a desert flower after a drought of forty days is more what it feels like. Blooming with stimulating ideas.

"I know who's got that map of Mr. Buster Malloy's place you want so bad," I say, hoping his greed will get the better of him.

"And who might that be?"

"Sneaky Tim Ray. I were you, I'd go get it from him right this minute and then ya could be rich and move away to someplace far, far away and . . ."

Circling his hands around my waist hard, he snarls, "Tell me where that boy's run off to and give me them pictures of Buster you stole outta my desk. I'm done messin' wit' ya." When I don't do what he's telling me to do, he kicks my legs apart. "Looks like I'm gonna hafta search ya." He'll find the .22. "On second thought." He looks skyward, reaches back for his handcuffs. "With this storm about to break loose, be better we did this in a more private place." (What he means is, he wants to take me off somewhere so he can whip it outta me without interruption.) "Why don' you and me take ourselves a little ride, Miss Gib?"

Now, if you woulda sped past us out on the road a few minutes ago, you mighta said to yourself, "Why, lookee there, it's LeRoy Johnson helping out that **N**ot **Q**uite **R**ight gal who has gotten her truck into a ditch. What a nice thing for him to do. He's for positive gettin' my vote come election time."

But oh, my dear, dear friend, that is the trouble with unmeticulous perceptions.

The limestone rock Cooter's got ahold of should do the job neat. And from behind me, in the woods, above the calling cicadas and dancing black gum leaves, Billy's new boots are creaking fast my way. Keeper, being so brave about the lightning, will have fetched him. I've wheedled my hand to the back of my pants. The gun is greased and ready.

We got this good ole boy surrounded. He just don't know it yet.

At the Gallop

We're all standing over him, including Keeper, who pokes him in the gut with his snout to make sure the sheriff is done but good.

"That was smart, sneakin' in the ditch like that, Cooter. Excellent bushwhack." If I had my leather-like I'd gold star him up but good. Where *is* my briefcase? In all the commotion, I . . .

"Gibby, could I have a word with ya?" Billy asks, with lips closed tight. Cupping his hand around my elbow, he guides me behind a tree. "What'd you *do*?"

"Whatta ya mean?"

"Last I heard"—Billy peeks around the bark at Cooter—"he was in jail and you were on your way to the hospital and then comin' right back for me."

"Ohhh . . . that's right." I hadn't really thought out how I was going to explain all this to him. "Ya know good as me, if somebody didn't get Cooter outta that jail right away, instead of lyin' here, the sheriff'd be fitting him for a rope necktie right about now. Ya want that on your conscience, fine, but I have no intention of burnin' in hell for all eternity. I'm ascared of fire. So I broke Cooter out and *then* I went to the hospital."

Billy kicks at a rock, sending it halfway to Madison County.

"I had to do it for Clever. You know how she favors him,"

I say, waggling a finger in his face. "And for Miss Florida. And Grampa. What about the cowboy way?"

"I might could understand you breakin' him out," Billy says, beginnin' to look basset houndish. "But what I *don't* understand is . . . why didn't you ask for my help?"

" 'Cause Clever was right when she said you'd try to stop me on account a you being so righteous, and I couldn't let you do that." I place my hands on his cheeks and make him look me in the eyes. "Ya understand, dear heart?"

Billy hooks my bangs behind my ear, sighs out in surrender, "Grampa all right?"

"Oh, my goodness, I forgot! What good news! You are not gonna believe where he's on his way to in a plane gettin' driven by your daddy and—"

Cooter, clearing his throat to get our attention, says, "Ya think y'all could hold off on catchin' up on the latest news?" He toes the sheriff. "He ain't gonna stay out forever, ya know."

"What you yappin' about, Smith?" Billy asks, struttin' toward him.

Now, to the best of my knowledge, these two haven't been spending time together in recent years. Not counting that night Cooter and Willard were chasing us through the woods looking for the treasure map, I believe this is the first time Billy's laid eyes on his old pal in a long while. Like I mighta mentioned earlier, Cooter used to hang out at Blackstone Cave with us in the old days. Georgie brought him around first, and then Cooter and Billy got pretty close, and then Clever and Cooter got even closer than pretty close. But nowadays, Billy's not what you'd call the social type. And even if he was, I believe Cooter grew up to be too much of a mischief maker for Billy's taste.

I'm back to staring down at the sheriff, who is NOT a sight for sore eyes. The rain's bouncing off his forehead, and the blood from where Cooter bashed him on the head is paling pink and flowing fast. "Boys?"

The both of them are too busy playing cocks of the walk to pay me any mind.

Cooter mumbles out to Billy, " 'Bout the other night. Stealin' the map. Weren't nuthin' personal."

"Y'all?" I got my two fingers against the side of the sheriff's blubbery neck, trying to find a pulse like I learned in the Red Cross First Aid Class. Don't know if I'm sad or glad when I find it beating like a tom-tom. "We should get him off the road, don'tcha think?"

Billy gives the sheriff a good long look and then commands Cooter, "Grab his other foot."

Me and Keeper following behind, the two of them drag his body into the woods and down into a shallow ravine, Billy helping himself to the sheriff's sidearm before he buries him with fallen branches and damp leaves but good. Standing right there next to him, I swear, even *I* wouldn't know that beneath this pile of greenery lies LeRoy Johnson.

I give Billy a glowing look. How talented is my knight in shining ardor!

He gets my meaning and says shyly, "Special Forces."

Indeed. Miss Lydia of Hundred Wonders will tell you there are ALWAYS special forces at work in the world. Never mind that we can't see them. They're there, guiding us, arranging for us to be in the right place at the right time. Gifting us when we really need a little help to get us through.

Look at Cooter, for instance. He didn't get drafted into the army the way Billy did. Miss Florida says it's on accounta his feet. "Flatter than an ironin' board." See that? The special forces knew Cooter had to stay home and work night and day so he could help his gramma out.

From back down at the road, Deputy Boyd's voice rings out of the county car's radio. "Ya there? It's me, Jimmy Lee. Sheriff Johnson?"

"That there is the sound of reveille," Billy says to Cooter. "Can you make it?"

Grimacing, Cooter tests his weight on his hurting leg.

Billy doesn't ask him again, just throws him over his shoulder like he's saving him from a horrible fate, which I s'pose he is.

All *my* nose is picking up on is the smell of green alfalfa hay and baling twine. I check with Keeper to see if he's sniffing up either hide or hair of Sneaky Tim Ray since my dog can whiff dubious intentions from an acre away. People can hide their badness from one another, but the scent of wrongdoing is pungent and unmistakable to our four-legged friends.

After Billy sets Cooter down gently on a pile of loose hay in Miss Jessie's loft, he takes out his army knife from his belt and rips through the muddy pants. Goodness. Cooter's leg is a rainbow of bruises. I touch my still tender ones.

"Could ya fetch that doctorin' kit from the tack room? And some alcohol," Billy calls over to me.

"Sneaky Tim Ray's usually got some stashed up here," I say, heading off toward where he beds down.

"Not *that* kind of alcohol, Gib, the *rubbin'* kind," Billy says, further inspecting Cooter's leg, pressing here and there. "But now you brought it up, the other kind might do some good. I gotta adjust this knee. I think it's dislocated." Sweat's waterfalling off every inch of Cooter Smith and his breathing doesn't sound regular.

Doin' like Billy asked me, I jump down the loft stairs two at a time, shouting over my shoulder, "Keeper, keep keepin' a snout-out."

The barn is still and cool. Smells like it oughta. The stalls are picked clean and the water buckets brimming. Some twangy country tune I never heard before is coming from the radio that Miss Jessie always leaves on, "to soothe the savage beasts." But there's something else . . . something like hushed-up talking is coming from around the corner near the wash tank. Must be Vern and Teddy, thank the Lord! Cooter will be happy to see his uncles, and I will, too. So in knowing those strong men will come to our rescue, *Surprise!* is on the tip of my tongue as I step into the open, and it sure as hell IS, because it is NOT my good friends the Smith brothers I hear yakking away over their aisle sweeping. It's Sneaky Tim Ray, hissing into the ham radio Miss Jessie keeps for when the phone lines come down after a storm, "I'm tellin' ya, Jimmy Lee. They's here! Turn your car around and get your dumb ass over here. And bring that reward money with ya."

Frozen solid in fear, I can't even speak, until something cracks deep inside me, and "Biiilly!" comes spurting out.

Hearing me, Sneaky Tim Ray lets out with a hoot and charges my way. But not for long. Billy leaps down the hayloft stairs, wrassles him to the ground, and with one good punch to the jaw, Holloway's out cold.

"Ya there? Ya there?" Deputy Boyd is calling tinny out of the CB speaker. "Tim Ray, answer me."

"He told Jimmy Lee where we're at," I cry. "What're we gonna do now?"

Billy gives a thoughtful look, then throws open a trunk in the aisle and begins unwinding one of the flannel bandages they use to keep the horses' legs from getting nicked up when they go for a trailer ride. "I'm gonna wrap Cooter's knee best I can," he says, sprinting to the loft stairs. "Pull out three of the horses. Get 'em ready."

Not daring to question, I dash into the tack room, check the nameplates on the bridles and yank them free. No time for saddles.

By the time the two of them make it down the loft stairs, the siren sound is coming down Tanner Farm Road. I'm already on top of Peaches. Cooter yelps bad as he swings his knee over the back of Dancer. Billy grabs the mane of Sonny and is up clean.

"Goddamn it all! I just remembered something," I say, sliding off the donkey's back.

"Whatever it is, we don't have time," Billy says in an SOS voice. He's pressing his leg against the chestnut's side, heading toward the barn's back door. Cooter's on his tail with his temple vein running blue.

Halfway down the aisle, I shout back, "It's Cooter they're after. They'll string him up they catch him, ya know they will!"

Billy presses the reins against Sonny's neck, spins around and commands Cooter, "Go on without me."

"No!" I holler. "Ya gotta help him, Billy. He's in no shape and doesn't know the trail. Go on. I'll be right behind ya. Sneaky

Tim Ray must have the treasure map on him. I gotta get it for Clever." I can see in his face that he's torn between abandoning me and keeping Cooter from getting strung up dead. "Ride, Billy, ride."

"I'll get him pppointed in the right direction, then I'm comin' bbback for ya," he calls, and the two of them charge out the barn, sucked up fast by the storm, Keeper out front.

Garnering my breath, I kneel down to where Sneaky Tim Ray's still passed out in the aisle and dig my hand into his breast pocket, just like he's done to me so many times. No treasure map there, but I steal back my locket. Maybe he put the map in his . . .

"Gotcha," he rails, latching his fingers around my arm and struggling to sit up, so pickled he doesn't even realize he's been beat up. "This what you lookin' for?" His hand slides down the front of his pants.

"No, it is not," I say, battling to break free.

"Ya sure 'bout that?" He pulls the map out from somewhere down there. Waves it in my face. "I got me a real good idea. What say me and you go fetch that treasure and take off for parts unknown, darlin'?"

This not being my first rodeo, thank Jesus, I know exactly how to handle this critter. I drop my tussling and put on an admiring tone. "Why, Sneaky Tim Ray, you really *have* repented. I'm so proud of ya for bein' willin' to share like that."

"Thought I'd sweeten the pot, ya might come to your senses. Near impossible to resist ole Tim Ray *and* a treasure," he says, giving me one of those shining smiles of his. "We could even get hitched, ya want."

So sure of his charms, he eases his grip.

"Well, as temptin' as that offer is, *darlin'* . . ." I reach back and remove the .22 from the back of my pants.

Tires crunch to a sliding stop. Out the barn doors, Deputy Jimmy Lee is jumping outta the car, shouting and gesturing to a couple of men. Not the law. They're bounty hunters come speedy for that reward on Cooter.

I take aim at the zipper on Sneaky Tim Ray's caked jeans. "Unless you're wantin' your precious pecker to be in the same situation as your eye, I suggest you hand over that map nice and easy."

Rain collecting in the brims of their black hats, the lanky bounty men are heading our way. I recognize the two of them, all right. They're well known for their tracking skills.

"I'm not foolin'," I say to Sneaky Tim Ray as I cock the gun. "Now."

Instead of him begging for mercy like I thought he would, outta his mouth comes the same phlegmy laugh he lets loose whenever he's got me cornered. "Ya ain't got the nerve. You and me both know you're nuthin' but a scared little retard with real nice titties." His hands shoot up to my double D's. Squeeze hard. "I got ahold a her, boys," he cackles.

I'm looking him straight in the eye, when I pull back on the trigger.

"Halt in the name of the law," Deputy Jimmy Lee booms down the aisle.

Plucking the map outta Holloway's fingers, I dash down the aisle and throw myself onto Peaches's back. "Git," I shout, heeling her hard into the downpour.

Behind me, Sneaky Tim Ray is squealing, "She shot me. She shot me in the pecker!" And the deputy is yelling, "Stop, Gib, stop." At the beginning of the trail, I spin Peaches around so I can see if they're coming after me. Jimmy Lee is kneeling down in the aisle, ministering to Holloway. But silhouetted in the barn door, those two bounty hunters are long and lean. And smiling at me like it's Christmas morning.

Farther down the trail, where the woods thin from oak to scrub, I can barely make out Billy coming toward me, that's how bad the rain is sheetin' down. I don't dare call out to him. Those black-hatted bounty hunters back at the barn? They're the Brandish Boys. And they got ears bigger than Peaches's. Well, one of them does anyways. Even as far away as Tennessee, they are legends. I heard a story about when the Boys were hunting a bail-jumping feller from two counties over. By the time those two dragged him into town, that poor man was missing an arm. Word was the Brandish Boys ripped it clean out and near beat him to death with it. Even Grampa, the least jumpy man I know, swallowed hard when he told me, "Wouldn't wanna be the object of one of those Boys' searches. They hunt for the fun of it. Reward money's just the pork in the beans."

I reach down to swipe off the rain that's caught up in Peaches's mane, give her a pat for a job well done. The trail's so muddy, I don't know how she's managing.

"You okay?" Billy asks, drawing up close, trying to shield me from the punishing storm.

"Where's Cooter at?" I ask, peering around him.

"Keep's leadin' him. It's a straight shot from here to the cottage. He'll be fine."

He better be. Rosie needs a daddy. That's right, it's just come to me outta nowhere that it CAN'T be Willard that's Rosie's daddy. Even though Clever's sort of a birdbrain, she's smart enough to pretend that Willard's the baby's daddy so he'll take her back to New York City with him 'til tongues stop wagging. That rascal. She knows damn well if she births a baby of the opposite color around here, folks are gonna give her a flock of grief.

"We can't hide at the cottage long," I say. The trail widens enough here that we can ride the rest of the way together. "They'll figure that out, won't they, Billy?"

"We got a little time, I think. Jimmy Lee . . . ya know . . . that vat accident . . . he's kinda dumb."

"That's true," I say, looking up at him. "But the Brandish Boys aren't."

Billy whoas up in a flurry. "The Brandish Boys?"

"They were with Jimmy Lee up at the barn."

"Ya sure it was them?" he asks, surely hoping I'm not.

They're starving coyotes, those Boys, bunking down somewhere up in the woods between Cray Ridge and Appleville. I've seen 'em up close only one time. At the bait shop. One of 'em has a skin condition so his face is covered in angry pink craters and oozes. The other, like I said, he's got long ears and something not right with his nose. Lacks oomph. (Ya know how mamas and daddies warn their babies about the booger man to keep them in check? Around these parts, it's those misshapen brothers make children check under their beds.)

Billy says one more time, like he can't take it in, "The Brandish Boys." Might be his drenched shirt causing him to shiver. Think not.

"We got to get the four of us someplace safe," I tell him.

"Blackstone," he says right off.

"That's my thinkin', too." For now anyways. In Bolivia, they wear these types of jackets called *ponchos*. My man will look dashing in one of a deep wine color. Since I can perceive no way at all that we're gonna get out of our current predicament, I believe we're gonna have to pack our bags and move souther. *Pronto*.

Reaching the end of the trail, we trot across the road and go down a piece 'til we end up in the cottage's backyard. The rain'll make it harder to track us down, but then again, it *is* the Brandish Boys. What they lack in beauty they make up for in skill.

"We could do with some dry clothes," Billy says, dismounting and lifting the reins over Sonny's head, doing the same to Peaches as I slide off. Cooter's horse, Dancer, is already tied up under the wide tree. "We'll gather up what we can as fast as we can and head out."

Nearing the cottage, I can hear the sound of Grampa's boat rocking against the dock with a *knock knock* that makes me remember his apple-puckering lips. His grouchiness after getting up from a nap. His buttermilk pancakes and, well . . . just *all* the ingredients that get mixed up together to make a batch of Charles Michael Murphy. After he comes home, I'm gonna set him down in his lake chair with a glass of tart lemonade and tell him everything that's been going on while he was gone, and when I'm done, he'll push his cowboy fishing hat back on his head and say, "I'm proud as punch of ya, Gibby girl. Ya done good." 'Specially after I tell him what I'm about to tell Billy. Grampa'll give his knee-slapping laugh.

"I mighta shot off Sneaky Tim Ray's pecker."

Billy swipes the rain off his face and grunts. "Saves me the trouble."

(I know, I know. I should be feeling ashamed. But it felt so damn good to pull that trigger, not wicked at all.)

Coming around the corner of the screened porch, I hold up for a minute to watch Clever and Cooter, their heads bowed together, but then Keeper gives off a welcome whine, and Clever turns my way, yelping out when she sees me, "Goddamn it! Goddamn it! I thought ya was dead," throwing open the screened door and herself all over me.

"I'm fine . . . I'm fine," I tell her with a pat. "C'mon. Let's getcha outta this rain."

Billy heads into the cottage, probably following up on his plan for dry clothes, and Cooter follows.

Once I get her back seated on the sofa, Clever says, "What the hell happened?"

"What do ya mean what the hell happened? I broke Rosie's daddy outta jail, just like I told ya I would."

Bringing her eyes up to mine, she locks and loads 'em. " 'Zactly how long ya known?"

"Figured it out on the ride over."

Maybe until she just admitted it, it was nothing but wishful thinking on my part. Willard is such a dope that I didn't want Clever having his baby, who would then grow up and go off spreading that dopiness throughout the world by breeding. (Miss Jessie says it's important who you pair up with when it comes to the spraying of seed, otherwise you could end up with a foal that's got some low tendencies.) What the heck has happened to Willard anyways? I bend forward to eye his place. His "contemplating" hammock is hanging half off the yellowwood. He's a loose end, that damn Yankee is.

Clever is working hard to get control of herself, but as we all know, even though the word is it *does*, I'm here to tell you, hard work *doesn't* always pay off. "Miss Florida's gonna beat me 'til I'm blue when she finds out Cooter's the daddy," she splutters. "Ya know how she lectures about mixin' blood."

I want to tell my sidekick she's wrong. I really, really do. But she knows well as I do that I'd be lying. "Don't fret. I got a plan."

"Ya do?" she asks, skeptical.

"Remember from our movie how all the folks down in Bolivia are sorta coffee with two creams in color? Well, soon as this is all over, the five of us'll move down there after all. Rosie'll fit right in." They can't stay here. 'Cause not only would there be **Reprisals: Avengement** from both the white *and* the brown folks, there'd be nobody to help them out with raisin' the baby. Maybe Miss Florida would pitch in after she calmed down, but only a fool'd count on Janice to do her job of grandmothering. If Grampa stays alive, I know he'd protect them, but what if he . . .

"Butch?"

"Yeah?"

"I know this may not be the best time to be bringin' this up . . . and I feel real bad about ya not gettin' to investigate for that important Mr. Buster is dead story because ya got so busy with the jailbreak . . ."

I completely forgot all about ***Buster Malloy Found Dead on Browntown Beach!***

"But," Clever says, "I believe . . . I'm beginnin' to have the laborin' pain. I think Rosie Adelaide's comin'."

Back to Blackstone

Cooter could barely ride himself, so Billy held Clever steady in the saddle while steering us through the storm away from the cottage and toward Blackstone. Having hid in jungles for months upon months, my man knows better than any of us what we got to do to keep the Brandish Boys off our scent, so soon as he knew we were high and dry, he rode back down the trail to cover up any evidence of us being there.

Snug in the cave, when I'm done sortin' out some of the clothes Billy and Cooter grabbed out of the drawers in the cottage, I pull Clever's soaking-wet shirt off over her head and shimmy on a dry one. My goodness. Her cups do runneth over.

Experiencing what appears to be tremendous pain, Clever is not in what you would call a jovial mood right this minute, but I'm gonna try to rectify that. I've been saving this tidbit for a moment just like this. "Knock knock," I say, rubbing her hair dry.

She cannot answer 'cause she's biting on her hand, so I reply for her in a different voice, deeper, "Who's there?"

I go back up the scale again. "Is Sneaky Tim Ray's pecker home?"

"Sorry," I bluster, "Sneaky Tim Ray's pecker ain't home. Ain't ya heard? Gibby McGraw shot it off."

se birthing pains must hurt something fierce because

what Clever's doing would only be considered grinning if you look at her upside down.

"That true?" Cooter asks, buzzing around us . . . not sure where to land. "Ya shot that boy's pecker? Off?"

"I believe so."

After the pains have ebbed, Clever shoves me on the shoulder and starts laughing her lungs out. "Ya always did have skills with a gun, Butch. Ya'd *have* to be good to get a bead on something that small."

"Clever!"

"What? I seen it a few weeks ago over at the Tap. Holloway was airin' it out, tryin' to interest Janice."

(Please forgive her. Being lawless and godless like she is, Clever can be not appropriate at all. Even when she's trying. Which she isn't.)

But now that she's brought up her mama, this is when I probably should tell Clever about how I found Janice in the drunk tank down at the sheriff's station. But I'm not gonna. Cooter knows what I'm thinking and I can tell he agrees. That's just plain good manners, not reminding your sidekick that her mama has a better relationship with Mr. Jim Beam than she does her own girl.

"Speakin' of airin' out, guess what? I got the treasure map!" I say, trying to keep her good spirits on the rise. "So y'all are gonna be okay now."

Clever says, "Dang, *you* are, too. In all this upset, I forgot to tell ya. While you were gone breakin' out Cooter, Miss Jessie called up to the cottage all the way from Texas. She told me to tell ya that Grampa is doin' just fine."

"What do ya mean?"

"The heart attack?"

"I recall that, but I don't know *where* and *why* Miss Jessie is with him and I'm not."

" 'Member? They took Grampa to Texas in Big Bill Brown's airplane and they're gonna give his heart an operation."

"No, that's not right," I say, befuddled.

"Is, too," Clever says, gettin' short. She despises her word to be questioned. "When I called down to the hospital lookin' for you when you didn't come right back, I made that varmint Darlene Abernathy tell me. She said the operation's supposed to make his heart steady and that—"

"Shhh . . . ya hear that?" Cooter whispers, haunches hackling.

Hard to hear much of anything with the thunder giving off its best licks, so I check to see if Keeper's gone into point, which he would if something wicked was coming our way. He's not paying a bit of mind, too busy giving himself a lick bath. Straining to hear what Cooter heard comin' up the trail, I finally catch it on my love radar. "Oh, that's only Billy."

Not a minute later he rides back into the cave, slides outta the saddle and says, "I covered our tracks best I could and didn't see . . . *them*." Can't blame him for not wanting to say their names out loud. That'd be akin to evoking the devil. But ya know, I don't think that's fair. We need to tell Cooter and Clever, let 'em know that what we're up against is more'n just the sheriff and his dumb deputy. Like Grampa says, "You can't win a fight 'lessin' ya know who your enemy is."

So I clear my throat and announce, "When Billy says he didn't see *them*, what he really means is, he didn't see . . . the Brandish Boys."

"The Boys?" Clever says, giving a willies tremble. "Who they huntin'?"

I jut my chin toward Cooter. "Sorry to be the bear of bad news . . . but there's a reward on him, Kid."

(Ya know how I mentioned earlier that she ain't afraid of anything? I forgot about the Brandish Boys.) Clever is letting loose with one of her ear-piercing wails and Cooter looks a whole lot less colored, that's how bad he's waning when he finds out the bounty the Boys are comin' for is none other than himself.

"No sense gettin' all worked up. We're safe for the time bein'," Billy says, jabbing Cooter in the ribs, none too gently, maybe still mad about him holding that gun on him in the woods the other night. "Why don't ya tell us why everybody wants this treasure map so bad?"

Cooter, trying to recover from the shock that it's *you know who* that's coming after him, says, "Ya ain't gonna believe me if I do."

"Try us," Billy insists. He sure does smell good. Safe, and a little muddy.

Cooter stabs at the map that Billy lays out on the ground in front of us. "Ya see those red lines? *That's* the treasure up at the Malloy place."

"We already figured out *where* it is," I say. "What Billy's askin' you is . . . what the hell IS the treasure?" I am picturing us draped in pearls and ivory and sequins and silver. "It's gold, isn't it?"

"Yeah, it's gold," Cooter admits.

"Bless Patsy! That just about solves all our problems, right?" I shout, reaching for Clever, who looks so relieved.

Cooter adds, "Wish it was, but it ain't the kind of gold y'all are thinkin' it is."

What I'm thinking is, to the best of my knowledge, there IS only one kind of **Gold: A valuable yellow metal.**

Clever asks, "What kind of gold *is* it then?"

"Hemp," Cooter says.

Me and Clever and Billy—the three of us look a lot like we just heard the world is flat after all.

"I'm sorry, I believe I misunderstood you. Did you say hemp . . . h-e-m-p?" I ask him.

Cooter nods. "It's a special kind of gold-colored weed that comes from Colombia."

"That's in South Carolina," I tell Clever, since she's not so good in geography.

"Not *that* Columbia. There's another one," Cooter says. "In South America."

Right where we're headed?

"This kinda hemp is real strong," Cooter continues. "Willard says he can sell it Up North for a lot of money to folks who wanna get high."

"That's nuthin' but dumb Yankee talk," I tell him, already beyond losing my patience. "Everyone knows ya can buy a hemp rope at Ready's Hardware if you need to climb high."

Cooter says, "I'm not meanin' the climbin' kind of *high*. I'm meanin' the kind of *high* ya get from smokin' weed."

Billy says knowingly to me, "Smokin' hemp can make ya feel real relaxed. *High* is just another word folks use to describe that feelin'."

I already knew that relaxing part from observing my next-door neighbor. Willard's the poster child for relaxation. "So you're tellin' us there's no emeralds or diamonds or candelabras buried up at the Malloy place? That the treasure we've been COUNTIN' on for Rosie is just some . . . some dumb old weed that gets ya *high*?"

"Tha's right," Cooter says. "Willard and Bishop planted the seeds in the spring."

This sounds so completely off. "How did Bishop Malloy happen to meet up with somebody like Willard?" I ask.

Cooter says, "Don't know 'bout that. All's I know is that come next month they's gonna harvest the hemp, dry it in the old barn, and take it back up to New York to sell in a place called the Village."

I'm not sure how everybody else is taking this news, but I feel like I got drug into a wet hole and left. Even if we all went up there to the Malloy farm, and stole the hemp out from under them, Clever can't very well go draggin' off to New York to sell it to villagers. Mothers, good mothers, the kind Clever's gonna be, not like *her* mother, they don't do those kinds of things. They paint watercolors and at night they stroke you with so much tender that you fall asleep in their arms breathing in their lily-of-the-valley scent.

"The sheriff's in on it, too," Cooter adds.

Surely, Cooter *is* mixed-up. "Well, if the sheriff is in on it and Willard was the one planted it, then they know right where that hemp is, so what the hell they need the map so bad for?"

"They don't need it to *find* the hemp. They wanna get the map back to make sure nobody *else* finds out about what they're doin'."

Clever, just getting her breath back from a pain, asks Cooter, "How did ya get messed up in all this anyways? With Sneaky Tim Ray?"

He says, not ashamed at all, "Holloway got wind of what Willard and Bishop were up to and came to me suggestin' we figure out some way to cut ourselves in. I told him gettin' ahold a the map'd be the first step. Not sure how Holloway found out y'all had stolen the map from Willard, but that's why we was trackin' ya down that night." He shrugs. "I needed money. Gramma's gettin' elderly."

"Wait just a cotton-pickin' minute. First things first," I say, trying to mask my disappointment behind an enthusiasm that I DO NOT feel. No treasure? I'd been thinking once we dug it up, we could keep a tiara for Rosie and maybe a couple other geegaws and sell the rest of it to Miss Montgomery at her downtown shop called Precious, which, amongst other things, has got a lot of fancy bracelets and broaches in the glass case right up front. We coulda used the cash she'd give us to buy boat tickets to Bolivia. Since that's not happenin' now, we gotta come up with another plan. My friends are not trained investigators or as perceptive as I am. It's my professional duty to take charge. So after thinking on it a spell, *focusing* to make this picture clear as can be, I announce, "I know what we have to do. We gotta . . . number one on our very important things to do list . . . we gotta get Cooter clear on these charges. Prove that he didn't murder Mr. Buster Malloy. We should forget about the treasure for the time bein' 'cause what good will it do us if the Boys catch up with him, right?"

Our breathing sounds like a treed barbershop quartet.

"But how we gonna do that? Prove that Cooter didn't murder Buster." Billy's got a funny look to himself when he says that. I don't know what I'd call it exactly. Maybe **Duplicitous: Feeling one way, but acting another.**

I musta forgot to tell him. "Show 'em, Cooter."

He reaches into his back pocket and pulls out the photos of dead Mr. Buster Malloy on Browntown Beach. After he passes them over to Billy and Clever to take a gander, their faces light up like the Fourth.

Billy says, "We gotta get these pictures to somebody fast 'fore—" He stops. Too late. We all know what he was about to say. They'll shoot first, ask questions later.

Relentless: The Brandish Boys.

As dark draws deeper into the cave, Clever and me are cuddlin', consoling each other over the—there ain't no treasure 'cept for some stupid gold weed that gets ya high—news. The boys are a ways off, opening tin cans, slicing cornbread, and speaking in whispers. We can't build a fire 'cause Billy says the Brandish Boys will spot the smoke, so we have to eat cold grub. After we get something into our tummies, we're gonna decide what our next move should be. Keeper's at the mouth of the cave, his snout twitching.

Even though Clever says her stomach feels like somebody reached in and pulled it out, nothing can stop her from vigorously sniffing on the dead Mr. Buster pictures. "Ya know who I think murdered him?" she asks me.

"Who?"

"Miss Loretta."

"Why'd *she* wanna murder Mr. Buster?" I ask, more than a little curious.

"Well," Clever says, using her storytelling voice, "I was gettin' me some peanut brittle last week when Buster came into the shop to pick up a bag of his butterscotch candies."

(She means she was stealing some peanut brittle last week.)

"When Miss Loretta apologized for not having them done up yet, Mr. Butter got real ugly with her," Clever goes on. "Told her, 'Ya better get on the stick, Retta, or I'll take my business elsewhere,' and slammed outta the shop. And Miss Loretta, when she was stickin' her little tinker bell back up to the door, she said, 'I could wring his stinkin' neck, that's what I could do. Goes and gets hisself elected governor and now he thinks he's even *more* better than everybody else.' " Clever flashes the pictures of dead Mr. Buster in front of my face. "And look here . . . that's just what somebody done, wrung Mr. Butter's stinkin' neck but good."

That's just so goddamn dumb. Miss Loretta of Candy World is always rantin' on like that. It's the heat in her kitchen melts her patience away. Everybody knows that it's best to go and buy your sweets early in the morning 'fore it gets so hot in that shop. I don't point that out to Clever though. She can get awfully ratty.

"Ya doubtin' me?" she asks, when I don't pipe in to agree with her.

"Not doubtin' exactly."

"Ya ain't callin' me a liar, are ya?"

"No . . . no, I am *not* callin' you a liar." Trying like the devil to keep her calm, the way Billy told me I should, I think fast. "Hey, Cooter told me something real dishy!" (This'll calm her down. She'll eat this up. Dirty gossip about high-and-mighty folks is Clever's most favorite thing in the whole world next to shoot-'em-up movies, and stealing, and roses, and funerals, and I guess now, Cooter.) "On the way home from the jailbreak, he told me that he believes that Georgie Malloy didn't die of natural drownin'. Cooter thinks Mr. Buster murdered Puddin' and Pie!"

"Already knew that," Clever says, yawning in my face. "Suppose ya don't know either that Buster was not only Georgie's *uncle* but also his *daddy*."

Laboring a baby must make you temporarily insane! "Poor

ole girl. That's just not possible," I explain to her slow and pronounced. "It's common knowledge somebody can't be somebody's uncle and at the same time his daddy . . . that is just not humanly possible."

"Ya think I'm dumb, don'tcha? Ya think just 'cause I didn't finish high school. Well, I got *news* for *you*. Buster forced hisself on Miss Lydia one night when he was drunk, and nine months later out popped Georgie!"

"Billy!" I yell. "Come quick. Ya gotta ride Clever over to the mental institute at Pardyville."

"Why, you little . . ." She lunges for me, her hands clawed up and ready to give me one of her dreadful Indian burns.

"Y'all quit! This ain't no time for you two to be jumpin' on each other," Cooter shouts, rushing over to separate us. "We gotta stay calm. 'Specially you." He passes Clever a plate full of chow that she turns her nose up at. "What she's tellin' ya about Mr. Buster forcin' hisself on Miss Lydia is true, Gib."

"But . . . how . . ." This is just too much information for one almost **Q**uite **R**ight reporter to take in! My brain feels like it's under one of those attacks Billy's always flashing back on. Only the sky's not sheeting bullets, but news. Miss Lydia was taken advantage of by her own brother Buster Malloy? And she bore him a boy? And that boy was Georgie Puddin' and Pie? No wonder she likes to listen to that opera music so much. (Even though they're well known for their excellent salad dressing, there's always something tragic going on with those Italian folks.)

"Ya absolutely sure 'bout that, Cooter?" I ask, taking my supper out of his hand. "That Mr. Buster took advantage of his own sister?" Everybody knows these types of family unions happen from time to time in the hollers, but here in Cray Ridge?

We got a larger population to choose from when it comes to courting.

"Just as sure as I am that a lot of folks gonna be happy as hell Buster's dead," he says, digging in. "Gonna be hard to find out who *actually* murdered him since just about everyone hankered to."

Uh-oh.

It's just occurred to me that I may have overlooked a few things.

"Whoever it was that murdered Mr. Buster, the importance of perception in meticulous investigation says in the means, motive and opportunity chapter that a person would have to have all three of those things in order to commit a crime," I blurt out.

Clever frowns. "I already told ya. Miss Loretta murdered Buster. Stabbed him with that sharp fudge-cuttin' knife and then wrung his neck with those powerful candy-makin' hands a hers."

"Clever," I say, "the knife and her hands are the *means*, and I'll give ya the fact she knows where Browntown Beach is, so I guess she had the *opportunity*. But what'd be Miss Loretta's *motive*?" I can tell by the way she's cockin' her head at me that she is not familiar with the meaning of that word. "Motive means a damn good reason for doin' something. Just 'cause Mr. Buster irritated her some in the heat of the day, that is not a damn good reason for Miss Loretta to kill him. Hell, if irritation was a good motive to murder, half the town'd be dead!"

I mighta said that all a tad **Condescending: Displaying a superior attitude**, because Clever snipes, "Goddamn you, Gibson," and claws up her hands again. Thank heavens an awful birthing spasm stops her in her tracks. Billy checks his watch. Because he's delivered a lot of foals up at High Hopes, he explained that when the pains don't have much time between them it'll be time for Rosie Adelaide to make her way out. He's brought sheets from the cottage and has got his trusty army knife to cut the cord that'll be attached to the baby.

"Please accept my deepest of apologies for gettin' you all worked up," I tell Clever once the pain's straightened out. "During the course of my investigation, I promise I will question Miss Loretta."

She gives me back a *rumpf*.

I break off a piece of my cornbread and toss it Keeper's way. Bet he's wishing as much as I am that it was a trout pulled straight out of the lake this afternoon by my peg-legged-fishin'-cowboy-whittlin'-bird-watcher. "It's just . . . I'm so worried about Grampa and Mama isn't resting in peace and—"

"I know, I know." Clever won't straight out apologize for her part of the spat, 'cause that's not her way, but she *is* making a peace offering when she says, "All this chasin' and jailbreakin' and drownin' and birthin', this is just like one of our western movies, isn't it, Butch?"

What she really means is, it's just like OUR western movie. "Only difference is this story is true and that one's made up," I remind her.

"There's no way you're tellin' me Mr. Paul Newman and Mr. Robert Redford are not the best of friends. 'Course they are. Tried and true. No matter how dumb one of 'em gets actin'." Firing off an ornery look at me, she says, "Cooter, why don't ya go ahead and tell us what ya think Mr. Buster's *motive* was to drown Georgie?"

"Y'all know anything 'bout politics?" Cooter asks, showing off his college.

I don't believe I do, so I say, "Uh-uh." So does Clever. Billy is keeping his lips padlocked. He is being awfully excellent at that this evening. What's troubling him?

Cooter says, "Well, right before Georgie died, that was about the time Buster'd begun to talk about throwin' his hat into the ring."

Clever and me give him our *huh?* look.

"Throwin' your hat in the ring is another way of sayin' ya want to get involved in politics," Cooter explains. "And when ya do that, ya gotta make folks want to vote for ya by makin' sure that you're lily white."

I say, "Everyone already knows that ya gotta be white to be governor."

"Lily white—it don't mean white on the outside, like your skin. It means you gotta be clean. Without a bad mark in your morals," Cooter says, warming up to the subject. "You cain't have nuthin' goin' on with you or your family that folks might consider not right. Like rumors goin' round about breedin' up your own sister? That might not go down so smooth with the upstandin' voters."

For the millionth time, I am left simply breathless by what I don't know.

"So what you're sayin' is, ya think Mr. Buster drowned Georgie so he could get some more lily white votes 'cause he was desirin' to get elected for something?" I ask.

"That's 'zactly what I'm sayin'," Cooter says. "Once Georgie was dead, Buster had himself what ya call an out-a-sight-out-a-mind situation."

This is the most bastardly idea I have ever heard!

Bringing his plate up to his mouth, Cooter licks the last of the beans off. "And then everything just fell into place even better for Buster when Miss Lydia developed, ya know, mental area problems. That way nuthin' she said about her havin' her own brother's chil' would be held up like truth."

I guess Cooter feels about Miss Lydia same as Grampa and, truth be told, a lot of the other folks in Cray Ridge. Miss Lydia's gifted ways frighten them so they say she's got problems in her mental area and tap their temples. I'm used to that. I even understand it. Miss Lydia has taught me that people are always ascared by what they don't understand.

"Oh, Mama . . . ," Clever wails, balling up again.

I lean behind her back and whisper to Billy, "Seems like they're comin' faster now. Ya sure we shouldn't take her to the hospital?"

"We can't do that. The sheriff knows she's 'bout to have a baby. The posse might be watchin' for us. They could come down on us. Take Cooter back to jail. Or worse."

Thoughtfully, he left out the part where they would take me away, too. Not hang me, I don't think, but I wouldn't put *anything* past the sheriff at this point. He's already ticked off at me for breaking Cooter out of his jail and stealing back my pictures of dead Mr. Buster. And he's probably gonna blame me for pulling that stunt on the road when he got knocked out with that limestone rock. (Getting outsmarted by an imbecile who's dumb as anthracite coal ain't exactly a boost to your manhood, is it now?)

Wiping off the beads of sweat that keep popping up on Billy's forehead, I ask, "You feelin' all right?"

"I'm fine," he says, looking up at me, but then turnin' his attention back to his watch. Not fast enough. I saw his lyin' eyes. Mr. Howard Redmond in his chapter entitled **Determining the Guilty Party** explains that one of the things guilty people do, besides lie and fidget, is they perspire a lot. Though my man is well-muscled, he is quite sensitive, so earlier this evening I thought it might be all the sad reminiscing about his old pal Georgie that was makin' Billy damp. Or the Brandish Boys comin' for us, that'd make an ice cube sweat. But I was mistaken. He definitely had the *means*. True, I have no idea what his *motive* might be for murdering Mr. Buster, but he certainly had the *opportunity*. He's always prowling around, sight unseen. I also understand now why he was the only one believed me right off about finding Mr. Buster dead on Browntown Beach.

Oh, my sweet, sweet Billy. What have ya gone and done?

At first light, Billy shakes me awake. I only drifted off for a bit, worryin' like I was about Clever, who spent the whole night groaning, moaning, wishing for her mama to magically appear with a heart full of caring. And my guilty Billy, I fretted about him, too. A whole heap. "Gib, get up," he says, tense.

Groping for the .22, I ask, "Is it the Boys? Have they come for us?"

"It's Clever. She's burnin' up with fever."

I glance over at the two of them entwined near the back of the cave, the coolest part. Clever's face looks like it might burst into flames. Cooter is dabbing the sheen off her with his kerchief.

"Gotta get her to the hospital," Billy says, reaching for his boots.

"But they'll get us. Just like you said, they'll have the hospital staked out."

"I know what I told ya, but I gave this all some thought through the night. The truth is," he says, "they're not really coming for Clever. Or me."

Not yet anyway. But once Cooter is let off from murdering Mr. Buster, they WILL be coming after you, my honey bunch. Somebody's bound to notice how Mr. Buster's neck was about twisted off. Somebody will remember your Oriental neck choppers. And how your army knife could do a fine job making those four holes in his chest. Like I said, I don't know why he murdered Mr. Buster, but knowing how Billy feels about killing people in general, he musta had a damn good reason. (And you, my dear friend, knowing me the way you do by now? You gotta know that I CANNOT let the law cart off my man. I just got him back. No. He and me will head to the border. We'll send for Clever and Cooter and Rosie once we get settled in the rolling hills of Bolivia.)

"I want you and Cooter to stay put. I'm gonna ride Clever back to the cottage and call my daddy. He can take us to the hospital," Billy says, taking charge. "I've got the pictures of Buster dead on the beach and I'll also make sure he gets them into the hands of Judge Larson. Once the judge sees those snapshots, he'll know the sheriff is up to no good and he'll call off the hunt."

Judge Larson is older than Cumberland Mountain, but has always been fair. He's a checkers-playing friend of Grampa's.

"Wait a minute. Isn't your daddy gone? Flyin' Grampa to Texas for his operation?"

"He'll be back by now," Billy says, pulling on his other boot. "That don' take that long."

I think on it all for a minute. "So the plan is you're gonna take Clever to the cottage and call your daddy, who'll take her to the hospital and make sure Judge Larson sees those pictures of Buster on the beach, and ya want Cooter and me to stay here until the coast is clear?"

"That's good rememberin'," Billy says, admiringly.

I say thank you with a kiss on his cheek. Keeper does the same.

Billy lifts his powerful Vietnam binoculars out of his pack and hands them to me. "Once we head down the trail, get outside the cave behind the rock, and if you see the posse comin' . . . we sh . . . sh . . . should go while it's still a little dddark."

I press against his chest. "Don't get all worked up now, ya hear? Cooter and me'll be just fine. We'll meet up with ya at the hospital later."

"Butch?" Clever calls weakly.

Billy says, "I'll leave the rifle."

"Butch?"

"I'm comin', Kid." Getting to where's she balled up in the corner, I can feel the heat roiling when I kneel down next to her. See her eyes darting, trying to flee the pain. "Hey, you."

"Is this what birthin's s'posed to feel like?" she asks with cracked lips.

"Ya just got a little fever, is all. Remember that time you got the Scarlett and I had to pack you in frozen peas? This is just like that," I say, smoothing her hair off her face. "Don't ya worry none. Billy's gonna ride ya back to the cottage and call his daddy and he'll come in that beautiful Cadillac a his and drive ya to the hospital. Miz Tay Lewis, you know her, you like her, she did good nursin' of Grampa and she'll give you some nice medicine, too. Everything's gonna be fine. You'll see."

Clever, latching on to my wrist, whispers, "But sidekicks . . . sidekicks don't *ever* leave the other one in a bad situation."

My heart gets awfully snarled having to look at my wild child like this. Her ascared so out in the open. "I got your back. I promise."

Cooter kisses each finger on her floury white hand, lifts her gently into his arms. "We haveta get you and the baby safe."

"But . . . but . . ." Clever struggles, so worn and warm. "They's comin' for ya."

Cooter lets loose with a laugh that echoes off the cave walls. "Ya think me and Gib can't take care of those Brandish Boys? Lordy, ugly as they is, they's not bulletproof," he says, setting her softly onto the saddle.

Billy swings up behind her, gathers the reins. "Just in case, don't ffforget the bbback way out," he says, pressing his leg against the horse's side. "I already tttied the animals up there for ya."

Cooter and I follow them outta the cave. Whatever coolness the rain brought, it's evaporating along with the night. Steamy clouds are rising off the treetops. "They're gonna be all right," I tell Cooter as we watch them head down the trail that'll end close to the cottage. "Billy'll take care of her. Them."

Cooter, on the brink, says, "I feel so helpless."

Being better acquainted with that feeling than most, I know nothing I can say to him will make him feel better, but a hand on the shoulder can be steadying. We watch quiet together 'til Clever and Billy are almost outta sight of the naked eye and Cooter swallows hard and points off to my right, asking, "What's that moving around over there in those thin trees?"

I lift the binoculars up to my eyes, adjust the wheel.

"It's *them*, ain't it?" he says, panic coming into his voice.

Cooter can't perceive that this is far worse than he knows, 'cause he's not looking through the glasses. But I can see that our true loves are riding too near the posse, who're coming toward the cave on that parallel trail. Looks like only yards away. If Clever gives out a birthing shriek, the Boys'll be on 'em like wolves on sick calves. And I don't care what Billy says, I know the sheriff. Even though he's not chasing after the two of them, he'll make them suffer if he catches them.

Backing up, tripping, Cooter says, "We gotta get."

"Not quite yet," I say, lifting the .22 out from my back. Mr. Howard Redmond in his excellent **Creating Diversions** chapter states: *There will be times when an operative may be forced to draw the attention off of himself/herself/others by creating what is known as a diversion.*

"Ya gonna shoot one of 'em?" he asks. "Ya better use the rifle." He limps back over to Billy's bedroll and slides the gun out with a sharp snap. I don't really need something this powerful for what I'm intending to do, but the rifle feels like home in my hands. It's the kind Grampa taught me on. A Remington. "Aim at that one with the big ears, wing 'em maybe," Cooter coaches as I wedge the 600 into my shoulder.

I reconsider for a moment. That'd be a twofer, all right— warning Billy AND giving us more time to skedaddle. But you know how pissed off animals can get when they're wounded?

Through the scope, I can see their black lathered horses down to the nose hairs as I squeeze the trigger back easy, aiming at the treetops.

"Ya missed. Go lower and to the left," Cooter gasps, running his hand down his endangered neck.

No matter how **NQR** I am, my Billy knows I wouldn't be drawing attention unless it was a matter of EXTREME emergency. Like if the enemy was bearing down on him. So he's doing just what I hoped he'd do. Veering off the trail he's on over to another one that lets out at the edge of town. Being accustomed to making quick decisions in the field of battle, my Billy's made his mind up to take Clever straight to the hospital himself. Atta boy.

Of course, the diversion shot got *their* attention, too. The sheriff's pointing our way, waving to Deputy Jimmy Lee Boyd, who's riding in front of him. The Boys are in the lead.

Peering through the scope again, I can see that the one Brandish—not the one that's got only holes for a nose, the other one with the oozing skin craters—he's tall in his stirrups and has his rifle up, too. We got a bead on each other. Until he slowly, slowly lowers his gun. Grins with his gums. Run, he mouths. Run.

The Importance of Perception in Meticulous Investigation: Following Directions: *Paying close attention to directions given by others is important if an operative wishes to keep his relationships running smoothly.* So me and Cooter and Keeper are doing just what Mr. Redmond AND the oozing Brandish Boy directed. We're running. Smoothly as this overgrown back trail will allow, anyways. We'll follow it past Miss Lydia's, where it hairpins back to town. If all goes as planned, me and Cooter should show up at St. Mary's Hospital just in time to sing, "Happy birthday to you, dear Rosie Adelaide."

Riding single file down the hill, then beneath this canopy of trees that welcomes you to the beginning of it all, I can't help but perceive that there's something different about this light. It's not falling in a careless way across the branch tips and creek water. No. The light here is humble, like it's worshipping. Can't blame it really.

Land of a Hundred Wonders Cemetery is surrounded by an iron-wrought fence with spear-point tops and a sign green with age. Especially during summer evenings, there's almost always somebody doing rubbings here since we got some well-known graves, like the one belonging to Benis M. Frank. Born 1801, died 1801, a baby grave. Two stones down from Benis is where Miss Lydia does her nightly CRYING UPON, which is a sharing communion that the living can do with the dead. Laying her body down on top of her dead boy's mound, she weeps and weeps until the grass beneath is moist with her missing. I also perform CRY-ING UPON with her some nights. The two of us together, me holding her burned-up hand in mine, we get down on my mama's grave and that makes me feel so regretful. *I've let you down, Mama. I know now that I shoulda chose entering that public Scrabble tourna-ment they hold on the first Sunday of every month over in Appleville to impress you with my **Q**uite **R**ightness instead of the writing an awfully good story plan. Near as I can remember, you were fond of Billy. Ya don't expect me to report to the whole town that he's the one murdered Mr. Buster, do ya?*

"No time for ruminatin'. We gotta keep movin'," Cooter says, trotting past me.

This graveyard is where Grampa will be buried. I hope later rather than sooner. Right over there next to Gramma Kitty and Mama.

"Hey," Cooter hollers back at me. "Y' all right?"

I'm really not, but like Grampa always says, "Go ahead and cry . . . nobody's listenin'."

"We could use her phone to call over to the hospital. Ya think she's home?" Cooter says, when I join back up with him. He's try-ing to lighten the mood. Everybody knows Miss Lydia never sets foot off her property. She's sworn to tend to the spirits day and night. "Cannot fall asleep at the wheel," is what she'd tell ya.

"Man, the place looks a lot worse than the last time I was over here," Cooter says, gingerly lifting his hurt leg over Dancer's back and sliding down.

It's true the shutters are half off the house. The paint back-bending. And a couple of the boards on the front porch are missing, but that's only because Miss Lydia doesn't care that much about what she calls "the Corporal," which I have figured out has not a thing to do with the army, but means the *outside* of things. No. What she's mostly concerned with is "the Private," which means the *inside* of things.

Land of a Hundred Wonders—I don't care what everybody else thinks—the parlor where my spiritual advisor does her crystal readings and fortune-telling . . . the baptizing creek . . . the grave-yard . . . the honey and potion stand—is more than just a tourist attraction. It's my **Sanctuary: A sacred place of refuge.** Think **Divine: Beautiful. Blissful. Hallowed.** Now triple it.

Colored glass hangs from every bush, mostly red, since that's the color well-known for its awe-inspiring properties. And there is good growing dirt where healing herbs are thriving. Plants when ground up or liquefied or baked in the oven will help people feel better about being alive. There's plenty of *bush basil* for nervous headaches and wandering rheumatism. *Balmony* for piles. *Daisies*, whose roots you can milk boil and feed to pup-pies so they'll get no bigger, thrive along her rickety fence. And there's so many *sunflowers*. Their seeds get brewed into a drink that ya can give to babies suffering with whooping coughs. (Re-member Miss DeeDee from the Miss Cheryl and Miss DeeDee story? Miss Lydia helped her eyes by making her a potion out of baby carrots.)

But despite my spiritual advisor's vast and miraculous pow-ers, she doesn't have something for *everything* that ails. "Ya got a plant for *memory* you could give me?" I have asked her time and time again, 'cause I don't remember 'til it's too late that she'll always reply, "Sometimes not rememberin' . . . it's a blessin'," looking sad beyond anything I previously thought was considered sad-looking. A kind of sorrowfulness so vast, so churning, that if you're not careful, you could lose your footing and slip into it.

No matter what the rest of the place looks like, the Hundred Signs of Wonder that line the front of her house in no particular order are always painted fresh and easy to read. Each one more deep in its thinking than the next.

WONDER # 57
THY MUST SUMMON COURAGE UPON ENCOUNTERING THE EVERLASTING FLAME

WONDER # 26
SINNERS MUST MAKE RESTITUTION FIRST IF THEY SEEKETH REDEMPTION

Like everybody else who comes to Miss Lydia for spiritual advice, I've spent hours upon hours pondering her words of wisdom. I bend down to straighten:

WONDER # 15
THE HIGHWAY OF LIFE HARDLY EVER TAKES YOU TO WHERE YOU'RE HEADING

"Ain't that the God's honest truth," Cooter says, reading over my shoulder. He's tied the horse and donkey up to a sycamore branch, leaving enough rein so they can graze.

"Gib?" Miss Lydia calls out from her porch in that raspy voice she's got. "Cooter?"

"Yes'm," he calls back. "It's the two of us."

Miss Lydia looks like a left-behind rag doll in the wide-back chair. She'll never talk about it, but I heard she used to be quite a bit taller. The explosion she was in melted her some, I guess. Like always, she's got on a gauzy scarf of purple, the forgiveness color, that wraps around her head and hides the side of her scarred face. She NEVER takes that scarf off. Says it gives her an air of mystery.

"Where's Keeper at?" she asks as we come up the steps to her veranda.

I look both ways, shrug. "Thought he was right behind us," I say, not really bothered since I know that dog can take care of himself. So does Miss Lydia. (Just so ya know, even though she will not admit to it, I believe she was the one left Keeper back out next to the Dumpster at Top O' the Mornin' for me to find right after I got home from the hospital. *After* teaching him his few good tricks.)

The lavender shawl I crocheted her is set on her shoulders 'cause even though it is sopping warm, Miss Lydia is almost always on the chilly side. Shuckin' beans into a white bowl she's got on her lap, she tells me, "Your mama's been missin' you." And then to Cooter, "What happened to your leg?"

"The sheriff."

Miss Lydia puts her bean bowl off to the side and goes through the door of her house, leaving behind the smell of the camphor oil she massages into her puckered skin, wind chimes tinkling in her wake. There's gotta be a thousand of 'em hanging off of every tree. (Besides their favorite—soul music—Miss Lydia tells me the dead truly appreciate hearing the wind stroking the willows.)

Cooter says to me, "Don't get comfortable. The posse's gotta be on our tail."

Coming back out the screen door, Miss Lydia's holding one

of her special poultices that she makes out of clay and pepper-mint oil. "This'll draw out the pain," she tells Cooter. "Bring me your knee." Removing the bandage, she smooths on the mixture in gentle strokes, and asks me, "Billy do it?"

"WHAT?"

"The knee, Gib," she asks. "Did Billy doctor the knee?"

Miss Lydia's just been making mannerly conversation since we got here, 'cause a course, she *already* knows the sheriff was the one that messed up Cooter AND that Billy was the one who doctored his knee. That's because she is **Omniscient: All know-ing.** E.G., she can hear things only an animal can. Knows when a storm is coming days before the wind changes direction. And if you are still doubting her mystical powers, this should convince ya. Miss Lydia knows things about the crash and she wasn't even there.

"What's troublin' ya?" she asks me, still applying the poultice.

I hardly know where to begin. "Well . . . Grampa is in Texas and Clever is havin' her baby and the Brandish Boys are comin' for us 'cause the sheriff lied and told them that Cooter is guilty of murderin' . . ." She might not know about the deceasing of her brother, Mr. Buster Malloy. Then again, she's got extra-strong communication with the spirits, and they've probably already in-formed her that Buster has joined up with them. NOT the ones residing in heaven. Not after what he did to her. "We gotta call up to the hospital to check on Billy and Clever. May we use your phone?"

"Ya could if the storm hadn'ta knocked it out," she says, wip-ing the leftover clay onto the grass and replacing the bandage. "Ya better put the animals in the shed."

"Pardon me?" I say.

"They're comin'." She pats Cooter's leg, and he doesn't wince at all. "Git now."

Ya think she's right in her head or wrong in her head, Miss Lydia is not the kind of person you question, so Cooter scurries even faster than me toward Dancer and Peaches. Of course, this is the moment Peaches has chosen to show off her stubborn. She's dug in.

Miss Lydia calls from the porch, "Leave her, Gib. Go quick."

The shed's just a piece from the house, closer than the barn. Cooter's already halfway there, dragging Dancer behind him, and swearing a streak.

I hear the posse now, too, on the other side of the trees. They're arguing about what direction to go off in. They could head toward Cray Ridge, Browntown, or make the turn our way. Above the rustling, the grunting, the sneeze of a horse, the sheriff hollers out, "Looks to me like the tracks lead off to Lydia's. We got 'em now, boys."

I can imagine him fingering the rope on the side of his saddle. Bet Cooter can, too, 'cause I barely get the door closed behind us and he's off in the corner, attempting to shrink invisible. This shed is where Miss Lydia keeps her gardening tools and old tack and worn-out bushel baskets and plows but nothing large enough to hide either under or behind.

The sound of hooves and leather comes roaring into the yard.

One of the Brandish Boys—it has to be one of them because neither the sheriff nor Deputy Boyd has got a voice that sounds like a bone getting ground up in a disposal—shouts, "Well, ain't this convenient." Peeking through a wormhole in the shed door, I can see the one with the seeping skin condition pointing up at the Hundred Wonders Cemetery sign. "We can string him up and bury him all in the same place," he shouts again, following up with a laugh that is tremendously **Bloodthirsty: Encouraging violence.**

"Mornin', Lydia," the sheriff says, pulling his horse up to the porch steps.

"LeRoy," she says politely, but doesn't look up from her shuckin'. "What can I do for you and your friends this fine after-a-storm mornin'? A calmin' elixir, perhaps?"

The Boys' heads are swiveling like a pair of lazy Susans.

"The McGraw girl or Cooter Smith been by this morning?" the sheriff asks as he steps down out of his stirrup.

Cooter wails softly from the corner of the shed. "Can ya see 'em? Are they comin'?"

"*Shhhhh* . . . they're gonna hear ya."

"What ya do to your skull, LeRoy?" Miss Lydia asks, her eyes still not meetin' his. "Might have a little something for that."

The sheriff reaches up to where Cooter knocked him on the head with the limestone rock. The white bandage is dotted with blood. "Ya *sure* ya ain't seen those two?"

Miss Lydia strokes her calico cat with her long-fingered good hand. "Nobody's been by yet today."

The sheriff bends his leg onto the lowest porch step and with a bowing of his head says, "Ya know Buster is dead, don'tcha?"

Cool as one of her bush cucumbers, she doesn't answer him with words, just points off to the Wonders sign that LeRoy's standing next to, like she planned it, which she probably did:

WONDER # 12

ANGER IS AT ITS BEST WHEN BURIED

The Brandish Boys aren't paying any attention to this exchange of words between the sheriff and Miss Lydia. The other one's got off his horse now, too, and they're making their way over to Peaches, not so much walking like normal people, more like a kind of half slither. The long-eared one seems to be the boss, 'cause when he points down at Peaches's hoof, the other one obediently bends down and scrapes out what she's got collected in there, which is an old tracker's trick. Ya can tell where somebody's been by what your animal has collected in their feet. "This your donkey?" the Brandish Boy yells out to Miss Lydia.

His voice is . . . it's . . . it's . . . I can't really describe it, that's how genuinely horrible it is. Maybe swampish? Yes. That's what comes to my mind anyways. A swamp at midnight on Friday the thirteenth.

Miss Lydia lifts her eyes up to the sheriff and says from behind her purple scarf, "Any harm come to that girl, ya best be makin' sure your will is signed and dated. Same goes for Florida's grandbaby."

Ascared as a pumpkin on Halloween, but not being able to stand not knowin', Cooter joins me at the shed peephole. "They's worse close-up," he whispers. "Real worse."

Like they heard him, the Boys turn away from Peaches and start coming our way.

Miss Lydia calls to their backs, "Wouldn't go into that shed I was you."

The Boys flick her warning off like ya do a gnat.

"We got us a warrant." Sheriff Johnson passes it to Miss Lydia. "The Smith boy killed your brother and we're gonna see that justice is done."

"You and me both know that ain't true, don't we, LeRoy?" she says, letting the paper flutter to the ground. "On both counts."

The Boys can't be twenty yards from us now. Mouths hanging slack, they're eyeing the shed like it's fresh meat. I can *feel* their hunger, and I believe Cooter can as well. He can barely swallow.

Without one word, Miss Lydia reaches behind her chair so fast and brings out a double barrel that she lifts up to her shoulder, aiming at the backs of the Brandishes as she shouts, "Got a dog with rabies locked in that shed."

Either they don't believe Miss Lydia or the Boys'd purely relish a roll-around with a dyin' dog, 'cause they keep on comin'.

"Put the gun down, Lydia," the sheriff orders. "No matter how much you hated Buster he was still your kin. Don'tcha wanna see right done by him?"

"Call off the Boys now, LeRoy, 'fore I ventilate the both of 'em."

The sheriff comes up one more step, and it looks like he's fixin' to stroke her calico cat, but with a move so daring, he grabs out for the barrel of her gun and snatches it away.

I step back right quick, 'cause on the other side of the shed door, the pock-faced brother is reaching out his gloved hand for the handle. The metal latch swings up, but catches. Over and over. Hand to his heart, Cooter chokes out, "We gotta . . ."

I gesture to him to follow me as I move to the shed's back door. I know it's also locked, but from the *outside*. With a chunky wood latch held in a bracket. Hundred Wonders is our home away from home. I know its every nook and cranny. So does my dog. I realize now that's where he disappeared to earlier. He had to get himself into his lookout position.

Placing my cheek against the splintering crack in the back door, I instruct Keeper, "Open the latch."

The Brandishes got their eyes up to the grimy front window. They can't see us from there, but the next window they look through, they'll see us plenty fine.

"Use your snout, your snout," I urge Keep.

"What?" confused Cooter asks.

I must confess, to save my Billy's hide, I am tempted at this moment by my wickedness wave to let the Boys burst through that door and have at Cooter. Let 'em string him up for murdering Mr. Buster and be done with it, no one the wiser. But what about Clever and Rosie? Their hearts would be broke to bits, I allow anything to happen to him. Same for Miss Florida. If I let these bounty hunters string up her grandbaby, don't think I'd ever be able to eat another piece of her pie without crying all over the crust.

Yanking Dancer off the hay he's munching on, I boss, "Mount," and cup my hands to give Cooter a leg up.

"Cain't ya see the door's locked from the outside?" he chides, squirming his way onto the horse's back. Squaring himself, he reaches into his pants for the gun, ready to shoot his way out.

What's left of their faces is pressed up to the shed's side window. The Boys are beaming broad when the long-eared one smashes his rifle butt through the glass.

"Cooter, get a good hold."

Too scared to question, with no time left, he wraps the reins around his fist. Dancer is pawing, snorting and ready.

"Please quit goofin' around and finish up now," I tell Keep through the crack.

Seconds later, with the loveliest of creaks, the back door swings wide and reveals the ripe green of the woods.

Cooter, sobbing, extends a hand to pull me up behind him. But one travels faster than two.

"Give 'em my love," I say, firing the .22 into the air. And just like he was trained to do, just like I knew he'd do, ex-racehorse Dancer, hearing that shot, jumps through the back door like it's a startin' gate.

The Soul of the Matter

'm lying on my belly in the bushes back behind the shed as the posse, whooping and hat-waving, gallops past me. They're streaking into the trees hot on Cooter's trail. I'm not worried. He's got a head start and the best dog in the world leading him to his heart's desire. By the time Cooter gets to the hospital, Billy will already be there and his daddy will have called Judge Larson and told him about the pictures of dead Mr. Buster on the beach. Cooter will be **Exonerated: To be cleared from an accusation.**

I *should* be feeling real happy about all this, but the fact is, what I'm feeling is let down. I've reached **The End** of a whooper of a story I was hoping would have a *much* better ending. Especially for my Billy. Tomorrow he'll walk hands held high down Main Street, declaring himself guilty of the murdering of Mr. Buster Malloy to anybody who'll listen. That's just the kind of man he is. (I'm sure he was just waiting 'til we were all outta harm's way to do just that.) So instead of drinking coffee outta our shoes in the hills of Bolivia like I'd planned, looks like I might be spending the rest of my days bringing Billy pecan sandies in prison on visiting day. Well, like they say, that's the way the cookie crumbles. And I really *do* have a fondness for Cooter, so it's good that I didn't let my wickedness wave pull me under. His black fender hair has even grown on me some.

Miss Lydia hollers from the porch, "Ya can come out now, chil'."

WARNING: Do not be surprised by her saying this or anything else from this moment on. **Mystics: Folks who have the ability of attaining insight into mysteries that transcend ordinary human knowledge as by direct communication with the divine.** Miss Lydia knew I wasn't escaping along with Cooter, but hiding under one of her highbush briar berries.

"Comin'," I call back to her. With Billy and Clever and Cooter temporarily safe, my spiritual advisor and I, we got a little time to chat. I've been so busy dealin' with all of these messes, I haven't had a chance to stop by and I've been missing her. When we're through with our catchin' up, I believe I'll ask Miss Lydia to conduct a quick VISITATION with Mama. Then I'll cut some baby's breath to take along to the hospital for Rosie.

As I lower myself onto her porch step, she's shaking her head to and fro in a fed-up way. "I shouldn'ta turned my bad eye to him. I know better'n that. LeRoy Johnson's always been a slippery one. Even as a boy. Why, I could tell you stories that . . ."

While she's busy venting her spleen, I'm enjoying watching black-as-a-piano, slow-as-a-waltz Teddy Smith making his way down the path from Browntown. Too bad he didn't show up a little earlier. He woulda been a big help. (I may have previously mentioned, besides working up at Tanner Farm, Teddy also does heavy lifting with his chest and arms that are rippling in the sun for Miss Lydia.)

Getting to the front yard, Teddy doesn't wave like he usually does when he sees me. Instead he chirps, "Mornin', Gibber. Lydia."

"Hey," I call back with a lot of enthusiasm, as it is rare as a good porterhouse that he'll actually speak to you in that tweety voice of his.

Smelling the leftover smoke from the Browntown fire when it comes by on a breeze reminds me to ask Miss Lydia something that's been confusing me for the last few days. "Billy told me that he thinks the coloreds set the dump fire on purpose. The sheriff said so, too."

Miss Lydia nods in greeting at Teddy, and then says, "Billy's a smart man." Shucking now in a fiercer way, she adds, "Do you understand why they set the fire?"

I think on that for a minute. "Is it 'cause they'd like to get a brand-new dump that's farther away from their houses? The smell over there can get awfully pungent when the wind blows outta the north."

"While that may be true, that's not the main reason. They set the fire to call attention to the fact that they don't want to be treated different. The coloreds want to be treated equal to white folks."

Just about choking on a bean, I ask, "Like *how*?"

"With respect."

Now, I don't want to pooh-pooh Miss Lydia, her being all-knowing like she is, but that ain't NEVER gonna happen. White folks are awfully set in their ways.

"Did the fire bein' so close scare ya?" I ask, not able to stop myself from staring at the scars on her hands. "It did Billy and me." But right after I say that, I come to the realization that even though we just about got the poop scared outta us, I myself learned something wondrous as a result of that Browntown fire. It's only natural to stuff sad stuff away, like Billy's war and my crash, but listen here—if you expose those sorrows to the light of day, you might be pleasantly surprised by the outcome. Look how it all worked out for Billy and me. Can't be a rainbow without there first being a god-awful storm, right?

"The will of the Lord is strong and sure," Miss Lydia answers in that versed way she talks sometimes. "His flock need not be fearful. All wrongs will be set right when He seeth them."

"Is He seething now?"

"I believe He is."

Wheeling an empty barrow outta the shed, Teddy shouts, "I'm strippin' the stalls this mornin'," not knowing how relieved he should be feeling about his nephew Cooter getting away from the Boys like he did just a bit ago with no time to spare. I'm not going to say anything to him just yet. He'll find out soon enough, along with the rest of Cray Ridge, since I've already come up with my newest headline:

Cooter Smith Not Hung

(Don't worry. I perceive this needs a little work. Grampa will smooth it out once he gets home.)

The whole of the Land of a Hundred Wonders is sort of an antique, especially the graveyard. Miss Lydia *rarely* buys anything. Not 'cause she can't afford to, she does just fine with all her tourist business. But she preaches that it's best to do with what the Lord's already seen fit to give us, so I'm quite surprised when I see the shiny brand-newness of the pitchfork Teddy's holding in his hand. When I cleaned the stalls for her last week, the old one seemed to work plenty fine.

Miss Lydia calls back to him, "Careful of Holly, she's got a poor ligament in her right hind."

I just adore sitting on this veranda with her like this. Her flower garden smelling like Eden and the honeybees buzzzy at work. Cats cranking up their little purr motors figure-eighting between her red silky slippers. Since she can't wear regular shoes 'cause her one foot is damaged so bad that it's painful to feel anything rough rub against it, she wears these.

Tracing the dragon on the slippers with my finger, I ask her, "Ya know what I perceive?"

"What would that be?" she says, her gaze lingering on Teddy as he enters the barn.

"That settin' fire to the dump was a bad plan on the coloreds' part if what they were tryin' to achieve was that respect."

"Why's that?"

That's one of the things I love most about Miss Lydia. She listens to me like I'm not **NQR**. " 'Cause everybody is probably thinkin' even more disrespectful about the coloreds now for makin' the whole town stink of burned rubber. Wouldn't it a been more appropriate for them to've just quit pickin' tobacco? That woulda got everybody talkin' in a big way. And if he was still alive, well, that woulda got greedy ole Mister Buster's undivided attention. Ya didn't happen to kill him, did ya?"

I've been praying with all I got that I've made another bad assumption. That it wasn't my Billy that did him in. I've thought about it and thought about it and I can't come up with one single reason *why* Billy would want Mr. Buster deader than a store nail. Really, it's Miss Lydia who's got the best motive for stabbing up her deceased brother, him taking advantage like he did.

"For you," Miss Lydia says, without pausing at all, "I'll tell the sheriff I murdered Buster."

Boy, that's a relief! Since I believe Billy would never make it for long in a prison. Being closed up gives him the heebie-jeebies something bad, which wouldn't happen anyway because 'fore it did, I'd break him outta the sheriff's jail. I did it for Cooter. I can do it for my man. Besides, if Miss Lydia confesses to murdering Buster, both of us know that since just about everybody in the county believes she's touched in the head, the worst that'd happen to her would be she'd spend a few weeks in the mental institute crafting ashtrays, and Grampa can always use a couple more down at the diner, so this is not that big a deal.

Heavens to Murgatroid! I just perceived something.

"Since Mr. Buster is dead, you're gonna be the boss now. After they let ya out of Pardyville, ya can go back to live up at the farm." The second after I say it, I also perceive she'll never leave Georgie. Or Mama. Or the Wonders.

"I own the farm outright now, yes," she says, snapping a bean to smithereens.

"But what about what's his name . . . I forget . . . Mr. Buster's son? What's gonna happen to him?"

You don't see Miss Lydia smile all that often since people of wisdom see more of the bad in life than we simple people do, but she's giving it a try with the good side of her lip. "Appears that my dear nephew, Bishop, and that Yankee neighbor of yours got carted off this morning. The field boss found what the two of 'em been growin' and called the state troopers, who then asked my permission to burn those hemp plants down to the ground."

Well . . . well . . . well.

With Willard and Bishop outta the picture, the golden hemp treasure is fair game. Me and Billy and Cooter could go gather up that crop 'fore the troopers show up. We'll take it up to New York and introduce ourselves around that village while Clever is recuperating from the baby coming, and when we're done selling the hemp for lots of cash, I'll make a stop at the offices of Penguin Books to see if Mr. Howard Redmond is at his desk. I have been dying to ask him about—

"Ya can forget all that," Miss Lydia says, snippish.

(Told ya she can see my wheels working.)

"Did ya realize you got a birthday comin' up?" she asks, outta the blue.

"I do." I was thinking I'd have a party of some sort this year as I have not had one since . . . actually, I don't remember ever having one. "How old am I gonna be?"

"Twenty-one. That's a milestone birthday."

"Ya don't say."

"A milestone means it's an important event, chil'," Miss Lydia says, all of a sudden so supremely solemn. The breeze has stopped stirring. Birds have quit their twittering. Even the cicadas are stock-still.

I really do wish I had my blue spiral notebook with me because it's one of those times when something of great importance is about to happen. This is an almost daily occurrence at Land of a Hundred Wonders and always comes on fast like this. Miss Lydia is about to make one of her PRONOUNCEMENTS.

"The spirits have spoken," she says, setting down her bowl and floating up out of her chair. "The time for A FINAL RECKONING has arrived. Follow me."

What I really need to do is get over to the hospital to check on Clever and Rosie and Billy and Cooter, but since I trust Miss Lydia beyond reason, and would not ever disobey her, I go with her into the parlor that's dim with black curtains to protect her eyes that are so sensitive they can see into the future. Candles of white burn day or night, for they are soul cleansers. And ARTIFACTUALS OF PROTECTION are scattered across her tabletops, their chestnut faces and corn-husk bodies working just dandy to keep away evil spirits. I know there are four-leaf clovers lying beneath the cushions of her green cloth sofa, which is where we always sit when we have our VISITATIONS with Mama. And the ever-present vase full of lilies-of-the-valley looms large and reminding.

If Grampa would only come visit and see these pictures of Miss Lydia and Mama that hang on her every parlor wall, he would know how much love there is for his daughter here in Hundred Wonders. Maybe he'd stop being so bitter about everything. Maybe even his hope would spring back when he saw the snapshots of when they were blond enough to ride two to a pony. Little girls picnicking down at the lake with Gramma Kitty. Later when they are more grown, there is a photo of Miss Lydia gazing into my mama's eyes with such pure love that you can barely stand looking at it.

From underneath the sofa, Miss Lydia removes her tattered photo album with shaky fingers. We have spent day upon day, year upon year, looking at the two best friends glued forever on these pages. And me. I'm in these pictures, too. Baby Gibby . . . first day at school Gibby . . . braids down to my bottom Gibby. She removes a photo from the album. Gibby graduating from high school. My mama's got her arm around me looking so proud. And I'm smiling at her so **Quite Right**.

I say, "Did you know that back before the crash Billy and me were going to get married and . . ." Something like soul-shattering sorrow is sucking the air out of the parlor and taking my breath along with it. When I look over at Miss Lydia, to see if she's feeling the same, she's fingerin' that graduation picture and staring off into the distance. The sound of clattering chimes comes through the parlor window.

"Are you ready for THE FINAL RECKONING?" she asks. "Are you willin'?"

"I am willin'," I say, even though it has just occurred to me that maybe I'm not. I have no idea what THE FINAL RECKONING is. The room has drawn darker and the wind . . . it's unearthly sounding.

Miss Lydia's eyes close and she begins to chant, "Open your heart . . . open your mind . . . open your heart . . . open your mind."

I do.

"Breathe in my breath three times."

So honey sweet.

"Allow yourself to drift away to the night of the crash so—" She steels herself. "The spirit of rememberin' is comin' upon you."

I don't want to disappoint her, but I desperately do not want to go on with this. I am feeling floaty and faraway and frightened. Untethered. Because suddenly, I'm not in her parlor anymore. Not in Hundred Wonders. Not even in Cray Ridge. I'm back in the kind of night anybody in their right mind stays home and is grateful to do so, me and mine heading down here to start my summer stay. The rain is gushing down so bad it's erasing the highway line and our Buick's sprouted wings more than a few times. And the sky isn't the only one spittin' mad. My mama's saying in her crossest of voices, "We're not gonna outrun this storm . . . Lydia . . . get off at the next exit. Ya got talent at findin' motels, don'tcha, Joe? 'Specially the real cheap kind." Daddy's bellowing back, "Goddamn it. I'm warning you, Addy . . . for the last time . . . ," and Mama starts screaming. The driver of the car is burying her face in her hands when Daddy lurches for the wheel too late. And then there's an explosion.

We're never gonna outrun this storm, Lydia.

Lydia?

"It . . . it was . . . *you* drivin' that night?" I ask, trembling.

Miss Lydia reaches out for me, and when I pull back, her tears come. "Addy thought that it'd do me good to come visit y'all up in Chicago to get away from Cray Ridge for a bit, and then . . . then we'd all drive back down here together. I knew she and your daddy'd been havin' some marriage problems, but that whole week they fought something awful. The night . . . that night we were headin' back down here, they were so upset and outta sorts they asked me to drive, and I did . . . but then . . . in all their arguin' . . . the rain sheetin', I was wore out with their mad, and still feelin' so sad about Georgie, I closed my eyes, just for a moment . . . a moment is all . . . and then the bus . . ."

"I . . . I . . . Is this why Grampa doesn't want me to visit with you?" All this time I thought he was being so unreasonable. And that my daddy was the one driving. "Ya fell asleep at the wheel? Why didn't you tell me the truth?"

"I couldn't . . . I couldn't risk losin' ya like I lost Georgie and Addy and . . ." Miss Lydia breaks into the kind of banshee wailing she does when we do one of our LAYING UPONS on Mama's grave. "I'm sorry . . . I'm sorry . . . I'm sorry . . . forgive me . . . I'm sorry . . . I'm sorry . . . I'm sorry . . . forgive me. . . ."

"Y' all right in there?" Teddy Smith has come up the porch steps and is calling through the screen door. "Lydia?" When he pokes his head in and sees her balled up on the sofa, he rushes to her side, lifts her into his arms, and carries her off toward her bedroom, leaving me behind and alone.

All these years of believing in Miss Lydia with my whole heart and soul. How could she? That means the ACTUATIONS, and even worse, the VISITATIONS were a lie, too. And they were the only way I had to stay close to my mama.

I'm not sure how long I lay there on her parlor sofa letting the torturous sad spew outta me, or how long it took before I realized that my gulping breaths, they smell so strong of lilies-of-the-valley. But now I *am* sure that I can hear Mama's laugh that pealed like church bells resounding inside me. She drank coffee black. Melancholy was how she felt when she was done with one of her paintings. She adored applesauce cake with a sprinkle of cinnamon hot out of the oven. The warmth of her against the warmth of me, our heads sharing a pillow. The last thing she said to me 'fore I fell asleep every night, no matter how mad or sad or busy she was, "I love you forever, my little Giblet. No matter what happens . . . don't ever forget that."

That's when it comes to my mind that I've not been completely right about why my mama hasn't been resting in peace. It *is* because I'm **NQR**, but not the way I've been thinking. No. She isn't pacing heaven, wringing her strong but small hands 'cause I confuse my words and my mind wanders. Or even 'cause of the blue streak that runs through me. It's because, 'cept for a smattering here and there, I *did* forget about her love for me. And there's no way she can rest eternally until what's been lost is found and returned to its rightful owner.

So I pick up the picture of her and me at my graduation that Miss Lydia left lying on the table, and holding it to my heart, I trumpet loud enough that she'll hear me all the way up to the pearly gates, "Oh, Mama. Rest assured. Your little Giblet remembers."

Birthday

Could it be just this morning that I believed the nature sounds were so much louder here in Hundred Wonders? Like this is where it all begins and the rest of the world's gotta put up with hand-me-downs? Now the cemetery looks desolate like any other. And the baptizing creek's got some scummy weeds floating on top. Even the flowers don't smell as sweet.

Me and Teddy Smith are sitting side by side out on the wood bench across the road from Miss Lydia's house. He's staring off yonder and I am struggling to fit together the pieces that got me to where I am right now. Mama. How right it feels to have her back cozy in my mind. And Miss Lydia, I'm thinking on her, too. I don't believe I'll *ever* be able to forgive her. Even if I wear purple every day for the rest of my life. Not 'cause she was driving the car the night of the crash. That was just an accident. That coulda happened to anybody. But having your trust snatched away from you like that? That's gotta be about the worst thing there is. Makes me feel like I lost my grip on a trapeze, knowing I've got no net below. Maybe many, many, many moons from now, I'll be able to say to her, "It's all right, ya made a mistake, Miss Lydia, let's have a kitty cuddle." But maybe not neither.

"Ya know, don'tcha," Teddy says, extending his arms, "that this, all of it, come 'bout 'cause of you and your mama? The signs.

The healings. The baptisms. All of it goes back to that night of the crash."

I figured some of that out while we've been sitting here staring at the Wonder signs. Like plucking off artichoke leaves to get to the heart of the matter, all of a sudden I understood what they *really* meant. Especially:

WONDER # 100

SAVING THE INNOCENT IS THE JOB OF THE ONE WHO'S
GOT HOLD OF THE WHEEL

"That's how she got herself burned," he goes on. "Lydia's the one pulled you away from the fiery car. If she hadn't stumbled into a creek after the exertion of it all, she'd be 'side your mama right over there."

I lift my head to look where he's pointing. The graveyard. "Just like all the other lies she told me, it wasn't a miracle that I survived the crash," I say, bitter.

"Well, *I* believe, like beauty, that miracles are in the eyes of the beholder." I could tell from the way he cradled Miss Lydia that it wasn't the first time he had. And what she nicknamed him—the Caretaker—that name has a whole new meaning for me now. Teddy here, even if he is slow on the uptake, it's clear to me he's lightning quick to keep Miss Lydia safe. Would do just about anything to snatch her out of harm's way.

"Nice visitin' with ya, but I gotta get over to the hospital," I say, starting to stand.

He clamps his hand down upon my shoulder. "She don' want me to say nuthin' to ya, but I figure long as ya know the rest . . . Too many secrets been held too long." Once my bottom meets bench, Teddy gives my shoulder a squeeze like a reminder to stay put. "Ya was over here visitin' with Lydia that night. Heppin' her jar up preserves. Blueberry."

What's he talking about? Does he mean the night of the crash? No. That's not right. We were coming from Chicago *to* Cray Ridge that night. "What do ya mean by *that night*?" I ask, hardly caring.

"The night . . . a bad storm was comin'," he says, tellin' the story like I'm not even here. "When ya got done with the jarrin', Lydia sent you out to the barn to fetch me so I could walk ya back to the cottage 'fore the rain came. But I was busy, pitchin' the late hay, so I told ya to go back up on the porch and that I'd be there right off. And ya said, 'I sure 'nuf will, Teddy. I'll wait right there for ya,' and off ya went. After I finished off the feedin', I hurried back to the house, but when I got there you were gone. I thought ya left without me, so I ran toward the path to catch up, callin' out your name. I was in such a state, I didn't even notice I still had my pitchfork in my hand." He swallows hard. "When the thunder stopped rumblin', jus' for a lick, that's when I heard your dog barkin' and yowlin' over in the graveyard. That's where he was waitin'."

"Well, a course he was waitin'. Keeper always does that," I say, wondering why this would upset Teddy enough to make his eyes shine.

"Weren't Keeper. It were . . . 'member?"

Closing my eyes, I wait for the memory of that night to appear. Surprisingly, it doesn't disappoint. Coming to me is the aroma of just-picked-that-afternoon blueberries on the stovetop simmering away in sugar. And the feel of the smooth rubber rings from the canning jars. And there's Miss Lydia, swaying to her opera music, the wind of the approaching storm shoving around her white kitchen curtains. But that's where the memory fades. "I . . . nuthin' . . . *who* was waitin' in the cemetery?"

Teddy's breathing out all right, he just can't seem to breathe in.

"It's all right," I say, patting his hand. "Ya can tell me."

"It were . . . Buster."

"Mr. Buster Malloy?" I ask, stunned.

"I shoulda walked ya straight home," he says so hollow-hearted. "None of this woulda happened if I hadda."

"None of what woulda happened?"

Teddy shifts his eyes over to the cemetery. "By the time I got to ya, he already . . . he was drunk. He was . . . Buster was tryin' to do to you what he did to Miss Lydia all those years ago."

Oh my goodness.

That night . . . that night . . . yes. Me and Miss Lydia were working together in her daisy-papered kitchen. When the jam jarring was just about done, she said, "Time to get ya home," while she bustled around the kitchen putting the preserving supplies back into the cupboard. "Bad storm's comin'. Go out to the barn and ask Teddy to walk you home, chil'. And take a scarf, it's already startin' to sprinkle. I send ya back with a wet head, your grampa will be fit to be tied, won't he."

Knowing she was right, I did do that, took a scarf out of the basket of purple ones she keeps next to her front door. After I wrapped it around my face, just one eye peeking out, I looked at myself in her hall mirror and thought, Look at me, why, I look just like Miss Lydia. And I did go out into the barn and ask Teddy to walk me home, and then came back to the porch like he told me to. And I rocked in her chair while I was waiting for him to finish feeding, until outta the darkness, a nightingale warbled over in the graveyard, which was Mama's favorite bird, so I figured it was a sign that she wanted me to come snuggle with her a bit, so I made my way over to the graveyard. And I was bent over, giving her stone a smooch the way I like to do, when I heard from behind me, "Well, look who's come to visit," and the voice sounded so much like . . . I got confused.

"Georgie?" I called into the pitch of the night. "That you?"

I squeeze Teddy's hand real hard, but he does not yelp out. Somehow he knows that I need to hold on to him so I don't drift off into a sea of ascaredness, because this is bad, this remembering of that night. This is real bad. 'Cause after I realized it wasn't Georgie talking to me from THE GREAT BEYOND, I shouted, "Who's there?" and that's when he came stumbling outta the shadows.

"Evenin', Mr. Buster," I said, not surprised, figuring he'd come to pay his respects to his dear nephew. Lots of folks like to come around that time of the evening to visit their departed because Miss Lydia says that's when their spirits are the liveliest. "You come to say good night to Puddin' and Pie?"

Mr. Buster broke out bawling, and was so disheveled, his eyeglasses hanging off one ear, and I felt so bad for him because I know what it's like to miss a loved one so bad that you just can't even be bothered to comb your hair. So I came and knelt down next to him, patted his back. But it wasn't comfort he was seeking, not that kind anyway, because I could see by the light of the lantern that hangs off Georgie's stone that Mr. Buster's pants were already half down, candies tumbling out his pocket. Keeper was crazy barking and snarling, so Mr. Buster picked him up and threw him at the pointy fence and drug me to the ground and pushed my legs apart, held them open with his smooth little hands, letting loose only once to pluck at my panties. "Lydia . . . Lydia . . . Lydia," he chanted.

I cried, "No, Mr. Butter, you're confused. Put your glasses back on. It's me, Gibby McGraw." Teddy was calling for me in the distance, and I tried to shout back, "Here I am, here I am," but Mr. Butter closed my mouth hard with his hand that smelled of butterscotch and booze.

"By the time I got to ya, he just about had his . . . ," Teddy says. "I pulled him off and pierced him with the pitchfork and he fell back onto Georgie's tombstone and broke his neck."

So that's how I got those bruises on my thighs. They were from Mr. Buster holding me down. And that's why Miss Lydia had to stitch up Keeper's head. 'Cause he got thrown up against the graveyard fence.

I lay my head on Teddy's shoulder. "Ya killed him for her, for Miss Lydia, on account of what Mr. Buster did to her, didn't ya?"

"And for what he done to her boy," Teddy says so mournfully, like her pain is his. "And for you, Gibber. Ya know I've always had a fondness for ya."

I bring his hand that has held me steady up to my lips. "Thank you for savin' me, Teddy. That was real brave."

We sit there still together for some time, until the investigative reporter in me comes calling. "I didn't find Mr. Buster dead here in the graveyard. I found him over on Browntown Beach." Teddy is strong, but I don't think he could've lugged that fat man all the way over there by himself. "Did ya use your wheelbarrow to get him over there?"

"By the time Lydia got your dog sewed up, Billy'd come lookin' for ya. He hepped me carry Buster's body over there."

My guardian angel really does need to work on his punctuality.

"Billy brought along the pitchfork and swam it out into the lake so I'd never have to see it again," Teddy says. "He wanted to take Buster's body out there, too, weigh it down so nobody'd ever find it, but I told him, no. Let him lie dead and cold in the same place as little Georgie." He pulls back his sloping shoulders. "Ya best go now, Gibber. Tell 'em in town that I'm the one murdered Buster. I was fixin' to turn myself in right 'fore ya broke Cooter outta the jail anyways."

My voice is so pitchy sounding, practically matching his when I say, "Ya know, I don't believe I'm gonna tell anybody in town anything of the sort. *You* know and *I* know and *Miss Lydia* and *Billy* know that you did in Mr. Buster, but that's all that do. In my opinion, that sorry excuse for a man deserved to die. And even though everybody in Cray Ridge will agree with that in their hearts, when it gets down to it, at that county courthouse, you'll be found guilty 'cause you are not lily white, and I say the hell with that."

I get up off the wood bench to pluck the sign out of the muddy earth and bring it back to him.

WONDER # 33
IF SILENCE IS GOLDEN, THEN FORGIVENESS IS PLATINUM

"Everybody can go catch a green rabbit, for all I care," I tell him.

Teddy doesn't say a thing for a piece. But then reminds me, "Important to keep in mind that I weren't the only one saved ya."

I know he means *her*. But I can't. I just can't.

"Ya know what ya should do now? You should go into that house and make her a cup of that dandelion tea she's so nuts about," I say, trying to dam up the tears. "And could ya tell her . . . tell her that I'm not ready just yet, but I hope like hell she's right about thyme healing all wounds."

Teddy doesn't answer me back, just looks awful desolate when he runs his hand down my hair that covers my scar, then gets up and walks off. But if I know the Caretaker . . . he'll do his job.

was thinking of ridin' Peaches, but changed my mind. I feel like walking to the hospital. Feet touching the earth one right after another, there's something real grounding to that, and Lord knows I'm in need. Mr. Howard Redmond states in the last chapter of **The Importance of Perception in Meticulous Investigation: Writing the Story:** *The concluding part of an investigation can be overwhelming, particularly in an important case. All investigative reporters worth their salt must take their time to thoroughly examine the facts before they begin to write their story.*

So that's what I'm gonna do. Take my time to sort this all out. But NOT because I need to get my facts straight. As I wind my way down this wide-as-a-ribbon trail that leads away from Land of a Hundred Wonders toward town, like I already explained to Mama, I know that I'm not *ever* gonna be able to report my awfully good story. I really only have the headline: **Buster Malloy Found Dead on Browntown Beach**. I can't tell my loyal *Gazette* readers *who* did it or *why* or *where* or *when*. Which means I'm not ever gonna become well known enough as a reporter to travel to Cairo, but that's fine. Billy wouldn't like Egypt. He's not so good with sand, I'm not sure why. He just really despises the stuff. And now that I know he's innocent of murdering Buster, we won't have to relocate to Bolivia, which I got to admit is kind of a relief, since I was fairly certain we would have to kidnap *Senor* Bender so he could translate for us down there and Billy's also not so good with that Spanish teacher. Thinks a man that gets manicures is smarmy.

And Grampa. He's gonna need me here to take care of him. Setting him up on fresh-laundered pillows out on the screened porch so I can go off to cook us a big fish over the fire. Even though he never cut *me* any slack when I first got out of the hospital, my mostly 100% lovable self is figurin', for a nice welcome home from the hospital present, I'll let him whup me in Scrabble.

So with the case solved, but not being able to report it, and Clever having a baby, but us not having the treasure to buy diapers and such, and Miss Lydia not being so miraculous after all, well, I'd describe how I'm feeling right this minute as . . . bittersweet. Like one of Candy World's green caramel apples. Now don't get me wrong. I still got hope. After all, it does spring internal. (*Even though I know that you're resting in peace now, me getting* **Quite Right** *again'd be the dusting on the doughnuts for us, wouldn't you agree, Mama?*) And I got so much else to look forward to. Like Billy and me gettin' married, and baby Rosie's toes, and I bet Grampa'll be back home soon.

So I'm thinking about picking some of his favorite bluebells for him when outta the woods up ahead somebody yells out in a last-chance voice, "Come on out or we're comin' in after ya."

"Yeah," somebody else calls out.

Thinkin' it's me they're hollering at, I flatten down to the ground until another voice shouts, "I'll be back with her mama," and then I realize it can't be me they're talking about because, as you well know . . . Well, lookee here! I bet all this commotion is breakin' news of some sort. Thank goodness. I sure could use another awfully good story right about now.

Skittering fast down the trail, trying to blend in like Billy taught me, I get a good look at what's unfolding on the other side of the trees. The angry voices are coming from the old Hamilton place, which has been abandoned ever since Mr. Garr Hamilton got dragged back to jail for moonshinin'. Years ago, I was friends with his girl, Martha Jane, who went and lived with her auntie out west once they carted her daddy off. I haven't been up here since. The clapboard house looks like it's shrugging now. Ya can't even tell that it used to be painted a dawning-sky blue. Focusing on the front-yard tree, the one that's got the tire swing still hangin' off it, I can see the sun glinting off a gun barrel poking through the minty leaves. And over to my right, there's Deputy Boyd trying to conceal his chubby self behind a skinny outhouse.

What the heck is goin' on here?

Ohhh . . . I get it.

Once Billy and Clever got away from 'em, and Keeper led Cooter safe down the trail to the hospital, the posse, all worked up like they were, musta went looking for somebody else to sink their yellow dog teeth into. That's what's gotta be happening here. They got somebody cornered.

Martha Jane and me used to play cowboys and injuns in these woods, and I remember 'em well enough to be making my way closer to the house on my best buffalo-hunting feet. Arriving behind a wide-trunked maple, I get a view of the side yard of the old place. There's bushes that haven't been trimmed in years and a scraggly apple orchard and grass so long that it's up to the knees of the horse that's grazing like he died and went to heaven. If I didn't know better . . . wait . . . *is* that . . . Dancer? How'd he end up here at the Hamilton place instead of at the hospital where he was supposed to deliver Cooter just in time to see Rosie

Adelaide make her way into the word? Did Dancer spook and throw Cooter off? Or maybe Cooter's leg got bothering him so bad that he couldn't stay mounted and had to make the rest of his way to St. Mary's on foot or . . . OH MY GOD IN ALL YOUR GLORY!

It's gotta be Cooter the posse has run to ground! They got him trapped inside the house! What's happened to Keeper?

I'm about to call out for my dog, the hell with the posse hearing me, when the sheriff's car sweeps into the circle drive and comes to a halt on the lawn. Knocking down the old birdbath with the door of his squad car, LeRoy barges out, saying something spiteful sounding to somebody in the backseat. Then he squats and bellows, gun pulled from his holster, "This has gone far enough y'all. This is your last warnin'."

Y'all?

I'm weaving amongst the trees, attempting to get a better look, when I see tethered to a tree that's growing new in this old place, Sonny, lapping cloudy water from a puddle.

Oh no . . .

Clever and Billy never made it to the hospital! That means Billy didn't get to show the pictures of dead Mr. Buster on the beach to Judge Larson and so . . . "Oh, sweet, sweet Jesus," I say, falling to my knees and begging for His help. My eyes looking heavenward, that's when I see my Billy and he sees me. Up on the roof of the house, there's what you call a cupola, that's what he's hiding behind. Sniping. He's holding up a warning finger. *Wait,* he's signaling.

"I said, come out NOW," the sheriff yells through his bullhorn. "This is your last chance."

Billy better have a real good plan to end this standoff 'cause furious fumes are coming off LeRoy Johnson when he reaches back into the squad car door and yanks out Janice Lever by her wrist.

I've gotten even closer by belly-crawling. Billy told me to wait, and him knowing so much about warfare, that's what I'll do for now, but I got my .22 already drawn.

Within earshot, LeRoy Johnson threatens Janice, "Ya tell your girl to bring that boy outta the house with her, and I'll let her go. If not, I'll have her and that baby she's about to birth incarcerated."

The sheriff's talking blustery, but he gets an ascared look on his face when a voice wet with excitement comes out of the top of the tire swing tree, saying, "Time's up." It's one of the Brandish Boys up there in the hunting blind. The one who sounds swampish.

The sheriff shoves Janice closer to the house. "Do it," he commands her.

"Carol? Carol, honey? It's Mama," she tries to shout, but her voice, weak from her yesterday drinking, won't barely rise. Her hair is tumbling to the side and she's wearing the same clothes she had on in the jail cell when I broke Cooter free. "You gotta come out, baby. They's gonna burn ya out, ya don't."

To my left, I hear a sneer, actually hear it, I tell ya. Carefully, so carefully, I peek. The long-eared Brandish Boy, he's secreting himself a few yards away from me, behind a gnarled oak, so I can smell the gasoline just fine. And hear him flicking a lighter off and on, off and on like he's so hungry to see that house gorging itself on flames.

For a piece, all is quiet, 'cept for the cicadas, but then a voice comes muffled from inside the house, "Don't shoot. I'm comin' out." When the front door swings open, it's Cooter, hands waving in surrender.

Keeper's not by his side.

That's when I hear the Brandish Boy cock that rifle from up in the tree. Seein' what's about to unfold, I shout, "No! Cooter! It's a trap!" And hearing me, he starts to turn back, but then, something I never woulda imagined . . . like in some awful, awful final scene from one of them shoot-'em-up movies, Clever's mama takes off runnin' toward the front door the exact same moment the Brandish Boy pulls back on his trigger.

I scream, louder than the sheriff, who's aiming his rifle up to the tree the shot came from, booming at the Brandish Boy, "Drop your gun and get down outta there. You're under arrest." And then, not taking his eyes off the branches, LeRoy orders over to the outhouse, "Jimmy Lee, the other one's makin' a run for it. Get after him."

From atop the roof, Billy, slipping and sliding down the shingles, shouts, "Gibby, run!" and I almost do, but the blood from Janice's head is gushing down her neck and onto her chest.

"Stay still, stay still," I cry, hurrying to where she's collapsed on the grass. Picking up her pointy-nailed hands and cradling her head gently in my lap, all I can think to say is, "Why? Why the hell did ya do that, Janice?" Amidst all the yelling and the distracting smell of fresh gun smoke, I can barely focus enough to hear her struggling to say, "The Boys." She's striving for, but not attaining, one of her snotty smiles. "I know 'em real well. They . . . they was gonna shoot Cooter for the reward no matter what." A bubble of pink comes floating to the corner of her pale lips. "I had to stop them . . . I . . . every girl should have a daddy. My grandbaby is gonna have hers."

Pressing my hands to the side of her head, I'm trying to push the blood back where it belongs. "For crissakes, don't die, Janice," I say, at the same time the awfulest keening comes from outta the house.

When I look up, there's Clever standing in a broken-out top-floor window, Cooter by her side. Our desperate eyes meeting as she screams out, "Mama. I'm comin'. Don't let her go, Gib."

But after Janice in a barely-there voice says to me, "I told ya . . . I told ya I'd make it up to her someday, didn't I?" I know it's too late. With a flutter, like a petal falling from a flower, nothing more, Clever's selfish, selfish mama is already gone.

With all her funeral-attending experience, Clever was able to pull together a real attractive one for her mama. She came to me a few days after Janice's passing and asked, "Ya mind puttin' some words together for her stone? Something *nice*," she tacked on, because she knew that even though I admired Janice sacrificing herself for Cooter, and her wonderful waitressing skills, I still got some leftover feelings about her overall poor mothering performance. Did the best I could.

Janice Lever

(1937-1973)
MAMA OF CLEVER
BATON TWIRLER
TWO-TRAY SERVER
HEAVEN DESERVER

Miss Florida musta baked a hundred pies. That's what the coloreds do when somebody makes their trip to the Promised Land. Throw 'em a goin'-away food and music party. Janice Lever, if she hadn'ta been gunned down, woulda been Cooter's and Miss Florida's kin, so once Miss Florida got over her initial blood-mixing madness, she explained to me as we baked those pies together in her Browntown kitchen, "Since she ain't got no other family, Carol has given us the go-ahead on buryin' Janice the colored way." So everybody was gnawing on pork ribs in their funeral best, keeping a beat to that lowing saxophone music after the ceremony at First Ebenezer, remarking how awfully attractive Janice looked in her old twirling costume, which Clever insisted on buryin' her in, sparkling baton and all.

Clever and me are at the cottage, out on the pier, legs hanging long to the water, shooting skimmers in the dwindling light. Pink balloons are sagging off the dock after today's shindig. We're celebrating my belated twenty-first birthday and Rosie Adelaide's one month. Cooter and Clever got to the hospital in plenty of time after the showdown for her to deliver a baby who resembles a box of colors with her burnt umber skin and cornflower blue eyes. She's curled up in the cottage in her daddy's arms. In Grampa's old bed.

As usual, Keeper's at my side. Snubby tail wagging at nothing I perceive. His back leg is still bandaged and maybe he won't be able to use it again after he got it caught up beneath one of the Brandish Boys' horses when he was trying to lead Cooter to the hospital. The fact he can't bound into the lake and retrieve these skimmers is just about causin' him to go blind.

"Tell me again what Mama said to you right before she passed," Clever says, landing a three-skipper.

"She said that every baby should have a daddy and her grandbaby was gonna have hers." I musta told her this story a bazillion times, adding on as I go, "And that she was sorry for treatin' you like she did. And that you were the best daughter in all of Kentucky. And that she knew you'd be the best mama. And that you were extremely good-lookin'."

I can practically see my sidekick's smile coming clean through the back of her head when she says, "That really was something, her taking that bullet for Cooter like she did."

"It sure was, Kid."

I gotta admit, I was somewhat shocked by how broken up Clever was after Janice's passing. More than I thought she'd be. But she's settled down some now 'cause after they set her mama in the ground at Land of a Hundred Wonders Cemetery, her and Miss Lydia have become quite close, their shared interest in the dead being the thing they have in common. They've been spending a lot of time having VISITATIONS and discussing in depth:

WONDER # 12
TRANSMUTATIONS OF THE HIGHEST ORDER

"Ya think that's possible?" Clever asks.

"Do I think what's possible?" I'm remembering the last time we were out here on the pier. It was right after Grampa's heart attack.

"Transmutation of the Highest Order," Clever says, looking *almost* thoughtful. "Ya think a soul could crawl into another body so it can finish off any business it didn't get to when it was alive?"

I haul back my arm and let loose, delivering a four-skipper. "Before I answer with what I think, why are you askin' me?"

Clever looks sheepish. "I swear, sometimes Rosie reminds me an awful lot of Mama."

"She's not askin' ya to pour Mr. Jim Beam into that baby bottle, is she?"

Clever cups her hands, moving into Indian burn territory. When I'm done swatting her off, she says, "Miss Lydia's taken to wearin' black almost every day. She's missin' ya something awful, ya know."

"I heard she's got Teddy and Vern managin' the tobacco farm. That was smart a her." After all, one of them *is* the Caretaker, and the other one reads. Once that hiring news got out, agitated Browntown relaxed.

"How do ya think the white folks are gonna feel 'bout that?" Clever says, knowing we're not the only ones that enjoy throwin' stones.

"What choice do they have but to at least pretend it's such a fine idea, bein' that Miss Lydia is the second-richest person in Grant County now?"

"Shoot. I forgot. She gave me something to give to ya." Clever pops up dripping, runs off to the picnic table, and brings back a shoe box. "Open it," she says, bossy as ever. I lift off the top, and beneath the white tissue paper there's a bouquet of dried forget-me-nots held together with a purple ribbon. "She said you'd know what that meant."

"Gibby?" Grampa shouts out. He's making his way toward us from the old Fleming cottage. The one that damn Yankee Willard rented out. That's where Grampa's been living since he got back from the Houston hospital. That's the way he wanted it. Said me and Clever and Rosie should stay in our cottage and he'd move over there. After he aired out the hemp smell. When they're married, though, him and Miss Jessie will live at her farm. Cooter's been bunking down with Billy for the time being in the tent in the woods. We're all gonna have a ceremony right here on the cottage lawn when the maple leaves reach their reddest. This is what the *Gazette* headline is gonna announce in next week's "*All You Need Is Love*" column:

Comin' Soon . . .
A Trifecta Wedding!

We haven't worked out all the details yet, where everybody's gonna be living *after* we've tied the knots, but for sure it'll be here in Cray Ridge and not Bolivia. Which is good, since Loretta Boyd from over at Candy World told me this afternoon when I stopped by to pick up a sack of chocolate-covereds that *Senor* Bender would NOT be available to do any *Espanol* work in the near future 'cause he's run off with the Spanish Club's treasury money. And Miss Darlene Abernathy. (I haven't told Clever about that last part. She'll be too disappointed. She stole a rusty shovel from somebody and gave it to me for my birthday, promising, "Tomorra we'll head over to the hospital and beat that varmint Darlene to death on her lunch break.")

"Ya hear me, Gib?" Grampa calls out to me again in his hut-to voice.

"Hard not to, Charlie."

Turns out his heart attack wasn't as bad as the doctors first thought, so he didn't have to get his chest opened up with a saw down in Houston. "But," Miss Jessie explained on our way home from the airport a few weeks ago, "he's had a complication." (I'm embarrassed to tell ya that made me snort, and say, "Ya think HE'S had a complication. Lord. Ya have no idea.")

Once we got him back home, the four of us, Billy and me and Clever and Cooter, took turns telling him the best we could about what's been going on. Slow, so he'd understand. Because his complication is called a stroke. (Just in case you're not famil-iar, this has nothing at all to do with swimming. It's a medical condition that happens when some of your brain blood doesn't get where it's supposed to and your body can go sorta slack on one side and your understanding of words can get messed up.) He said to me yesterday morning when I was gettin' him dressed, "Guess the thoe's . . . on . . . the other foot now, huh, Gibby girl?" See how confused he gets? His shoe was right where it was supposed to be.

While Grampa's been rehabilitating, he's turned over the everyday running of Top O' the Mornin' to Miss Florida. Some folks got their dandruff up 'bout that, but I have a lot of faith in the persuasiveness of her black bottom pie. The customers are also having to get used to new waitress, Clever Lever, who is displaying the familiar snotty behavior of her mama. She's already got down the two-plate arm handle, so it looks like waiting tables is in her blood. Cooter's also back in the kitchen part-time helping out.

"Got thomthin elth I forgot to give ya," Grampa says, still making his way over from the next-door cottage. The hospital doctors told Miss Jessie that it's important to his recovery that he does things on his own, so I don't rush over to help.

"Hey, Grampa," Clever calls to him as he lowers himself into his chair to take the evening breeze on his face. "I can tell you're fond of that baby, so ya can quit pretendin' ya ain't."

"That baby . . . that baby looth like a frog." He gifted Rosie a whittled red-wing blackbird at the party today. (Until he gets his strength back in his right hand, everything he's been working on looks a lot like everything else, but he said it was a blackbird, so there ya go.) To get him stronger, Grampa and Clever work every morning in the rose garden as well. He's named a real pretty miniature pink rose—Rosie A. That made Clever do her air-raid siren crying. And, of course, the other part of his rehabilitation means I take him out on the boat every day.

"Mr. Bailey came by and mentioned that the fish been bitin' all week in Carver Cove. So if you wanna go over there tomorrow, we can. But we have to get an early start," I tell him slow. "I'm doin' something important in the afternoon. Whatcha got there?"

"Happy birfday," Grampa says, taking a vanilla envelope out from behind his back.

"Sounds like somebody needs me," Clever says, running her fingers down my hair as she walks past me toward the cottage. Like her, I can tell by the sound of that cry that Rosie's hungry. There's not a doubt in my mind that Miss Lydia didn't lie about one thing. Yes, what we're witnessing here is an honest-to-goodness Transmutation of the Highest Order. Rosie's piercing, wailing demands remind me EXACTLY of Janice. *She* doesn't like to sleep in her own bed, either.

"Open it," Grampa says.

Inside the big envelope there's a birthday card that says in his new scrawled-out-like-a-ransom-note writing:

Knock knock
Who's there?
Little lady
Little lady who?
Little lady who's about to get a
mysterious visitor from the east

When I look back up at Grampa, he's apple-doll puckering. (Even more than usual, factoring in the sag he got from the stroke.)

"I don't get it," I tell him, studying both sides of the card.

"Look inthide the envelope. There ith thomething elth."

Blowing it open, I palm out a large glossy picture of my hero, smoking a wood pipe in a tweedy jacket with patches on the sleeves and looking nothing at all like I imagined he would. Not rugged and sly, more bookish with horn-rimmed glasses. Down on the bottom in professional handwriting:

Finest regards, Mr. Howard Redmond

"Gosh," I gush. "I can't believe he made the time to get a picture taken and then sign it so personal. Isn't that something?"

Grampa half smiles, and so does Billy, who's done doing the dishes and has joined us out on the lawn. He looks adorable in Grampa's Chief Cook and Bottle Washer apron. (On the airplane trip home from Houston, Texas, Grampa had an old-man-to-old-man talk with Billy's daddy. Told him to quit being such a horse's ass. That he had a fine son. A soon-to-be Vietnam veterinarian. Big Bill Brown is still not buying that. But that doesn't seem to upset Billy like it used to. We're his family now.)

I open my leather-like briefcase and slide in the picture of Mr. Howard Redmond below his fine book, **The Importance of Perception in Meticulous Investigation**, which reminds me that I'm not done for the day just yet. "I got a little more work to do. Don't let the bedbugs bite," I say, bussing both my men on top of their sweet heads.

Keeper limps after me up the lawn and into the screened-in porch. (I'd pick him up, but he takes after Grampa in this respect.) After fluffing up my pillows, I take out my blue spiral and read aloud this week's top story.

Brandish Boy and Sheriff LeRoy Johnson Set to Go to Trial

As you probably already heard, Janice Lever was shot dead by one of the Brandish Boys, who'd been offered a dandy reward by Sheriff LeRoy Johnson to track down Mr. Cooter Smith, who it turns out did NOT murder Mr. Buster Malloy dead at the dump like the sheriff told everybody he did. Eyewitness, Deputy Jimmy Lee Boyd (Sheriff of Grant County elect), says that he was too ascared to mention it early on, but he witnessed LeRoy Johnson and Sneaky Tim Ray Holloway throwing dead Mr. Buster on the burning dump on the night in question. The sheriff had no choice but to admit his guilt. "I found Buster on the beach while I was makin' my daily rounds. Figured I might be able to blame his death on the Smith boy somehow, but not havin' a ready plan on how to do that, I hauled him into the woods for safekeepin'. When the coloreds started up that dump fire, it was like the Lord himself was tellin' me, LeRoy, if'n you throw that body atop those flames, everyone will think Cooter Smith did Buster in on account a that's where he works. It's your Christian duty to put that rabble-rouser where he belongs once and for all. Behind bars." (The sheriff smiled lunatically when he said that, so I suspect he might be spending some time up at the Pardyville Institute.)

So who was it murdered Mr. Buster Malloy? Will we ever know? This reporter thinks not. I believe that murder will always remain one of life's little mysteries. (In case you haven't noticed . . . life is chock-full of 'em.)

Next week Tuesday, the Brandish Boy, the one with the

oozing pocks that shot Janice Lever dead, will stand trial at the Grant County courthouse. The other Brandish Boy, the one with the long ears? Nobody's seen him since he ran off after the showdown at the old Hamilton place.

In other news . . . After a slew of encounters involving Sneaky Tim Ray Holloway's hands and my double D ninnies were described to Judge Larson, charges were not pressed against this reporter for shooting his pecker. (Not off, but close.) Holloway is presently taking his meals at the jail. It appears "the old bat" that he stole the cookie jar money from earlier on this summer over in Leesburg is none other than the mayor's dear grandmother.

Setting down the blue spiral, I ask, "Well, what do ya think?"

My dog gives me a slurpy kiss of approval. The best of all his couple of good tricks.

"Ya know, now that I've had some time to dwell on it, I believe Teddy Smith might be right, don't you, Keep?" I say, lowering the lantern light. "Miracles really *are* in the eyes of the beholden."

His ticktock tail lets me know that he couldn't agree with me more.

The two of us side by side, we're getting lulled by Billy's and Grampa's low voices conversing out on the lawn. The *who . . . whoo . . . whoo*ing of the horned owl, the boat knocking bashful against the dock. The crickets are performin' a solo tonight 'cause I'm not sure when the cicadas disappeared, but they won't resurrect 'til years from now. And right on the other side of my wall, there's one of the best sounds of all. Precious baby cooing.

"Night, Mama. You, too, Daddy. By the way, I'm gonna use some of that money I inherited on my birthday from the Champion Bus people to pay off that cheating debt you owe that art dealer up in Chicago. Thought you'd like to know."

Wait just a cotton-pickin' minute.

Reaching back under my pillow for my blue spiral, I flip to the page that's got my **VERY IMPORTANT THINGS TO DO** list. It needs immediate updating.

Using my No. 2:

1. ~~Solve the murder of Mr. Buster Malloy and write an *awfully good* story so Mama can rest in peace eternal and~~ I can get **Q**uite **R**ight.

2. ~~Check out apartment listings in Cairo.~~

Well, much as I'd love to visit a bit more, I need to get me some shut-eye 'cause tomorrow's the first Sunday of the month. Got that public Scrabble tournament to attend over in Appleville.

(Not to brag or nuthin', but I'm a shoe in.)

Photo by Richard W. Bublitz

Lesley Kagen is a writer, actress, voice-over talent and restaurateur. The owner of Restaurant Hama, one of Milwaukee's top restaurants, Ms. Kagen lives with her husband in Cedarburg, Wisconsin. She has two children. Visit her Web site at lesleykagen.com.

Land of a Hundred Wonders

LESLEY KAGEN

This Conversation Guide is intended to enrich the
individual reading experience, as well as encourage us
to explore these topics together—because books,
and life, are meant for sharing.

A CONVERSATION
WITH LESLEY KAGEN

Q. Kentucky is an uncommon location to set a novel. Why did you choose it?

A. I've always been intrigued by the South. The language, the culture. My daughter goes to school in Virginia and has recently married a wonderful man from Georgia, so I've spent a lot of time down there in recent years. I absolutely adore it! I also wanted the story to unfold in a small town because of the interesting dynamics that go on in that sort of setting. Folks who have known each other for years and years create lifelong relationships that are fascinating to me. I've lived in big cities for most of my life, many times not knowing my neighbors. Guess I'm a country girl at heart.

Q. Why did you set the book in 1973?

A. The seventies were a time in American history that signaled a significant change in our society. Mores were shifting, racial tension bubbling, the Vietnam War raging, and the drug culture surfacing. It was interesting to visit all this unsettledness onto sleepy little Cray Ridge.

Q. Your protagonist, Gibby McGraw, has suffered a traumatic brain injury and as a result her perception of life can be both hilariously funny and sad as can be. Why did you choose to write from the perspective of a young woman whose life is so different than the norm?

A. You know, I'm becoming increasingly suspicious about this word "normal." We all claim to be, but who really is **Q**uite **R**ight? I know I'm not. And I grow weary with the effort of proving that I am. Why can't I go grocery shopping in my jammies? Why can't I walk in the rain without my umbrella? Maybe we could all agree to be who we are and from now on that will be called "normal." Do you know who I could speak to about that?

Q. Describe Land of a Hundred Wonders *in one sentence.*

A. A love story.

Q. Awww . . .

A. I know, I'm a fool for love and all its many manifestations. The love of a parent for a child and vice versa. The love between a man and a woman. Best friend love. Forbidden love.

Q. Your love of horses and dogs is clearly an important element of the book. How did this love affair with animals get started?

A. After reading *Black Beauty*, I talked my mother into getting me riding lessons when I was seven years old. I've been crazy about these gorgeous creatures ever since, and passed that love on to my daughter. Same with dogs. And cats, I like cats, too. And bunnies and . . .

Q. One of the parts of the book that I enjoyed the most was the underlying cowboy theme. How did you come up with that?

A. I grew up with shoot-'em-ups. The simple themes of good guys versus bad guys easily identified by the color of their hats, the hunky guy capturing the heart of the damsel in distress, and the immediate dispensation of justice. Life is so complicated now. This down-to-basics stuff sorta makes me swoon.

Q. So you're a romantic?

A. Yeah, I guess I am, in a covered-wagon sort of way.

Q. Who is your favorite character in the book?

A. I adore Gibby's tail-wagging enthusiasm. Her heart of gold. Her courage inspires me.

Q. Least favorite?

A. Sneaky Tim Ray Holloway. Can there be anything more despicable than the theft of innocence on any level?

Q. The story has many underlying themes, one of which is the belief in miracles. Do you believe?

A. With my whole heart.

Q. Can you describe your writing process?

A. Gosh, I have no idea how I come up with this stuff. I think it might be something you're born with, blessed with. Like singers. Or artists. Of course, you need to develop that talent. And discipline. I'm up every morning when it's still dark to write.

Q. Your debut novel, Whistling in the Dark, *was a national bestseller and met with critical acclaim. What has been the most exciting part of the past year?*

A. My little book seems to have resonated with so many people, on so many levels. I hear from readers who love the nostalgia in the book, others who lost a parent, and some who were sexually abused as children. The booksellers have also been phenomenal. And the book clubs. I've had the opportunity to talk with them via phone and in person. It's fascinating to answer their questions and hear their thoughts, many of which I never even considered. The whole experience, every little bit of it, has been so much more than I could've ever imagined.

Q. What's in store for the future?

A. I'm still busy at my restaurant. And doing my voice-overs. I've also discovered that no matter how old your kids get they still need you, so they keep me on my toes. I'm also working on my next novel.

Q. Anything else you'd like to add?

A. Yes! A million thanks to everyone who has contributed to the success of *Whistling in the Dark*. You've made it possible for a whole new world full of unexpected adventures to open up for me at a time in my life when I had anticipated nothing of the sort. I'm so very, very grateful.

QUESTIONS FOR DISCUSSION

1. As a result of her brain injury, Gibby interprets the world in a slightly different way than the rest of us do. For instance, the filter that "normal" people employ to keep themselves from saying things that are "inappropriate" is not fully functioning in Gib's brain. Do you ever wish you could be as honest as she is?

2. What is a miracle? Gibby believes. Do you?

3. What are the advantages and disadvantages of living in a small rural town like Cray Ridge?

4. Life has given every major character in the book lemons. Have they successfully made lemonade?

5. We all experience painful loss in our lives. Do you believe the adage "What doesn't kill you makes you stronger"?

6. Gibby's relationship with her departed mama is as alive as her other relationships. Do you believe in life after death?

7. Much of the relationship between Gibby and her grampa is based on his desire to keep her safe. How do you balance your need to keep your children out of harm's way and yet encourage them to be brave?

8. Clever is a wild child. What do you envision her future to be?

9. Many of Gibby's observations of the "colored" characters in the book would now be considered politically incorrect. What do you think of political correctness? Does it at times keep us further apart rather than bring us together?

10. How do you think the Vietnam War affected us as a country? On a personal level? Were you supportive or did you protest? Why?

11. Gibby finds spiritual solace at Land of a Hundred Wonders. How do you nourish your soul?

12. The relationship between Gibby and Clever is at times adversarial yet you sense that they'd defend each other to the end. Although not related by blood, the two of them function as sisters. Does your relationship with your sister at all resemble the characters'? Do you have a friend with whom you have this sort of relationship?

13. In keeping with the old-time cowboy theme, a few of the

characters in the book are stereotypically black-hatted. Do you think people can be born evil or do they behave this way as a result of their experiences?

14. Gib endows Keeper with almost magical powers. Why do you think that is?

15. Miss Lydia is a complex character. Discuss her function within the story.

16. Gibby's memory, or the lack of it, plays a substantial role in the novel. Can you imagine what it would be like to lose your memory? How much of who we are is based on our past?

17. As Gibby says, "Hope springs internal." Has there ever been a time in your life when you felt you would not have had the courage to go on without the belief in a hopeful outcome?

18. Janice Lever surprises us in the end. Have you ever known anyone whom you believed to be of questionable virtues do a complete turnaround?

19. At one point in the story, Gibby dispenses eye-for-an-eye justice and is not punished for her actions. Did you find this righteous or offensive?

20. Certain relationships within the story were considered taboo during the early seventies. Do you think times have changed?